D0115300

BABE'S BIBLE
GORGEOUS GRACE

BABE'S BIBLE
GORGEOUS GRACE

KAREN JONES

DARTON · LONGMAN + TODD

First published in 2012 by
Darton, Longman and Todd Ltd
1 Spencer Court
140 – 142 Wandsworth High Street
London SW18 4JJ

© 2012 Karen Jones

The right of Karen Jones to be identified as the Author of this work has been
asserted in accordance with the Copyright, Designs and Patents Act 1998.

ISBN: 978-0-232-52920-3

A catalogue record for this book is available from the British Library.

All characters appearing in this work are fictitious. Any resemblance to
real persons, living or dead, is purely coincidental.

Printed and bound in Great Britain by Bell & Bain, Glasgow

CONTENTS

*To my daughter Sophie, who has often
been known to say that she's heard
it all before and that the
Bible is boring.*

ACKNOWLEDGEMENTS

To Bill Cahusac who, after a sermon class at Wycliffe Hall, Oxford in 2005, thanked me for my sermon attempt on Matthew 9:1–8. He suggested that I write a book in a similar style.

To Elaine Storkey, who inspired me with her insights during a lecture on Luke 7:36–50.

To Susie Bishop, who has faithfully read all my attempts at writing this book over the last two years and has never stopped encouraging me.

To my husband Si, who has always believed in me, even when I haven't believed in myself.

To my children Sophie and Sam, who keep me from getting comfortably complacent and keep me thinking creatively.

To all the women over the years with whom I've journeyed, loved, laughed and cried.

To Jesus, my Prince, who has fiercely commanded me not to put my hope in any other princes.

1. CONNECTION

The woman caught in the act

Grace watched with interest as Chloe drank her first glass of wine in one go. A glass or two was neither here nor there on a girls' night out, but it was the speed at which it disappeared that was surprising.

It was getting dark outside the Italian restaurant. The group of women were at their favourite table by the window, where hanging baskets danced outside in a light breeze. Trailing tendrils of summer flowers cast their shadows across the table as shop lights winked in between. The six of them were secluded, but could still watch people go by. They'd ordered food and their waiter had just filled their glasses. He was young, maybe in his mid-twenties; everything about him cried 'recent-holiday-somewhere-hot', with tanned, well-muscled arms and his chest partially on view at the open neck of his crisp, white, linen shirt. He smiled confidently as he made eye contact with a few of them. The flickering candlelight glowed through the wine and masked the heightened colour in some flattered cheeks. Good friends, good wine, good food and, of course, the good waiter. What more could women want, other than perhaps more of the waiter?

Grace returned her attention to her friend. It struck her that there was a lot more that Chloe wanted. She watched her curl a stray strand of dark hair behind her ear, thoughtfully touching the simple diamond stud that Mark had given her for their tenth wedding anniversary. Grace remembered how excited Chloe had been when she'd shown them off to her a few months ago. She watched Chloe press her earlobe between her forefinger and thumb, and then run her hand down the side of her neck. Wisps of hair fell from a loose knot at the back of her head, making her look like she'd come from a strenuous dance class. She could have been Spanish, with dark eyes, thick arching eyebrows and olive skin. She was in her mid-thirties, the telltale signs of which were beginning to show round her eyes and mouth.

Grace knew that Chloe liked her right side profile and would always make sure she presented it in photographs. She didn't like her left profile because a large, dark mole nestled there near her nose. She'd told Grace she disliked them both – criticising her nose for being too wide and the mole for having the audacity to exist at all. She also thought her forehead was unfashionably high, envying women in magazines with lower foreheads. But they'd laughed over those things they didn't like about themselves, and Chloe had said that her sister had told her she'd grown into her face as she'd got older. Neither of them was sure if this had been a compliment or not. However, being optimistic people, they had decided that it was – they were women coming into their own.

Three or four glasses into the evening, and having hardly touched her food, Chloe's conversation began to turn to what was on her mind. Grace was relieved – she knew only too well how close Chloe could play her cards to her chest at times. 'How are you getting on with Tom?' she asked Grace.

'Fine thanks. He's a good detail person. I like that.' She paused. 'You've been working with him a year now, haven't you? How about you?' She eyed her friend speculatively.

Grace had been glad when she started her curacy that there was another woman on the staff at St Matthew's. Friendship had quickly blossomed between them through a shared sense of humour. However, Grace was aware that Chloe was slightly in awe of her ability to hold her own so confidently among their male colleagues. She was also aware that she was a bit of a novelty in the village, nestled in London's commuter belt. People who went to university from here rarely returned because it was too expensive for first-time buyers, so there weren't many people her age with her qualifications in the parish (she had an undergraduate degree and a Masters in Literature from Cambridge, as well as her degree in Theology).

She had gone to theological college later in life, having had a promising career in journalism with a national paper based in London. It had taken much soul searching and had caused many issues in her marriage to Peter, her graphic designer husband who was not a churchgoer at all. He'd been married once before and had been widowed, so was nearly ten years her senior. Grace knew that it was something to do with his first wife's death that kept him from God and the church, but they never spoke of it. Their love for each other helped them bridge any differences in their worldviews and they eventually triumphed, enabling their marriage to survive her ordination.

Peter commuted to work in London, where they'd met, and rarely got involved in the parish, except at Christmas and Easter. Chloe told Grace that it was a good thing she was married because when the flower arrangers, banner-making-ladies, Mothers' Union members and other clergy wives saw her, they were reassured to know that she was not a single female priest who might lure their husbands away.

It was true that more women than men generally attended church, but it was still the case that the majority of Anglican ordained clergy were male, especially in the conservative, evangelical tradition that had been (until recently) the tradition of St Matt's. Women clergy were still considered slightly odd, and usually were. But Grace didn't fit the stereotype. At a glance, she might have been mistaken as Swedish (her mother was Dutch), being 5'10" with naturally curly white-blonde hair that fell about her face in soft corkscrews. For someone so delicate looking, her strong-minded and forthright personality was a disconcerting contradiction. Her mother had always said it was a particularly Dutch trait. Despite this, Grace was never as sure of herself as she sounded and, of late, had been trying to adopt a more measured approach. She had quickly realised that thinking out loud didn't always go down as well in the church community as it had done in journalistic circles. She'd learned a lot from watching Chloe's amenable and accommodating manner when relating to others on their team. Grace envied her easy-going nature, wishing she could be as relaxed as her.

When Tom, the present incumbent, had arrived, Charlie (the youngest of Chloe's three children) had just started school. Tom had invited her to become the church's full-time youth worker and to come onto the payroll. That had been only six months before Grace arrived.

'A year ... ' Chloe gently squeezed her right shoulder and then let her hand fall to the table to find the stem of her glass. 'Has it really only been that long?' she marvelled, swirling her wine around.

'So you like him then?' Grace asked.

A slow smile crept over Chloe's mouth as she responded: 'I think he's pretty amazing ... gifted ... insightful,' she looked up at Grace who noticed her friend's eyes weren't moving as fast as they normally did. 'It was him who convinced the PCC to take me on full time and pay me. I'll always be grateful to him for that. He takes time to meet with me regularly – at best it was sporadic with the last guy. We have such a laugh together and I've really enjoyed praying with him for the young people. He's so spiritual ... not like Mark,' she said, muttering the last part of her sentence.

'Did you say, "not like Mark"?' Grace asked, leaning forward and tucking a curl behind her ear.

'Yeah, I did!' Chloe rubbed her nose and fixed Grace with an affronted stare. 'Mark never prays with me. He doesn't even ask me about my work anymore. I come home on Wednesday and Sunday nights, and he's glued to the TV.'

'Oh dear, that doesn't sound good,' Grace frowned, knowing that Christian couples probably should pray together, but never having expected or experienced anything like that in her own marriage.

'No, it's not. See – I am right about this, aren't I?' It was a rhetorical question. 'I used to love coming home to him. He'd have cleaned up the mess from dinner and sorted out the kids so I could be free to run youth groups two nights a week. I'd positively glowed with his affirmation of me. I'd snuggle up to him to watch the end of whatever he was watching and we'd often end up making love on the sofa or the living room floor,' she tipped her head back, laughing at the memory. She slowly lowered her head, a sad expression settling over her features, 'But not so much any more – something's changed.'

'Are you going to do anything about it?' Grace asked pragmatically.

'Well I've already been doing something about it,' Chloe's sad expression escaped into a smug one, 'I've been praying about it with Tom.' Chloe reached the bottom of her glass and smiled – a secret sort of smile. Grace wanted to know what it was about, but Chloe shook her head and laughed again.

'Where was I? Oh yes,' she reached unsteadily for the wine bottle and poured herself another glass, 'I was saying ... I like him – Tom. He's a very caring vicar. He seems to know when I need a hug or an encouraging handhold.'

'Really?' Grace felt growing alarm, raising her eyebrows and piercing Chloe with an incisive blue stare.

'Oh no, not like that at all,' Chloe frowned, annoyance flashing in her dark eyes.

Grace quickly said she was sorry. 'He hasn't ever been that cosy with me. Mind you, most ordained men I know are so confused by me being among their number and terrified of sexual impropriety that it's hard to get them to look me in the eye, let alone give me a hug.'

'Well he's a real pastoral type,' Chloe said rather too emphatically, 'and you must agree that everyone's enjoying the changes he's brought to the parish. Maybe he doesn't think you need any pastoral care – you can be a bit scary sometimes, you know. Anyway, the Mothers' Union simply adore him. I'm sure he hugs all of them too.'

But Grace detected a tremor of doubt in her friend's voice, along with a concerted effort not to slur her words.

Chloe continued: 'Only the other day I was sharing with him how difficult it is being in leadership in the church and feeling that Mark doesn't really understand the pressures I'm under. He touched my hand with such empathic understanding … it was quite moving.' A confused look crossed Chloe's face and then was gone in an instant. 'He gave me a book about the stresses of Christian leadership on marriage.'

Chloe rallied and looked down at her cold food. 'What a waste,' she said, '– a bit like how I feel. Here I am coming into my sexual peak and Mark doesn't even want me, doesn't even look up when I come in. At least I've got the youth weekend away to look forward to in a few weeks' time. I can't wait. He's coming with us.'

'Mark?'

'No, Tom! Isn't it amazing that he is so committed to the youth?'

'Don't spend too much time alone with him, will you,' Grace said, uncomfortably aware that she was sounding like her mother.

'For goodness sake,' Chloe snapped, 'we're both married with families and committed to Christian ministry. We wouldn't do anything stupid. Anyway,' she glared at her friend, 'he isn't even good looking.' She rubbed the back of her hand gently, where, Grace guessed, the fingers of their spiritual and understanding boss had recently been. 'I just want to be wanted,' Chloe muttered, wiping away a drop of wine from the corner of her mouth with the back of her hand.

One of Chloe's voluntary youth assistants called Mo, a twenty-something single mum who was sitting on the other side of Chloe, turned and engaged her in conversation. In the lull, Grace sipped her wine and averted her gaze from the oh-so-fine waiter whom she had caught looking at her several times. She was jerked back to reality by Chloe asking, 'Do you ever feel like you made a mistake in marrying your husband?' It was now very clear that Chloe was well over her limit.

'Well, yes, probably about once a month,' Grace laughed, shaking off her anxiety for Chloe. 'Poor men,' Grace continued, feeling mildly guilty and thinking fondly of Peter.

'Poor men?' Chloe looked indignant. 'Poor us! We endure their endless football games, their burping and farting, their snoring, their insecurities over their receding hairlines and their inability to talk about their feelings. And sex? Well, there's a design fault if ever there was one. Remember when they wanted it four times a night ...

'Four? That was just the once then, was it?' Grace interjected, making Chloe raise a knowing eyebrow as she went on.

' ... and we had the body and the energy for it, but hadn't quite figured out how to get *there?*'

'Well, other than on your own,' Grace quipped, sending Chloe into a fit of laughter.

'How did you ever get ordained? No, listen! Now we know how and we're interested, they're glued to the TV, the kids are always there and the house is made of plywood anyway, so any noise made in any room can be heard by everyone.'

'It's not sexy, is it?' Grace shook her head, laughing.

They were giggling uncontrollably by this stage. Mo leaned round Chloe, her long beaded cane-rows slapping against Chloe's bare arm.

'Ouch!' Chloe exclaimed, rubbing the red welts that instantly appeared on her skin.

'Sorry, luv,' Mo said. Chloe accepted her apology with a slow nod. Mo looked at them astutely, sucking air in through the gap in her front teeth, 'You talking about sex again?' Her east-end accent assailed them like her plaits.

'Yep,' they said in unison.

'Well, just be glad you're getting some,' Mo took a big gulp of her wine. They were instantly sorry.

'Oh, Mo. Your time will come and when it does, that man won't know what's hit him! It's just good to come out and have a laugh about some of the annoying things about being married.' Grace's guilt grew as she realised she hadn't been very pastorally aware.

'I'd give anything right now to be annoyed and married,' Mo smiled and forgave them. 'So, anyway, what were you whinging about?' she said, looking at Chloe. Other conversations had stopped round the table and everyone's attention focused on Chloe.

'Oh, it's nothing really ... probably just me,' Chloe's face reddened. 'Oh, go back to your own conversations,' she shooed them with her hands. 'You hear the word "sex" and you're all ears.'

'I didn't hear the word sex,' said a forty-something woman called Val, sitting opposite, 'and if I did, I wouldn't be interested anyway. So much fuss and bother, over what? I'd rather have a cup of tea and a chat.'

'You serious?' asked Mo, incredulous.

'Yes,' Val's face was solemn.

'Have you ever enjoyed it?' Mo asked. They were all leaning in, thinking of Val's poor husband who mustn't have been getting any for some time now. Chloe was glad they had forgotten about her.

'When I was young I was pretty wild,' Val disclosed with a wink.

'So what changed?' Chloe asked.

There was a pause. Then Val leant back in her chair and breathed in deeply. 'Life,' she said, letting out a rush of air with the word. She returned her gaze to her friends from a point in the distance. 'And don't you all be thinking that poor Jack doesn't get any –'cause he does, when I've had a drink or two and ol' Ruby comes out to play.' She raised her glass and smiled cheekily.

'Ruby?' several of them chorused.

'Yes, my alter-ego hooker,' she laughed tipsily.

Grace felt uneasy and wondered if Val was going to regret telling them this in the morning. There were squeals of laughter round the table as someone started singing a Kaiser Chiefs song by the same name.

'No, no,' Val interrupted, 'I got her from Kenny Rogers.'

No one knew who that was, so Mo raised her glass and said, 'Whoever inspired her, we give thanks to them on Jack's behalf, because his luck's in tonight!'

They all raised their glasses, cheering raucously, but Grace sensed that Chloe was only half-heartedly entering into the fun.

As they were leaving, Grace caught her arm. 'You OK, Chloe?'

'Yeah, I'm fine,' she smiled sloppily.

Grace helped her with her coat. 'If you want to talk, I'm here.' She squeezed her friend's shoulders affectionately.

'Thanks,' said Chloe, shrugging her off.

The waiter made a beeline for Grace and held her coat for her. As she slipped into it, she heard him murmur 'Bellissima'.

As she walked away she glanced through the window to see if he was still looking. He was. She smiled, '... If only you knew,' she shook her head, her hair bouncing gently against her cheeks.

As she sat on the bus home she was thinking about Chloe, her mind flitting fitfully to the waiter's interest in her.

※　※　※

Chloe rang her a few days later. She said she'd been praying about things with the vicar and that she was feeling much better.

Another couple of weeks went by until they met for coffee at Grace's. Her house was just up the road from the church office. Chloe was bubbly and energetic. She and Mark must have sorted their love life out, Grace thought. Chloe was looking good. But when Grace asked her about Mark, a cloud crossed her features. Nothing had changed there, she said, and moved swiftly on to talk about the youth weekend – they were heading off tomorrow, taking thirty kids to the beach for the bank holiday weekend. It was the only thing that was keeping her going. She jokingly said she'd be careful not to spend too much time alone with the 'understanding vicar', as she wouldn't want the magnetism between them to pull her in too close. He could be very charismatic.

'Yes, you've said,' Grace replied. 'So how are you going to manage this magnetism when things aren't so great between you and Mark?' she asked bluntly.

'Oh, don't be ridiculous. We're both adults. We know the score. I may be at my sexual peak and Mark's missing it, but I'm not hanging around moping. I'm channelling all this energy,' Chloe gestured towards her chest, 'into ministry.'

'Stranger things have happened, Chloe. It's human nature doing its thing. "Know thyself," and all that,' Grace smiled anxiously at her. 'I love you, babe. I wouldn't want you to end up in a mess.' They hugged as Chloe headed for the door.

'You are such a worrier. I won't do anything stupid.'

※　※　※

Well, Chloe was true to her word. She didn't do anything stupid, oh no. She did something spectacularly devastating.

'Spiritual and understanding vicar' was going through hell. His wife had left him, taking the children with her to her mother's. He was under clergy discipline, his job suspended, and would soon have to vacate the vicarage. What had he been thinking? Maybe that was it – he hadn't been thinking. Well, not with the thing between his ears anyway. Or maybe he really had fallen head-over-heels in love? How had he thought he could get away with an affair in his line of work? Maybe he'd bought the whole 'old-boys-club' spin on clergy. Maybe he thought it would only be a misdemeanour worthy of a raised eyebrow and a surreptitious sweeping under the proverbial diocesan carpet. At least he and his wife were going for counselling together. Grace didn't know how it would turn out, but she hoped they would make it through. She felt angry and sorry for him at the same time. She knew she had a lot of work to do in sorting out her own emotional reaction to it all.

What had Chloe been thinking? Had she really fallen in love? They shared a passion for youth ministry – was that what had confused her? Or had she deceived herself by calling the need to be wanted by some worthier name?

Mark booked them in for counselling sessions too. At least he didn't throw her out. Grace wondered if maybe he understood more of what she'd done than he was letting on. He went to see Tom. Grace laughed as she told Peter about Mark's 'tough love', when he pinned Tom up against the wall.

But the children – both families' – they were traumatised; they were all at the same school.

It had been one of the youth group, who happened to be off 'sick' one day, that discovered them. Bored and aimless, he had made his way up to the youth office and caught them in a rather compromising position. The boy ran straight home to tell his Mum who, in turn, didn't ring the church wardens as she should have. Oh no, she went directly to the top; she rang the bishop's office. She'd always wanted to have something important to tell the bishop. After that, she also had to ring her best friend who couldn't carry the burden of this knowledge alone and shared it with her colleague at the Church of England school the children attended. Sadly, Lottie Stanton – a year five pupil – was listening at the reception desk window. She was very short for her age and couldn't be seen from the secretary's seated position. On hearing the story, she forgot why she was standing there and ran back to her classroom with the news that was sure to make her the most popular girl in school. The whole school was buzzing with the gossip by the end of break time.

Grace went straight round to Chloe's to give her a hug. Chloe clung to her in her kitchen, sobbing and shivering for the wrong she'd done to their children. She hadn't thought of them at the time.

As for the church kids – well, that was another problem altogether. The bishop asked the associate vicar Trevor to galvanise his team and join in clearing up the mess. Trevor was to run the church while the matter was being investigated. Grace was to address the young people's disillusionment and work to reinforce their connection with God. She listened to their feelings and thoughts. Some of them were angry; others seemed to have aged with a new cynicism; several said they weren't interested in God and church any more; a few of them met with Grace privately to wrestle prayerfully through their hurt.

Because of her friendship with Chloe, Trevor also asked her to take on the bulk of the pastoral care for Chloe. He would see Chloe and Mark together at regular intervals, if they were willing, and would ensure Mark got the support he needed. Tom would come under the supervision of the head of pastoral care for the diocese.

Chloe was scared of meeting churchgoers; she'd been hiding at home. Her kids hadn't been to their church groups for several weeks either. Mark had stayed at home on Sundays, not because he was afraid, but because he was standing by his wife. Two of his mates he prayed with sporadically had been coming round every Sunday during the church service to listen to him and pray.

Grace cupped her hands round the mug of morning coffee Chloe had given her. She noticed that Chloe's hands had become very thin and realised that her whole frame had shrunk. Her cheeks were hollow, her eyes dull. She said she couldn't eat, she felt sick all the time. She said her youngest, Charlie, had been wetting the bed. Each time it happened, she wanted to die. Grace didn't know what to say.

'You know how things that happen on holiday aren't really real?' she asked in a monotone. Grace didn't answer. 'Do you remember how before you were married you just thought being married was the same as going out with someone?' she paused. 'I've been such a fool. Who was I kidding?' She slowly shook her head .

Grace still didn't comment.

Eventually Chloe spoke again: 'It was during the youth weekend. We'd been chatting outside, sitting on deck chairs while the kids built a human pyramid. The chemistry was brewing. Then everyone wanted to go down to the beach. We said we'd stay and sort out kitchen stuff or something. The other leaders had no reason to be suspicious and left us to it. He asked me if I wanted to go for a drink. We took a walk to the local pub, talking all the way. We sat watching the sun go down; the wine went straight to my head. At that point, wild horses couldn't have dragged me away. We kissed and … well, he couldn't walk for a while,' she smiled ruefully. 'We were laughing like kids playing a stupid game. But after we got home I couldn't wait to see him. When we were alone, we were all over each other. It was so exciting.' But there was no thrill in her voice, just relief in the telling of it. Chloe's eyes moistened; something of her isolation was diminishing.

'How long would I have let it go on for if we hadn't been found out? I don't know. And now,' she breathed deeply, 'now, I'm appalled at myself. I can't bear to be in my own skin. Will my kids ever heal from this? Will Mark? Because of me, three little boys might lose their daddy. Because of my selfishness, she,' she blinked and swallowed, unable to speak her name, 'has lost her husband's focus, maybe his commitment, to their marriage. I have to live with that now.' Chloe wiped a tear away.

Grace moved closer and reached for her hand. She shrank away, 'Don't touch me,' she sobbed. But Grace moved closer still, not sure if she was doing the right thing but risking it anyway.

'You know the story in the Bible about the woman caught in the act of adultery?' Grace asked quietly.

'Oh, please don't get all religious on me now,' she laughed cynically through her tears. 'What possible use is the Bible at this point?'

'No, listen to me. Think about it,' Grace paused. In the silence they thought of the details of the story they both knew so well. 'I've been wondering how she got into adultery and how meeting with Jesus changed her – changed things?' Grace reached out and this time Chloe let her hold her hand.

'I've been writing a fictional story based on her. I know reading's probably the last thing on your mind, but you never know, it might help … Would you like to see it?'

'Not really – why would I want to read about someone else as stupid as me?' Chloe asked, sniffing loudly.

'Well, maybe I could send it to you and you could read it when you feel like it? I really think you might find it helpful. It's weird,' she hesitated, 'cause I started writing it way before all this happened between you and Tom.'

Chloe was momentarily surprised, and couldn't resist the offer from her well-meaning friend.

'OK,' she said slowly, 'but I'm not promising anything … ' She stared out of the large sash windows at the end of the lounge to her garden beyond. 'Do you want another cup of coffee?' she asked eventually.

'Yes, please – this one's gone cold.' Grace handed the mug to her friend as she got up slowly, weariness etched across her features.

※　※　※

It was 1.00am. Chloe knew it was no good – she was wide-awake. If she didn't get to sleep before midnight it was useless. But since the 'explosion', as she had begun to call it in her head, she'd hardly slept at all. Her mind kept running along the familiar track back to Tom's face, Tom's smile, Tom's arms. A surge of self-loathing propelled her out of bed, causing Mark to turn in his sleep with a sigh.

She wandered wretchedly downstairs, stopping along the way to listen at each child's bedroom door. When she got to the kitchen she decided to make herself a cup of coffee. She forgot to put milk in it. She wandered around cradling the hot mug in her hands, close to her chest. She ended up at her desk.

Are you online?

She opened her laptop and stared at the glowing screen for ages. She went to her emails, tension growing in her stomach. The only new mail in her inbox was from Grace. She frowned at it dismally and then dutifully clicked on it. 'Might as well read it … got nothing else to do.'

She rubbed her eyes and took a big gulp of hot, bitter liquid.

Hi Chloe,
Hope you don't mind – I couldn't resist.

Attached is a story I've been writing around the gospel account of the woman caught in the act of adultery. As I said, I started writing it long before I knew anything about you and Tom.

I haven't written anything other than sermons since I got ordained, but this story caught my imagination one day. I don't know if you'll want to read it, but it does seem as if I unwittingly wrote it for you.
Let me know if you do.
Much love,
Grace

Chloe's fingers hovered over the keypad. Ambivalent, she stared at the attachment for a while. Then she moved the cursor towards it and eventually clicked on it. The title read: 'Connection'.

To what or who? – she wondered, and despite herself began to read.

It was hot and dusty in the market place. Lila pulled her headscarf higher over her nose, trying to minimise the amount of dust she breathed in. She shifted the basket on her hip, heavy with the things she had bought. She was regretting buying the appliquéd, richly embroidered sections of cloth – they weighed more than everything else put together. With each step the weave of the basket bit into her skin. She pulled her skirt up, folding it over twice to give herself more padding. Then she began making her way through the Friday crowds again.

Jair would be home by dusk. She squinted into the sun. It was at its zenith. She reckoned she might have enough time to begin work on the dress she had in mind. Perhaps she could even start sewing before he returned. This strengthened her resolve to ignore the pain in her hip and to walk as fast as she could back to the house.

Soon the crowds thinned as she left the hustle and bustle of commerce behind her. The road narrowed, branching into a myriad of alleyways that ran like gullies from among the small houses and workshops of Market Street. Eventually, she came to the big sycamore tree that marked out the neighbourhood she'd always lived in. There weren't many trees in this part of the city; the houses were too closely packed to make room for them. But somehow this one had survived all the arguments about property boundaries and it stood tall and arching, like a guardian angel over all the homes beneath it. Lila's house was always in its shadow at noon, even in winter when the sun didn't rise as high. She liked that. She liked listening to the wind blow through its branches. She liked the cool of its shade as she walked through the door into what would have otherwise been a very stuffy little house.

She dropped the basket down on the baked-earth floor and went to the clay water pot in the corner. She lifted the lid and scooped out a ladle full of water, which she'd collected from the well earlier that morning. Drinking steadily, she was careful not to let any of the precious liquid dribble down her chin. She replaced the ladle and lid, and slid down the uneven wall; squatting on the floor, she closed her eyes as she leaned her head back. Perspiration beaded her smooth, dark skin. Her lips parted slightly as she breathed deeply. Jair's face formed behind her eyelids and her thick lashes fluttered slightly: low forehead, eyes closely set, pale skin stretched over the sharp edge of his nose, the small mouth surrounded by wisps of beard that looked like they didn't really want to be there. She lingered on his mouth and felt the familiar sinking feeling in the pit of her stomach.

What is that?

She was mildly surprised at her own question. Her hand involuntarily pressed into the feeling beneath her ribs and dared to wait for an answer.

I never stay with it long enough to know.

Her heart rate was slowing and her breathing was normal now, but still she waited.

Disappointment?

The feeling rose in answer to its name like a small wave and washed over her. She raised her dark eyebrows and sighed deeply. She had hoped she would grow to love his face more than she did. She opened her eyes and tossed her head so that her scarf fell onto her shoulders. Damp tendrils of wavy black hair fell forward and stuck to her oval face.

I knew that. Of course I did. What's the point of knowing it? There is none. That's exactly why I never stay with it.

She ripped the scarf from around her shoulders and irritably threw it onto their bed. She reached over and dragged the basket towards her.

Where are my beautiful embroidered pieces? If that bag of figs has leaked onto them … no, there they are. No stain. Why did I put the figs so close?

She pulled out the fabric and the embroidery that would make the breast and back panels and detail for the hem of the skirt. Rich purple, green and gold, contrasted with the black of the rest of the fabric. She ran one finger along the embroidery, enjoying the sensation of the raised silk thread over the soft cloth. It had cost so much – all her earnings since Hanukkah.

Cooking could wait.

She was cooling down now from the journey home. The sweat on her upper lip had dried into saltiness. She touched it with the tip of her tongue, enjoying the taste as she laid out the material flat on the floor. She got the pattern out from the box under the bed where she kept all her sewing things and began laying out the pieces.

When I wear this, Aaron will look at me again with that look. I know it.

A thrill of excitement ran down her spine. She paused, savouring it. He hadn't looked at her in the last couple of weeks. Mingling with the neighbours after synagogue was a dangerous time to look too long at anyone. Eyes were watching for the slightest impropriety and gossip was everyone's favourite pastime.

※ ※ ※

'Shalom, Jair, it's good to see you again,' Aaron said warmly, standing a little taller than the other men gathered around him. His open, confident face cracking into a broad smile as he greeted his old friend.

'It's good to have you back in Jerusalem, Aaron!' Jair clasped both Aaron's arms in his, shaking them as he spoke. 'How long has it been?'

'I think nearly twenty years this Passover. You were a single man then,' he laughed, eyes sparkling with a secret joke.

'And you too, my friend,' the joke seemed less funny to Jair. 'I hear you married also? Is your wife here?' he glided past the discomfort he felt.

'No, she has just had our fourth child – our second boy! So she is at home. She says she hears enough of me anyway,' he smiled, drawing a hand over his thick beard, as if for reassurance.

When Jair was concentrating, his eyebrows almost became one above his serious eyes. He seemed to carry the woes of the world on his shoulders. He hoped his face didn't give away any signs of the dark envy that wrestled within his guts. 'How wonderful for you! Congratulations!' he patted Aaron on the shoulder as he changed the subject. 'We need more good teachers like you these days, Aaron. You've certainly learned a thing or two while you've been away! Thank you for your thoughts today, I really enjoyed listening to you. Didn't you, Lila?' Jair looked over his shoulder at Lila who was appropriately behind him, inviting her into the conversation.

Lila involuntarily jerked her hand to fix her headscarf. She'd been miles away, thinking about the woman who had four children.

She focused her gaze on Aaron. He was a man that commanded attention. It was his eyes that attracted her the most. He was looking at her with interest. Not many men did that – after all, she was just a woman. Her father never had, unless he was drunk; the rabbi she cleaned for only spoke to her to order her around. Even when Jair looked at her, it was often as if he didn't really see her.

Laughter lines ran out from Aaron's eyes and crinkled as he spoke. She noticed he had strong hands that he used to express himself.

'Yes, I did. Shalom Aaron,' Lila spoke softly as she inclined her head slightly.

Aaron inclined his head in return and smiled.

'You don't remember me?'

For a moment Lila felt confused, but then she composed herself. 'How could I remember you? I was only a young girl when you left?'

'I remember you and your sisters ... weren't there six of you all together?'

'Yes ... there still are,' she smiled shyly. 'I'm surprised you remember me, I'm the youngest.'

'I know,' Aaron said simply. Lila realised he was looking deep into her eyes. It was an unguarded split second, a heartbeat's vulnerable connection. The pause yawned between them and then it was gone.

At first she felt shock, then pleasure, then self-consciousness ... *did Jair see?* He didn't seem to have noticed – he was talking about getting the younger men together with Aaron to explore some texts from the book of the prophet Isaiah. Aaron was focused on Jair now, as if Lila didn't exist. She felt foolish, smiled slightly and pulled back behind Jair, busying herself with an invisible stray thread on her skirt.

※   ※   ※

That had been six months ago.

She stood up and surveyed her work, arching her back to relieve the ache of having been bent over for so long.

Good. Still got time to start sewing that bit first ... then I'll cook.

She got out thread and needle and made herself comfortable on the bed, crossing her legs and leaning up against the wall so she could see out the only window. The tree was casting shadows that danced on the street outside. Some of the neighbourhood children were playing a game with stones, throwing increasing numbers of them in the air and catching them as the others counted loudly. If they missed, there was loud jeering.

The familiar pain in her heart surfaced as she watched them for a while. Her mind reached for comfort.

He wants me so badly. Last time I saw him I could feel it coming off his skin – through his clothes. Ah ... I had to fight my body to stay still and not move towards him. I've never felt that before. I make my body move towards Jair – it's my duty – well it was at first. Sometimes it's all right ... but he has never wanted me like this. He has never taken me with the passion I see in Aaron's eyes. Nor have I wanted him – not like this.

Her fingers hung suspended over her work as her mind lingered over this secret pleasure.

The pain was fading.

The last time she'd seen Aaron, they'd been standing side by side outside synagogue. Jair had been enthusing about the positive effect of the meetings they'd begun with the young men. To Lila it felt like a thick, invisible blanket was wrapping itself around her and Aaron. She couldn't hear what Jair was saying. She could only hear her own breathing and his; she could only feel her heart thudding in her chest. It was all she could do to stand still and focus her eyes on a small rock beside Jair's left foot.

A mixture of relief and longing engulfed her when they parted company: relief that she didn't have to concentrate so hard on resisting her desire for him, and a longing to be close to him again.

All the way home, Jair had chatted about the work with the young men, how wonderful it was to see them taking the scriptures seriously. Lila only needed to nod and smile every now and then in agreement with him. She was left to think about the slight touch of Aaron's little finger against hers. Hardly anything – an unconscious intrusion into personal space ... or was it? It had sent tingles up her arm.

She'd heard her oldest sister talk about these middle years. 'You wait, Lila ... then you'll know what all the fuss is about! You'll want it like you want to scratch an itch that you just can't reach,' she'd cackled through the gap left by a tooth that had fallen out.

Lila had felt revulsion back then at the thought. The only things she had known then about sex were things her father had done to her. She had hated the way he had touched her. She had endured his drunken fumblings in the small hours of the night when he thought everyone else was asleep. She had conflicting feelings of wanting to somehow erase herself along with each experience, but also wanting to please him, wanting whatever attention he would give her. She knew she was no good; that she was to blame and had never complained or ever told anyone.

She couldn't imagine ever enjoying sex. It was something that men needed, something you could become skilled at. The few things she had learned from her father had been added to by her sisters, showing her some skills they said she'd need. But skilful or not, it had to be done along with the cleaning and cooking – that is if you wanted to be looked after, have a roof over your head and of course, have the social status of children. The ache in her heart stung her eyes and they watered, blurring her vision momentarily. The needle jabbed into her finger.

'Ow!'

She stuck it in her mouth quickly to stop the blood from falling on her precious fabric. She looked out of the window again, but the children were gone. The shadows were longer and, with a start, she realised the time. She folded everything up and put it under the bed, dusting the lint off her skirt. She sighed deeply and moved into the smaller room in the house that served as the kitchen, dragging the basket of food with her foot across the floor.

※　※　※

A week later, she wore the dress she'd made. Jair had complimented her on her hard work. She'd done it so quickly, on top of all her other chores. He said she looked smart as his eyes flitted from the scroll he was reading to her and then back again. She didn't want to look smart, she wanted to look desirable ... but she said nothing. Their eyes met momentarily, but there was no connection.

Lila followed behind Jair to synagogue as usual, the monotony of the ritual broken only by the faint hope of meeting Aaron's gaze.

An argument broke out in synagogue about keeping the law. In the women's section a hush descended. The women stopped chatting amongst themselves and started listening for once. Back and forth it went about laws the Romans wouldn't allow any more. Aaron and some other Pharisees were strongly advocating that true Jews should carry out every Mosaic Law, regardless of what the present powers-that-be decided. Others were suggesting that the Romans were in power by the will of God and that perhaps they were helping to bring about progress. Others were incensed at the suggestion. The Pharisees and the rabbi argued forcefully, his remaining the most powerful voice in the debate. Lila noticed Jair was not taking sides. He was earnestly listening to all the views expressed and would often raise his hands in peace-making gestures to bring order when one or other speaker became too heated.

There was mention of the new teacher from Nazareth who had been causing quite a stir in the city with stories of miracles and healings. Apparently he had been flagrantly breaking the law, openly socialising with tax collectors and prostitutes, and yet he was considered by many to be a great teacher and possibly even a prophet ... maybe even, it was whispered, the Messiah? Someone spat after mentioning his name and a few applauded and laughed. But then Jair said he wanted to meet this man and listen to what he had to say before judging him. The rabbi nodded in agreement, taking this opportunity to regain control of the meeting and began reciting the closing prayer.

As Lila left the synagogue through the women's entrance she felt curious about anyone who dared to openly break the rules and socialise with prostitutes. She knew that many visited them secretly. Her father and two of her sisters' husbands had been regulars – she knew that for a fact. There was even gossip that the rabbi's son had been seen entering the house of a local woman of ill repute a week or so ago.

She walked round the corner of the synagogue to meet with Jair, her head down, deep in thought. She was watching the way the embroidered border of her skirt moved like ripples on water, enjoying the feel of the soft, heavy material against her legs as she walked. Suddenly, her breath caught in her throat as she recognised the two feet firmly planted in her path. She looked up into a gaze that sent heat surging up her neck and into her face. Neither of them spoke. A group of girls brushed past them, all talking at once. Lila quickly looked around to see who else was there. No one.

'You look … ' Aaron's voice trailed away as his eyes moved hungrily over her face and down. 'I like what you are wearing. I haven't seen it before, have I?' His eyes returned to hers.

Her skin was tingling. 'No, it's new.'

'Is the fabric soft?' his voice was husky.

Her eyes grew wide as they met his. She didn't trust herself to answer.

Suddenly there was movement behind him and Lila saw over his shoulder that a group of young men, deep in conversation, were coming round the corner. Quickly, she lowered her head and moved to one side as if to go past him. At the same time, the men saw Aaron and in unison called his name. Lila was invisible to them. She snatched a last glance at Aaron's face and saw frustration in his eyes that she'd not seen before. Then she was walking away from him; she could feel his body turning with the passing of hers.

'Brothers! What can I do for you?' she heard him making a huge effort to inject enthusiasm into his voice.

She turned the corner into the bustle of the Sabbath crowd, her thighs slipping against each other underneath the folds of her skirt. Somehow she was able to disconnect their exchange and her internal feelings from the reality around her. Nothing had happened; she was still a faithful, dutiful wife and Aaron a good teacher and husband. They'd done nothing wrong. So why was she feeling sickened and so sinfully exhilarated at the same time?

She nosed her way through to where she knew Jair would be

talking with the rabbi who was saying that several other rabbis from the area were planning a visit to the temple where they had heard the Nazarene teacher often went. She stood still near Jair, who acknowledged her with a slight nod. She focused on her breathing, taking air in slowly through her nostrils, holding it for a bit and then letting it out, little by little, through her lips.

She looked up at the rabbi's face, searching for any awareness that he might have of her. He was oblivious. Her eyes moved to Jair's face with little expectation; she wasn't disappointed. Her arousal began to die. Self-pity rose and washed over the last remaining embers of desire, leaving in its wake the worthlessness and isolation that she hated so much.

When will Jair tire of the rabbi's monotonous voice?

And then Aaron was there again, surrounded with his group of young men.

'Rabbi! Jair! Tell these young ones where in the scriptures the Lord is described as jealous. Something is pre-occupying me and I can't remember where it is,' he didn't even look at her when he spoke.

The rabbi quoted some of the scriptures and, enjoying being centre stage, began to expound them.

Then Aaron pulled Jair to one side, leaving the boys with the rabbi and Lila. She couldn't hear what he was saying. Then Jair reached over to her and pulled her in. Every muscle in her body tensed.

'Aaron's wife has not been very well lately. She has taken the children and gone to stay with her mother, where she can be properly looked after. These things happen, don't they? I didn't know what to do with you when you were ill in our first year of marriage. I was so glad your mother lived nearby. What would we have done without her?'

Lila nodded, her muscles relaxing again. She couldn't form any words in her mouth. It had gone completely dry. She instinctively knew what was coming next.

'Aaron has heard from the rabbi that you are a fine cleaner. He's wondering if you would be willing to come and clean for him while his wife's away. I think that would be good ... nothing is too much for an old friend, for a brother,' he smiled at Aaron.

'Of course, I would pay you,' Aaron said, one eyebrow rose as he brokered the unspoken deal.

'I wouldn't hear of it, Aaron,' Jair spoke for Lila. 'If we can't help our brother in a time of need, then what kind of people are we?' He clapped Aaron on the back and looked pleased with himself. He looked at Lila and smiled. The matter was settled.

Breaking boundaries; breaking faith; making a connection at last; obliterating loneliness; filling the aching void; sating the desire to be wanted: she knew the depth of deception that she was entering into as she looked into Jair's eyes and then into Aaron's. Jair's were oblivious, unseeing – happy at being in the position of doing a favour for a brother. Aaron's eyes were hooded, masking a glitter of greedy anticipation.

'When would you like her to come?' Jair asked.

'Could she come tomorrow?' The underlying strain in his voice was barely disguised. 'I will be there to let her in and show her what needs to be done.'

'That will be fine – she will come to you after she's collected water from the well.'

※　※　※

She had slept fitfully, waking with a jump every couple of hours. She didn't want Jair to know, so she had fought the restlessness that crawled down her arms and legs. Lying perfectly still she had eventually drifted off again into oblivion, until the next guilty lurch. At last the morning chorus began and slowly the patch of sky she could see through the shutters began to lighten.

She got up quietly and made herself ready to go to the well.

On returning, Jair was dressed. He met her at the door and helped her lift the huge pot off her head, as was his custom. Together they carried it to its corner in the kitchen. Lila first poured water into a blackened kettle and put it on the fire that he had kindled. Then she poured out water for Jair to wash with. She sat on the floor, watching him in silence as she had done so many times before. She heard the water beginning to bubble in the kitchen. As she walked, she felt like a puppet on strings being guided by unseen hands. She mixed some oatmeal with the hot water and added the right amount of honey. She brought it to Jair in a wooden bowl that he had carved some years ago. She watched him as he ate, passing him a cup of bitter black tea when he motioned for it.

'It's good we can help Aaron.'

Lila shrugged, 'He's a brother to you,' she forced a smile. *Do I matter so little to you? Do you have no fear that he might want me? Are you so naive?*

'Between you and me,' he sighed deeply, 'I think their marriage is not going so well. You know how some women seem to go into a deep sadness after they've had a child? Well I think that's what's happened to Aaron's wife after this fourth one.' He paused, then, 'I don't even know her name, do you?' he looked up at her quizzically.

She shook her head, hating the anonymous woman and feeling guilty at the same time. *You care more about her than you do about me.*

After he had gone, the battle within her grew to a frenzied height. She fidgeted around the house, kicking and flicking things with her feet, with her hands. Her frustration reached its peak as she hurled a clay cup against the wall, shattering it into pieces. A shard of it ricocheted off the wall, hitting her face and immediately she felt the warmth of blood pooling on her cheek. She burst into tears and grabbed a cotton cloth to staunch the bleeding, sobbing uncontrollably. She wasn't sure how much time passed while she rocked back and forth on the bed, but the bleeding had stopped and a calm descended on her.

She got up and brushed the broken pieces of pottery into a pile and scooped them into her skirt. She took them out to the back of the house and threw them into the basket of rubbish that leaned up against their back wall. Returning indoors, she dragged out the box that held her few articles of clothing and quickly put on the skirt and tunic she'd made.

You wanted to know if it was soft.

She pulled on her headscarf as she walked out the door, shutting it firmly behind her, closing down that part of her life.

It took longer than she had thought it would to get to Aaron's house. He lived in the wealthier part of the neighbourhood. Normally she would have felt intimidated by the signs of prosperity around her, but today she was a warrior woman going to get what she had been denied for so long. Anticipation made her bold and daring – an adrenalin rush to the head. She walked up the path to the door not looking left or right. She didn't understand her feelings – she didn't want to. She didn't want to know if anyone was watching either. She knocked once and he immediately answered the door, as though he'd been standing right behind it, waiting for her.

She came in and he closed and bolted the door. There was a momentary uncertainty between them as they stood still, looking at each other in the gloom. All his windows remained shuttered, even though the sun was climbing into the morning sky. She couldn't believe she was here, alone with him. She was trespassing. It excited her. Lila tore her eyes away from him and looked around the room. There were two low couches with cushions scattered across them and, in between, a rich Persian rug on the earthen floor.

Aaron explored her features leisurely. 'You've cut your beautiful face,' his voice was low and warm. He'd wanted to be with her like this so many years before, but how much sweeter to be here now, not with a girl, but with a woman giving herself freely to him. Her beauty, her need and brokenness, their deception – the combination was intoxicating.

Her hand went to the cut as she thrilled at being called beautiful. She traced the length of the gash with her fingertip. 'Yes. I was fighting with myself about coming here today.'

'Why fight?' his voice had dropped even lower and there was that grave huskiness again that created heat in the pit of her belly.

'We're reaching for forbidden fruit. I belong to Jair,' she replied, holding his gaze as feelings of terror and excitement crescendoed.

'Yes, we are reaching for forbidden fruit. But it seems to me that Jair cares too much about everyone else, when he should be looking out for his own. If you were mine, I would never let you out of my sight.' He dropped his gaze to look down at his hands as if something of interest lay there, then raised them unhurriedly, first to her breasts, then to her lips and finally to her eyes. Her heart was pounding. A slow smile spread across his face. 'We could stop now – not pluck the fruit. But then we'd never know what it tasted like. You would never know how desirable you are. You could actually clean for me. What do you think?'

His teasing lured a smile onto her lips. The thin scab on her cheek broke with the stretch of her skin and a tiny bead of blood formed at its edge. Slowly Aaron moved towards her. He cupped her face in his hand and wiped her cheek with his thumb. The sensation of his touch jolted through her. He slowly put his thumb to his mouth and pressed the tiny bloodstain to his lips, his eyes never leaving hers. She stared at his lips with her blood on them, as arousal washed away any remaining self-conscious restraint. They collided together like magnets let loose, slamming into the wall next to the door, their mouths locked. The ache she felt was beyond anything she'd experienced before.

'Don't wait … ' she heard herself gasp.

When it was over, they stood panting into each other's shoulders, Lila's left leg wrapped round Aaron's hips, fusing them together. Her leg muscles began to ache and she finally let him go. They both wove their way like drunks to the couch and collapsed together. Lila began to laugh and Aaron looked across at her curiously.

'What's funny?' He propped himself up on one elbow.

'Nothing … haven't felt this … ever,' as she spoke she could feel herself tipping over an edge into tears. She'd never given herself so freely, or been so connected. How could she feel guilty about this? But she knew she would. The tears rolled down her cheeks.

'You are wonderfully conflicted,' Aaron mused, reaching for her and drawing her to him. Her head rested on his chest and he stroked her hair as she sobbed out the fading pleasure. She curled up into his chest and allowed herself to believe she was safe.

✳ ✳ ✳

And so it had been. They lived from week to week for the next 'cleaning day'. They didn't look at each other after synagogue. The weeks blurred into a month and then another, with no word of Aaron's wife returning.

Jair would ask Lila how Aaron was, as he ate his evening meal of spiced vegetables and freshly baked flat bread. Lila would push against guilt and shame, making little comment, throwing in a fabricated detail of her daily chores to make sure the ordinariness of it would disinterest him. When Jair reached for her in the night, she found herself resenting him more and more. Any desire she'd had to connect with him was long gone. She'd given up trying to get what she needed from him and had found another way; an illicit, deceptive way. But that was part of its appeal.

※   ※   ※

One 'cleaning day', as she lay next to Aaron, he began talking about when he and Jair had been young and single.

'You know we made a bet that Jair would never be able to get you?' He turned his head towards her as he spoke.

Lila was surprised. She rolled onto her stomach and looked at him. 'What do you mean?' she asked.

'Well,' he paused, brushing the hair off his forehead. 'You had just had your Bat Mitzvah and Jair was lovesick for you. We used to tease him all the time.'

'I never knew that.' Little frown lines formed between her brows as she searched her memory.

'He'd been really ill when he was a boy and the doctors told his mother he wouldn't live very long. But he pulled through, to everyone's amazement. The illness left him frail and weak. An old woman came to see him once, on his mother's request. She was some sort of seer, you know.' Lila nodded. Not the sort of woman that the rabbi would approve of, but many still secretly consulted such people, as had generations before them.

'The old woman said that Jair would always be weak. She told him that the illness had cursed him with childlessness but that he would meet a powerful stranger who would break that curse one day. We used to tease him – it was cruel, I know, but we would tell him he could never be man enough for a girl like you. You were such a beauty, so vigorous and alive and he was ... well ... ' His voice trailed away and there was a long silence.

'Our family moved away but I heard that he had achieved the impossible and had secured your hand in marriage. I never really understood how he did it, but all credit to him, he did. If I could have stayed, I would have fought him for your hand.' There was that expression again in his eyes that she had seen outside synagogue.

Lila rolled onto her back again and closed her eyes. Why had she never known she was wanted? 'My father was tired of me.' She paused to push down the bitter feeling that rose in her throat at the thought of him. 'He wanted rid of me. The last of six girls, he was probably glad to accept any offer.' Her voice was flat, giving nothing away.

So Jair had been lovesick for her. Why had he never shown it? And all these years he'd known he was cursed? He'd never said. Maybe he hadn't believed it. Her throat constricted with anger.

❈　❈　❈

Then something extraordinary happened. She missed a monthly bleed, and then another. Unfamiliar waves of nausea washed through her on a daily basis. With growing amazement, she became convinced of the impossible. Excitement vied with terror in dominating her emotions. She didn't know if she wanted to tell Aaron or Jair first. She was mildly surprised at this realisation. She knew it was Aaron's, but that it would not be pleasing news to him. She found herself wanting to tell Jair – after all these years they had what they'd both longed for. Instead, she didn't say anything to either of them. It was her secret.

❈　❈　❈

At synagogue, Jair made his way towards Aaron who was talking with the rabbi. Lila followed behind him, to all intents and purposes a dutiful wife. They both stopped talking abruptly as Jair greeted them. Lila thought they looked slightly uncomfortable and a shiver of doubt ran down her spine, wondering if Aaron had confided in the rabbi. But then the moment passed; they were inviting Jair to come with them the following day to hear the teacher from Nazareth. This was becoming quite a regular excursion. The rabbi, Jair and Aaron had been up to the temple several times now with a group of rabbis and teachers of the law from the local area. They'd taken the young men from synagogue with them to listen to his teachings, argue with him and hopefully catch him out.

Lila knew from Aaron that there was a growing hope among the people that this teacher was the longed-for Messiah, the one who would come and establish Israel as a nation again and overthrow the Romans. He had great power over the people, with thousands flocking to him because of the miracles they'd heard about or seen him perform. The rabbis and teachers of the Law were very uneasy about his influence and wanted to bring an end to it. Aaron never seemed to remember what he said after going to hear him. Lila had asked him several times, but he was always vague.

On the other hand, Jair had also spoken of the new teacher. He found him fascinating and went into great detail about some of the things he'd heard him say. He also told her about the miracles he'd heard about and how he treated sinners with great compassion. He tried to disguise his excitement about the new teacher whenever the rabbi was around, as the mention of his name made him look like he was sucking a bitter lemon.

'What do you think, Aaron?' the rabbi asked, 'Shall we go up to the temple in the early morning?'

'Yes, let's do that,' Aaron replied.

Aaron then turned to Jair: 'Jair, can you go to work later and meet us at this end of Market Street just after dawn? We can all go up together.'

'Yes, that would be fine. I suppose you will be gathering the young men?'

'The rabbi will be doing that.' Aaron shot a look at the rabbi.

'Yes, yes … I will be doing that. Well, brothers,' he said, slapped both Aaron and Jair on the shoulders, 'we'll see what this supposed Messiah has to say for himself tomorrow!' With that, he began to walk away.

'See you tomorrow then, Jair.' Aaron turned to go quickly. He looked awkward. Then, almost as an afterthought, he said, 'Lila, I'd like you to come and clean for me first thing.' He smiled coolly at Jair, nodded at her, not meeting her eye. She nodded back, and touched the faint, anxious flicker in her belly under her shawl. The queasiness she felt whenever she hadn't eaten for a while was gnawing away inside her.

As they walked home, Jair was subdued. Lila was thinking of food. *I'll eat the lentil stew first, with bread, and then I'll have that yoghurt with figs and honey. I'll tell Jair soon. Soon. When? Soon. It will be our baby. Aaron's wife will come back and then everything will go back to how it was before. Only this time I will have no more shame. I will have a place, a purpose. The women will talk to me. I will have someone who will always love me. I will be worth something and no one will ever know but me. The empty years are over.*

With the child growing inside her, she no longer felt as needy and she sensed that Aaron had noticed the change. It was becoming more of an effort to show the same eagerness for him as she had shown at first. She had asked him last week if he had heard from his wife. They hardly ever mentioned her and she felt she was breaking an unspoken rule between them in doing so, but she had begun to want this faceless woman to come back.

Aaron had looked at her oddly, hesitated and then said that she would probably be returning at the end of the month, which was now only two weeks away. An uncomfortable silence had followed, as neither knew what to say to the other. Aaron eventually broke it with a shrug and a playful smile as he reached for her.

'We've not much time left, my goddess of love. Let's make milk and honey while we can, eh?'

❈ ❈ ❈

Lila arrived at Aaron's door as dawn was painting the sky, feeling nauseous and knocking only once. She didn't have to wait long. As soon as the door was closed, Aaron grabbed her, pushing her up against the wall. In his eagerness, he even forgot to bolt the door.

'Give me a moment,' she protested, forcing a laugh.

She pulled off her headscarf as he bit her neck. She pulled the scarf hard to get it free from under his chin. 'Ouch! What's the hurry? Why so eager ... have you really missed me that much?' Lila tried to hold him back from her, but she recognised the look in his eyes. She'd seen it in her father's. It told her that she was an object to be used and she had no chance of stopping him. She felt unnerved and tried to duck under one of his arms but he caught her round the waist and pulled her with him to the couch. She tried to gain a bit of space between them by pushing on his chest. She wanted to try and look into his eyes but he was on top of her, pinning her wrists above her head with one hand. She was a little girl again – helpless, silent, despairing.

'Come on little adulteress. Give it up, you know you want to,' he was breathing hard, his face flushed. His other hand worked at pulling up her skirts.

'I don't want to, Aaron. Stop it! You're scaring me!' She didn't like being called that name. It was very different from 'goddess of love'. Panic constricted her throat at this change in him.

'You're singing a different tune. You couldn't wait to have me at first. What did you say to me? Don't wait?' He was pushing her legs apart forcefully, his breathing rasping in his throat. She tried to get her knees together and push him away, but her muscles went into spasm.

The connection she thought she'd had with him had been a mirage. As it shattered, she broke away, detaching herself from what was happening.

He hasn't even taken his trousers off properly.

It was an absurd detail to focus on, but she focused hard on it as he worked viciously on her. She lay still like she used to with her father, wishing herself into nothingness.

The room suddenly exploded with light and a loud bang, as the door hit the wall with force. Shouting men filled the room. Aaron pulled away from her abruptly and stood up in one swift movement, his long shirt falling to his knees.

Lila was left stunned, lying on the couch, legs apart, skirts up round her waist. Men were swarming round Aaron, leering at her. She grabbed at her skirts and pulled them down, sitting up as shock turned to terror. She began to tremble as she looked at their faces. She recognised them all: they were her neighbours ... they were from synagogue. The rabbi came in, followed by the Pharisees, his face reddening with anger as he struggled to repress his own lust. He took an authoritative stand inside the door with his hands on his hips.

They will kill me ... they'll stone me ... my baby ... my baby won't ever get to live ... oh God, oh God, oh God!

She looked up at Aaron, pitifully hoping he would fight to defend her. Shock ricocheted through her as she looked into his eyes. She saw him disentangling himself from her, like a cobweb he'd got caught up in. His eyes hardened and grew distant. The men were getting themselves into a frenzy of lust and religious fervour. Their voices were blurring into one big roar in her ears as darkness began to creep in at the edges of her vision.

Breathe. Breathe deeply. Don't go unconscious. You don't know what they will do to you if you do. Breathe ... breathe ...

She sucked in air through her nose and slowly let it out through her lips as the shaking grew stronger in her legs.

'Woman, you have been caught in the act of adultery, the punishment for which is death by stoning,' the rabbi said, his voice rising, thick with emotion, above the voices of the other men. She looked up at Aaron again, reaching out for him one last time, but he wasn't there.

Woman? You've known me since I was born. You did my Bat Mitzvah ... you know my name!

'Aaron,' she whispered. Then louder, 'Aaron!' A sudden convulsion ran up through her torso and she vomited on the Persian rug. Someone spat on her, cursing her, cutting her with each cruel syllable.

The rabbi was arguing with some of the men nearest him. 'You will not stone her now!' he shouted. 'We are taking her to the temple where the man of the moment will decide her fate. Let's see what he makes of this!' he pointed his gnarled finger at Lila.

'You two – get a cloth and clean up this mess,' he ordered to two of the younger men, pointing at the vomit.

'You – get the woman and let's go.' He shoved one of Lila's neighbours towards her. He was a friend of Jair's. They often played cards together under the tree outside their home. Lila knew his wife. She would smile sympathetically at Lila over the drying washing, but they weren't friends. Lila's childlessness kept this mother of three boys at a respectable distance.

As her neighbour got closer she could smell sour wine on his breath and his face was twisted with rage and lust ... it wasn't the face she knew. He grabbed her by the hair, dragging her off the couch through her own vomit, her legs weak and her groin aching. She was barely able to support her own weight.

'Get up, whore!' he roared. Lila screamed with the pain in her scalp. The scream was suddenly cut short by a fist hitting her under the ribs – winding her. She gagged and retched and gasped for air, hanging suspended by her hair from her neighbour's grasp. She felt another fist hit her shoulder, another hit her head, and another, and another.

She heard the rabbi shouting, 'Enough! Enough! Take her to the temple first.'

They were out of the house now, somehow her legs began to work again and she was able to push up enough to alleviate the stinging pain in her scalp. Her neighbour mercifully lost his balance as they went down the path from the house to the road and let go his grip of her hair. When he regained his balance, he grabbed her arm instead, pulling, then pushing her through the growing crowds that were forming in the street. Lila was becoming disorientated with fear. Voices were magnified and slurred. The ground moved like the surface of the sea. She realised she was bleeding because she saw drops of blood landing in her long shadow. She reached her free hand up to her ear and felt a deep wound just above it. What had they hit her with?

The crowd were cramming themselves into the narrowing alleyway that joined Market Street from their sector of the city. As they came to the mouth of the alley, Lila remembered the conversation Aaron and the rabbi had had with Jair: 'See you at the beginning of Market Street,' Aaron had said. Was this all planned? Her mind recoiled from the thought. She frantically tried to see ahead through her hair, fear causing her to backslide against her neighbour.

Then she saw him: the familiar pale skin; the sharp edge of the nose; the close-set eyes looking on, concerned, bewildered and curious. A fresh convulsion wracked her body and she vomited again.

What have I done? What have I done? The words formed on her lips but only bubbles of saliva and acid came out.

'Jair!' shouted her neighbour, slurring the 'r' at the end of the name and pointing with his free arm. 'Jair – look what we have found!' Some of the men ran ahead and grabbed him. He was still oblivious of the devastation that was about to descend upon him.

'What's going on?' she heard him say in a shaky voice. She knew he would never have colluded with the humiliation of anybody. He had always rejected invitations by the more zealous members of synagogue to be part of punishments of women said to be breaking the law. She knew he would hate this spectacle before he even understood its impact upon his own life.

'It's your wife! She's been caught in the act of adultery – the whore!' roared their neighbour. Lila wanted to die. She stopped breathing.

Someone throw a rock at my head so I don't have to see his face!

But her face was grabbed by two sweaty palms, the rough nails digging into the sides of her head. Her face was shoved up towards Jair's. She did not raise her eyes, but she could see the wisps of beard on his chin: she was inches from him. She heard his sharp intake of breath. And then she saw something sparkle down his cheek. She watched the solitary tear hang on a hair of his beard and then drop, as if in slow motion, hitting the dirt and splattering across the edge of his sandaled toes.

She couldn't hold her breath any longer and let out a wordless howl.

He said nothing and eventually her neighbour yanked her away from him, disappointed with the lack of theatrics. He was cursing her under his breath as the crowd of men jostled them along. She felt a few of them pressing themselves up against her. They were aroused and thrilled at the opportunity to abuse a sinful woman in public. No one would care. She deserved it.

It seemed like forever before they got to the temple. The chaos around them was so great as they entered the Court of the Women that the rabbi was shouting and hitting people with a stick. In her mind, Lila hovered above the scene, distancing herself from the trauma. Memories of her grandmother bringing her here when she was a young girl drifted across her mind. She had liked listening to her praying; the rise and fall of her frail, old voice gently lulling Lila into daydreams. It had always been such a relief from her life at home. But images of her grandmother dissolved as the men around her grew more and more frenzied. The crowds of worshippers further away in the temple were now disturbed and curious. She saw people gravitating towards the scene, standing on tiptoe to try and get a glimpse of what the fuss was about. She found herself wondering how her judge was going to react.

She was jerked back down into her body by hands grabbing her and flinging her into an open space on the ground. She lay isolated, the figure of contempt, a stinking heap of bile, blood and dust, her hair sticking to her face where the blood had run. Her knees instinctively pulled up to her chest. There she lay in a foetal position, thinking of her secret; of Jair; of Aaron; of his wife – whoever she was. *This would never be forgotten, never forgiven. There was no way out, other than death.* Her mind recoiled from the thought.

My baby. My baby is innocent. What have I done? My baby.

Flies were landing on her to feast. The violent trembling that wracked her body didn't seem to bother them. 'Get up on your feet, woman,' she heard the rabbi shouting inches from her ear, his stick prodding her side. She obediently rolled onto her knees and slowly, painfully, stood up, her head hanging. She knew she was standing in front of the man for whom this had all been orchestrated. The pieces were falling together in her terrified mind. She was a pawn in their game, just like he was.

Then she saw Aaron in the periphery of her vision. She froze. He was standing in the same trousers and shirt he had worn when he had raped her. He was part of them, standing with his chest thrust out. He had his hands on his hips in a confrontational manner and she realised he wasn't even looking at her. He was focused on the man that she'd been brought to for judgement. Had he plotted it with them? Had he used her and betrayed her? With deep despair, she knew she had meant nothing to him. It had all been lies and he'd done this with no thought for Jair, his brother. Had they done all this to trap the Nazarene they were so jealous of?

A fresh wave of nausea shivered through her body. She doubled over and fell to her knees again, retching, but nothing other than a long drip of saliva came out, an elastic string hanging from her mouth. It swung there momentarily, catching the morning light as it dangled beneath her, making a dark line in the mud as it touched the ground. She dragged the back of her hand across her lips, breaking it as it clung to her knuckles.

She didn't raise her head to see her judge. She didn't want to. What would be the point? She sensed he was standing a few feet away. She heard the rabbi clearing his throat and banging his stick against the wall again. The noise began to die down around her. Soon a hush descended, stripping her of the cover of sound. Feeling naked, she wrapped her arms around herself.

The rabbi's voice rang out as he addressed the Nazarene. 'Teacher, this woman was caught in the act of adultery. In the law, Moses commanded us to stone such women. Now, what do you say?'

Even though she had spent most of her life pre-occupied in a spiral of self-pity, the horror of the moment had propelled her outside of herself. She found she was wanting to warn this man of their game. She willed him to guard himself.

Don't answer them. They want to trap you. They want to accuse you. They're jealous of you. They won't rest until they've ruined you. Whatever you say will be wrong. If you say, 'stone me', they'll report you to the authorities for breaking Roman law. If you say, 'don't stone me', you'll be breaking their law, as a friend of sinners. There is no way out ... no way!

Out of the top of her vision she saw movement. The man squatted down. She raised her head a fraction. He had his hands in the dirt and was writing something on the ground with his fingers. It wasn't what she expected – her judge in the dirt, down at her level. She was curious as to what he had written. The shivering stopped momentarily as she strained to see, but she couldn't. Somehow as she watched his fingers moving unhurriedly through the dust, her heart rate slowed. Watching the movement of his hands soothed her.

The silence hung over them. He had made no reply to the Pharisees and they began to harangue him, goading him into saying something – anything. The man slowly stood up, looking around at them all. In a strong, clear voice he said, 'Let any one of you who is without sin be the one to cast the first stone.'

Lila's head involuntarily jerked up. She could feel ripples of offence run through the men around her as they began talking amongst themselves. Realising she was looking directly at him, she cringed and lowered her head again. But in that split second she had seen a look on his unassuming face that arrested her. She recognised empathy – compassion – but there were other things there she was less sure of. Was there anger, anguish, frustration? She wanted to look again, but didn't dare. She turned slightly to see out of the corner of her eye the effect these words had had on Aaron. His hands were no longer on his hips – they hung at his sides limply, his chest no longer thrust out. She could see the bodies of the young men around him turned towards him, uncertainly questioning.

Is Jair here? Has he heard this? Her eyes darted about trying to see without raising her head too high.

There was movement in front of her. The judge was stooping down again. It was as though this was the more important place for him to be. He entered her small patch of ground once more, digging his hands into the dirt that she was covered in.

Why would you want to be down here with me when you are free to be up there with them? She watched the crown of his head in bewilderment. On impulse, she inched towards him on her hands and knees, somehow knowing she would be truly safe with him. The men were in disarray, deflated and nonplussed, shuffling their feet uneasily. They had come for a showdown but there was none.

Slowly, one by one, they began to back away through the crowd, the older ones first, until Lila was left alone with him. He reached over to her gently and lifted her chin with a dusty finger. She looked him full in the face. She couldn't look away. His dark eyes engulfed her. Fierce, tender, compassionate. He slowly stretched out his other hand to her. She took it and he helped her to her feet. She was exhausted, drained of all emotion; a limp sail. Her self-consciousness gave way to deep stillness as she searched his face, the trauma gradually evaporating from her like a passing mist.

'Woman, where are they? Has no one condemned you?'

Woman. How differently he says it. Woman ... not an object ... not a possession ... can he see good inside me, inside of this mess?

'No one, sir,' she whispered.

'Then neither do I condemn you,' the judge said. 'Go now and leave your life of sin.' The inflection in his voice was so fierce that everything in her wanted to do what he commanded. She stood transfixed. A burning sensation coursed through her from the top of her head down into her guts: forgiveness – love – goodness – dignity.

'Make me faithful,' she whispered. He smiled slightly and nodded. She was safe. She was connected.

2. SEEIN(

The prophetess

Grace looked at Chloe expectantly. 'So you read my story? What did you think ?'

They were sitting in Chloe's living room again. She still hadn't ventured out much. A tissue box sat empty beside her on the sofa. She was quietly shredding the last wet, crumpled one; soggy bits were falling on the floor.

'I'm not connected,' she whispered as a wisp of tissue fell to the floor.

'Oh, Chloe,' she reached over and squeezed her friend's limp hand. 'You still are, no matter what. Isn't the promise that he will never leave or forsake us?'

She slowly raised her bloodshot eyes to Grace's. A fresh surge of self-recrimination overwhelmed her as she sobbed into her hands.

'Don't do this anymore, Chloe. Don't resist his love. It's like you'll only let him love you when you think you're good enough. But the fact is you were never good enough. None of us are. His love doesn't depend on you keeping the rules.' Grace was reaching into the ether for the right words.

'You don't understand, Grace,' Chloe said, anguish in her voice, 'If it weren't for the kids, I'd kill myself,' her voice rose dramatically, as she hit her chest and dug her nails into the skin. 'I hate myself for what I've done, but I hate myself even more because ... I still want him. Yes ... see, you didn't know that! I lie awake at night and think about his body touching mine. What kind of person am I that, regardless of the devastation I've caused, I'd still be thinking like that?' Red scratch marks rose across her chest.

ght of a verse she'd read earlier in the week, *Though evil is
r mouth ... though you cannot bear to let it go ... yet it will turn sour
tomach.*

You're an ordinary human being, Chloe. We all have needs and drives
that can tear our world apart, left unchecked. That doesn't mean you're any
less loved than you were before you made a mess. Come on,' Grace urged
her in her blunt manner, 'let's pray. Let's ask God to come and meet with
you – to bring some good out of this.'

Despairingly, Chloe slid to the floor. Grace couldn't help thinking of
Lila. She brushed a tear away. Chloe closed her eyes, concentrating hard.
Haltingly, she began to pour out every squirming self-deception to the one
they both believed was invisibly present. Where else could she go?

After a long pause, broken only by several loud sniffs, she whispered,
'Please don't leave me, God. Help me in my weakness.' Her body shivered.
She lowered her head to the floor, turning her palms upwards.

They waited in the silence.

※ ※ ※

Grace stared into space. The room had grown dark while she'd sat at
her desk, oblivious of the passage of time. Peter had a deadline to meet
and would be home late tonight so she had blocked the afternoon and
evening out in her diary for sermon prep. But she hadn't been able to
focus, thinking about her time with Chloe that morning and the story
of Lila. Her Bible lay on her lap, opened at the passage she was to
preach on that coming Sunday. She'd managed to read it, along with two
commentaries that lay open on the desk beside her laptop, but that was
as far as she'd got.

A combination of sharing such a vulnerable moment with Chloe
and reading the short story about the old woman called Anna had
sent her mind spiralling back to the day when she had first given her
life to God.

She remembered coming undone like Chloe, kneeling with her Nana
at the communion rail of the old village church. She hadn't known where
else to turn. Going to her mum and dad was out of the question. But Nana
lived in Virginia Water, just on the fringe of west London, and Nana knew

about these things. Grace had jumped in her car and hurtled through the Saturday morning traffic in Richmond, crying all the way until she'd hit the M3. Only then had the tears temporarily dried up.

If Nana was surprised to see her, she hadn't shown it. She'd not asked questions, just held her and let her cry in the hallway. They had a cup of tea and Grace had haltingly told how she'd gone with a friend to a businesswoman's breakfast to hear a speaker that her friend rated highly. Grace hadn't known what to expect and was totally unprepared for what was to follow.

The woman shared her story of how she'd been led by God to work with prostitutes in Amsterdam. An organisation called YWAM had a centre there where they helped people come off drugs and change their lifestyle. The woman told story after story of redemption until there wasn't a dry eye in the place. At the end, she asked any women who wanted to give their lives to God to come forward and she would pray with them. Grace had found herself at the front, not really knowing how she had got there. The woman had asked her if she would like to give her life to Jesus Christ. This wasn't language that Grace was familiar with. The only religious experiences she'd had were formal affairs in school chapel services. Grace hadn't been quite sure what she meant by it, but was crying so hard that she had just nodded furiously. The woman had prayed a simple prayer and asked Grace to repeat each line after her. Grace had sobbed her way through it.

Her friend had been very excited and had uncharacteristically hugged her several times, but Grace hadn't really known why she was crying so much or what had really happened to her. She wanted Nana to explain it to her, because Nana would know.

Nana had smiled in her quiet manner and taken Grace by the hand. 'Let's go to the church,' she'd said. She was a churchwarden and so had a key. They'd let themselves in and she'd led her granddaughter in her bow-legged, old-lady-way up the aisle.

'This is where I have knelt and prayed for you all your life,' she pointed to a well-worn kneeler at the communion rail near the wall. 'When you were born, I knew that God was calling you to be His. My job was to pray you would hear his voice and come to him. And now you have – you've come home, my love.'

Grace knelt down where Nana's knees had made round indents in the velvet cushion and together they talked and prayed and cried, and talked some more.

That had been a holy moment. Just like this morning.

Grace sighed deeply. Nana had died that following week. Just died in her sleep. The old familiar sorrow swept over her and she slowly wiped a tear from her cheek. It was only then that she realised she was sitting in complete darkness. She reached over and switched on her desk lamp, lifting the Bible from her lap. She looked down at the passage again and read the description of Anna. So like Nana – only living long enough to see the thing she'd waited for all her life.

Grace opened her laptop and found her story of Lila. She read over the ending and felt excitement at how new story was forming in her mind.

'Anna means "grace" – Lila needs grace.'

She started to write …

❊   ❊   ❊

She'd felt connected once before – yes, a long time ago – right here, in this place. But when was it? She couldn't have been more than five or six? Memories of her grandmother came flooding through her mind again: grandmamma rocking gently to the rhythm of her whispery prayers; grandmamma, small and wrinkled like a soft prune; grandmamma, safe and loving, the only one who really cared. They had spent many happy hours here – the only happy memories Lila had of her childhood, as fleeting as it was.

As she stood in the temple courts, looking at the man who had saved her life, her grandmother's joyful face grew more vivid in her mind. It was clear that she was praising God in the way that she often had done, hands lifted, eyes closed, head thrown back, a gentle smile curving her mouth. Realisation dawned on Lila: she remembered – was it the last time they'd come to the temple together? The last time before … before … she'd tried so hard to forget.

❊   ❊   ❊

Lila always woke early to be ready for grandmamma. She'd brush her hair and firmly plait the wild curls into an orderly row at the back of her small head.

She was tired. She was always tired. She never slept well, dreading the sour smell of old sweat and cheap wine that dragged her into awareness of her father's presence.

Thankfully he'd not come last night. But still she'd been gripped by fear several times, lurching into wakefulness, with her heart hammering in her chest. It took so long to go back to sleep again.

She rubbed her eyes and waited by the door. When she heard the three light taps that grandmamma always made, she stretched up on tiptoe and silently slid the bolt back. She lifted the latch and pulled the door open, wide enough to let her slight body slip through. Her heart lifted as she looked into her grandmother's face. She closed the door behind her, listening for the click of the latch, a smile tugging at the corners of her mouth. She was free.

They walked in companionable silence, hand in hand through the narrow streets of Jerusalem, lit by dawn's light. Lila always felt a tingle down the back of her neck with the first glimpse of the temple bathed in new sunlight. She would impulsively squeeze grandmamma's hand and swing their arms a little.

Everyone at the temple knew grandmamma; she was always there. The priests treated her courteously, often taking time to sit and talk with her. Lila wondered why. She was only a little, old woman. Mama had told her that grandmamma was considered to be a prophetess and that's why the priests would sit with her and ask her questions sometimes. Lila wondered why mamma wasn't devout, like grandmamma, but she knew better than to ask; she'd been at the mercy of mamma's vicious temper too many times.

Once, Lila had mustered the courage to ask grandmamma why mamma was always so angry. She had said, 'She loved her father too much, and he her. She was our only child. I suppose we spoiled her. When he died, she was only six – the same age as you are now.

She never really recovered from losing him, poor thing. I devoted my life to trying to make her happy after that, but nothing worked. She turned down several suitors that I thought would have made her happy, and settled for the one who was larger than life, who promised much but has delivered so little.' Grandmamma sighed heavily.

Lila didn't talk about her father to grandmamma. It was wrong to speak disrespectfully of your parents and anyway, she hadn't wanted to make grandmamma any sadder than she already was about mamma's life.

'God has been a husband to me all these long years, and a father to her, but she will have none of it. It breaks my heart ...' grandmamma said, wiping the corner of her eye with her black shawl. Lila wished fervently that mamma could be like grandmamma. But wishing never did any good.

'Shalom,' grandmamma said to an old man seated on the top step near the Beautiful Gate, the entrance to the Court of the Women. It was Simeon. They were both surprised to see him there so early; usually he arrived after they did.

'Shalom, Anna, Lila,' he said, nodding solemnly in the serious manner to which Lila was accustomed. Lila liked him, but was in awe of him. She had never seen him laugh or smile in all the time grandmamma had been bringing her to the temple. He was very holy. Being near him made her want to walk on tiptoe.

'What brings you here so early?' grandmamma asked.

'The Spirit of God would not let me sleep,' he said, pressing his chest with his hand. 'I don't know why,' he frowned, 'but my heart keeps racing.'

'Perhaps today we will see the Lord's Christ?' grandmamma smiled. On hearing this, Lila felt her heart mysteriously skip a beat.

'Perhaps ... ' Simeon gazed up at her with a far-away look in his eyes.

As they climbed the last steps and made their way past Simeon, Lila tugged at grandmamma's shawl, 'Who is the Lord's Christ?' she asked.

Her grandmother stopped walking and looked down into Lila's

young face, 'He is the one who will bring redemption to Jerusalem.'

'What's redemption?' Lila asked guiltily, knowing she should understand these things by now.

Her grandmother smiled, sensing her granddaughter's discomfort. 'It's good to ask questions, Lila. Too many ask too few, in my view.' She stroked Lila's cheek with one finger. 'Redemption is like what happened when uncle Benjamin's ox got loose and gored their neighbour. Do you remember that?'

Lila remembered it well. News of it had quickly spread from the small town outside Jerusalem into the neighbourhood where they lived, inside the city walls. It had been at the height of summer and somehow the ox had got out of his stall, probably driven by heat and thirst, and had gone ambling over to the next-door neighbour's plot of land in search of water. Uncle Benjamin's neighbour had reacted badly on seeing the enormous animal and had begun shouting at it. The animal had charged. It had ended badly for the neighbour.

According to Jewish law, uncle Benjamin and the ox should have been stoned to death for the death of the neighbour, but because it was an accident – he hadn't wanted his ox to kill his neighbour – uncle Benjamin was legally allowed to pay a sum of money instead of being put to death.

'Well, uncle Benjamin redeemed his life – he paid a sum of money that meant he didn't have to be put to death. When the Lord's Christ comes, he will save his people from their sins – all the things that deserve death. He will pay a price for us – he will redeem us, ransom us, so we will be free.'

'How will he do that, grandmamma?' Lila asked.

Grandmamma looked up through the gate, into the Court of the Women, and on up to where the sacrifices were made, on the altar in the priest's court. 'I don't know, my love ... I don't fully understand it myself. But goodness knows, we need a saviour.' She looked back down at Lila and put her arm around her shoulders affectionately. 'Come, little one, let's find our spot in the sun, shall we?'

Lila wasn't satisfied with this answer but obediently went

with her grandmother through the Beautiful Gate. They came to the trumpet-shaped receptacles for the temple offering and grandmamma stopped and put some coins in. Then they moved on, into the Court of the Women. They made their way to the far wall, near the steps that led up to the priest's court. It was their usual place where, any minute now, as the sun rose in the sky, sunlight would pour down upon them. Lila settled herself close to grandmamma, leaning her head against her chest, eyes closed, waiting for the wave of warmth to wash over her face. It was God's presence, grandmamma said – God's presence pouring down on them.

It was glorious, as ever. Lila absorbed the golden warmth like a sponge as it made red splashes and patterns on the insides of her eyelids. Grandmamma began her lilting prayers that Lila could hear through the folds of her shawl. She often drifted off into peaceful sleep at this point – the only peaceful sleep she ever had. Today was no exception – she floated away on the undulating rhythm of worship.

Lila woke with a dry mouth and pangs of hunger. She sat up and looked at her grandmother. She had her eyes closed and was still lost in prayer. Lila wiped sleep-sweat from her face with her headscarf. She looked around at the crowds of worshippers that had grown in number as the morning wore on. She opened the little bag that grandmamma always brought; inside were some plums, bread and a skin of water. Lila drank first and then ate a small cake of bread. Grandmamma must have baked it before she'd come this morning; it was fresh and sweet.

Lila liked to play a people-watching game as she sat and looked on at the comings and goings of the temple. She would imagine what kind of work people did, where they lived and whether they were happy or not. Sometimes she would wander around the court and listen in to their conversations to see if she had been right about them. She looked round for someone interesting to begin with. No one captured her imagination. Her eyes wandered up the steps to the entrance of the priest's court. She would love to go in, but would never be able to. What wonders occurred in there while the priests sacrificed to God? In her mind she went even further, to the sanctuary, to see it for herself, even peek past the thick curtain that grandmamma had told her about. It hung there to separate the people from the presence of God; God was too holy for people to see – they would die if they did.

As she daydreamed about the mysterious God who hid behind a curtain, a curtain she would never see, she noticed a man coming out of the priest's court. He was carrying a baby in his arms. He approached a young girl who had been waiting at the entrance and placed the baby into her arms. They both seemed absorbed in the child. Lila watched them as they began to slowly make their way down the steps into the Court of the Women. She noticed the father's hands; they were rough and calloused – *a farmer or a carpenter,* she thought. The mother looked so young. Lila wondered what age she would be herself, when she had her first baby. They looked comfortable with each other – as if they'd been through some difficulties together that had bonded them. The father looked like he was a good man. Lila didn't know much, but she knew a bad man when she saw one, and this man was definitely not bad, she decided. There was something about the way he was looking at his wife that made Lila want to know more about them. What had happened that had drawn them so close together? What was the man feeling towards his wife? It looked like this was their first child. It must be a boy; the father must have taken him to be consecrated to God and to offer a sacrifice at the altar.

The couple stopped halfway down the steps. The noise of a commotion ahead had distracted them from their child. Lila turned her head to see what they were looking at. She saw Simeon making his way across the court, followed by a crowd of people. He was gesturing with his hands excitedly and shouting, 'I cannot believe what my eyes are seeing!'

Grandmamma had stopped her prayers and was leaning forward, shading her eyes from the sun to see what was going on. When she realised it was Simeon, she struggled to her feet. Simeon came to the bottom of the steps and raised his arms to the couple, beckoning them towards him.

They approached hesitantly until they were on the bottom step in front of him. Lila stood up too, enthralled with the unfolding drama and took hold of grandmamma's hand. She noticed that it was trembling slightly. For the first time ever, Lila saw Simeon smile. This rarity was bestowed upon the mother. He asked if he could hold the baby. She allowed him to take the child in his arms and the minute he held him he began praising God:

'Sovereign Lord,' he cried, looking down in wonder at the sleeping child, 'as you have promised, you now dismiss your servant in peace. For my eyes have seen your salvation, which you have prepared in the sight of all people, a light for revelation to the Gentiles and for glory to your people Israel.'

When he looked up at the parents, Lila could see tears in his old eyes. The mother smiled shyly at Simeon as he put her child back into her arms. Then Simeon reached out his hands, placed them on their heads and blessed them. The couple humbly accepted.

As he dropped his shaky hands from their foreheads, he spoke in a heavier voice: 'This child is destined to cause the falling and rising of many in Israel, and to be a sign that will be spoken against, so that the thoughts of many hearts will be revealed.'

The mother looked up at the father and then down at the child in her arms. Lila wondered what she was thinking. Simeon leaned in and said quietly, so Lila had to strain to hear, 'And a sword will pierce your soul too.'

Lila knew somehow that the mother had heard this before. She didn't look shocked or upset, she just accepted it like it was a bewildering gift that was somehow familiar, but she wasn't sure what it was for.

Grandmamma let go of Lila's hand and went up to the little group. Simeon saw her and nodded his head solemnly. He turned to the couple and said, 'This is Anna, the daughter of Phanuel, of the tribe of Asher. She lived with her husband for seven years and then became a widow until now. She is eighty-four years old. She never leaves the temple, but worships here night and day, fasting and praying.'

'I have been looking forward to the redemption of Jerusalem all my life.' Anna's voice shook with emotion. 'May I?' she asked, holding out her hands.

The mother looked at her husband who nodded and smiled at Anna, his ringlets bobbing gently either side of his bearded face. The mother lifted the baby into grandmamma's arms. She began to cry softly as she gazed down on him. 'I cannot believe what my eyes are seeing ... ' whispered grandmamma. Lila began to cry too, not because she understood, but because grandmamma was crying – she loved her so much, she couldn't help herself. She nestled into grandmamma's side and stood on tiptoe to catch a glimpse of the baby's face. She was disappointed – he wasn't especially beautiful, nor was he glowing as she had imagined. He was just ordinary. She looked up at grandmamma questioningly, but the old woman was unaware, she was caught up in worship.

Lila gazed at the peaceful, round face of the child. What lay ahead of him? How would he redeem Jerusalem? A feeling of awe crept over Lila's small frame. The more she looked, the more connected she felt. She wasn't sure what to, but she felt safe, like she belonged and was important, and felt like everything was going to be all right. The wonder didn't ebb away when grandmamma handed the baby back. The old woman lifted her hands, threw her head back and praised God. Lila felt it – an inexplicable joy.

The couple looked at Anna and Simeon with genuine gratitude and quietly excusing themselves, making their way through the small crowd that had gathered, towards the Beautiful Gate. Lila watched them go, wondering where they lived.

Grandmamma turned to Lila and hugged her tightly. 'Oh Lila, my love, we are blessed to have been here today. Who would have thought that God would choose us to see his anointed one?'

Lila said nothing, savouring the wonder.

Grandmamma spent the rest of the day talking to people in the Court of the Women. Lila had never seen her so gregarious. She was telling everyone about the child. Eventually, she seemed to give in to the tiredness of old age. She came and found Lila by the wall and sat down heavily beside her. 'Do you want some water, grandmamma? You haven't had a drink all day.' Lila reached into the bag and lifted out the skin of water, holding it out to Anna.

'No, my love … I have had food and drink today that I have longed for all my life,' she sighed putting her head back against the wall, exhausted and content.

Lila uncorked the nozzle and drank deeply. She put it back into the bag and rummaged around for a plum. 'Do you want a plum?'

'No, Lila,' grandmamma said in a whispery voice. 'I'm tired now … let me rest.'

Lila studied her grandmother's profile, lit by the afternoon sun. Her wrinkles seemed deeper because of the shadows. She watched as shallow breath blew a wisp of silvery hair that had escaped from under her shawl. It moved gently backwards and forwards. Lila liked the way the light caught the silver. She put the plum to her mouth and turned to watch the afternoon worshippers milling around. Grandmamma's head slowly lowered and rested onto Lila's small shoulder.

❀ ❀ ❀

Lila came back to the present with a lurch. She couldn't go any further in the memory; it was too painful, too devastating – even worse than what she had endured today. She had never recovered from that loss, from that realisation that her beloved grandmama had gone without saying goodbye. She felt like she was six again, standing in the Court of the Women, but this time it was before a man, not a baby; a man in whom justice and mercy had met, like two rivers, and tumbled down in a waterfall over her.

Could it be? Could he have been that baby – the Lord's Christ? She looked at him again – he was not glowing, he was not particularly striking. But he had rescued her. He had been her saviour today. Her grandmother's words reverberated in her mind: ' … but goodness knows, we need a saviour.'

Grandmamma's beloved face slowly began to fade from her mind. Tears caught in the back of Lila's throat and she let out a sob. Jesus was looking at her with a smile in his eyes. He nodded his head, as if answering her unspoken questions. Then she flinched, feeling an arm around her shoulders. She looked up to see who would dare touch her in such an intimate way in so shameful a situation. It was Jair. He must have been standing behind her all the time. At this, her legs crumpled beneath her and everything went mercifully black.

3. WEEPING

The women who mourned

Grace was asleep when Peter got home. He crawled into bed beside her and at his touch she woke with a jump.

'Oh, hello, darling,' she mumbled.

'Hello, my gorgeous Grace. How was your day?' His hand curled round her waist and pulled her to him.

She interlaced her fingers with his, pressing his hand against her flat belly, 'It was good ... no ... it was better than that; it was profound. How was yours?' she asked, nestling into him.

'Dull as dishwater,' he complained and kissed the back of her neck. 'Fancy doing something profound now?' She could hear the smile in his voice. 'You really should share some of that profoundness around, you know. It's not fair that I have to spend most of my waking hours with a bunch of jumped-up wannabes and their massive egos, when all I want to do is be with you.'

'You say the sweetest things,' she murmured, rolling over, wrapping one long leg round his hips and kissing him through her smile.

Much later, Peter quickly drifted into sleep, breathing deeply, but Grace lay wide-awake.

The sadness that she was usually able to keep at bay began to creep upon her. She tried praying, but the ache grew stronger; Nana had taught her how to pray. She tried a deep-breathing technique she'd learnt some years ago, but it didn't work tonight. On the back of the sadness came the memories that haunted her. Nana was the only one she had ever told. No one else knew her secrets. All hope of being free of them had died with Nana. She couldn't stop them from floating to the surface of her mind. She looked at the clock. It was 3.16am. She hated not being in control. She got up, went to the bathroom cabinet and found the box of pills that she kept for occasions like these. She took one, although she wanted to take two. *Saying the Morning Office with a slur would not go down well.* She smiled to herself, thinking of the condemning look Mrs Cooper would give her if she ever did such a thing. Ten to fifteen minutes and she knew she would be asleep again. As she waited for the chemicals to work their magic, she fielded the all-too-familiar images that made her sick to her core. One in particular kept coming to her tonight. As drowsiness descended, she could feel the choking sensation she dreaded.

'Oh Jesus ... help me ... '

❋ ❋ ❋

The next morning, Grace was in the church office printing off a service sheet for a funeral. She'd been chatting with the secretary about the deceased, a long-standing member of St Matt's. She'd just removed the sheets from the copier and was stacking them neatly together when there was a knock at the door. Predictably, the secretary didn't move. *Why do we employ her, I wonder?* Grace thought for the umpteenth time.

A man in an expensive suit pushed the door open.

The first shock was the smell of his aftershave. Grace immediately froze.

The phone rang and the secretary answered it.

He smiled. Big, white teeth against St Tropez tan. White streaks amongst the thick, well-groomed, gun-metal hair. Hard, calculating eyes barely disguised by a well-practised professionalism.

'Hello, I'm looking for the vicar. Have I come to the right place?' He was looking directly at Grace. The tenor of his voice sent a second shock wave through her torso. Grace looked at the secretary, but she was airily chatting on the phone.

She must speak. She tried, but couldn't. A rabbit caught in headlights. She tried again, this time managing to clear her throat.

Mild irritation crossed his chiselled features as he waited. Not a man who was used to waiting for anything. Did he recognise her? She saw the irritation turn to boredom. No.

'Yes, you have come to the right place.' She got back in control of her body, forcing her voice to be level and lower than normal. The secretary turned round, cradling the phone between her shoulder and ear and looked quizzically at Grace.

'Are you the vicar?' the man asked, incredulity and disdain crackling round the edges of his voice.

'No. We haven't got a vicar at the minute and the associate vicar is on leave. I'm the curate. Can I help you?' She realised she'd covered her throat with her hand, obscuring her dog collar from view. She let her hand drop to her side.

He stepped into the office, sliding his left hand casually into his trouser pocket. Grace felt claustrophobic. 'My wife and I have recently moved into the area. We've also just become parents for the first time and would like to discuss the possibility of having our son Christened here.'

Grace's heart sank, but she forced a smile, 'Congratulations, on both counts.'

'Thank you,' he reciprocated the smile. He was studying her. She wanted to run. 'Have we met before?' he asked.

'No, I don't think so,' Grace lied.

'There's something ... no, never mind.' He shook his head and laughed. 'James Martin,' he thrust out his hand and smiled charmingly. He had captured the secretary's attention. She had to ask the person on the other end of the line to repeat something they'd said.

Grace stared at his hand before moving towards him and taking it in hers, shaking it briefly. 'Reverend Hutchinson,' she said, quickly stepping back from him. She felt sick.

'I'm sorry for turning up unannounced. I've been working from home today and felt the need for a breath of fresh air. Thought I'd come and check out the parish centre of operations.'

Grace forced another smile, 'That's no problem. Lucky for you I was here. Normally it would be better to phone. We are quite a busy parish.'

'So it seems,' he looked ironically at the secretary who was leaning back in her chair still chatting on the phone.

Grace felt the first flush of anger emanating from her guts. She breathed deeply and, with fresh energy in her voice, said, 'We ask all those bringing their children for baptism to come for three baptism preparation classes before the service. We also ask that both parents attend weekly services in the run up to their child's baptism as well as afterwards. If you're happy to comply with these requirements then we can proceed.'

'Steady on,' he joked, 'that's a bit serious, isn't it?' He was trying to flirt with his eyes now.

She just looked at him steadily. No, he wouldn't recognise her. She'd had dark hair back then and she used to straighten it. She'd also worn coloured contact lenses. He would never recognise her in this context. She felt herself relaxing slightly.

He looked uncomfortable for the first time. *Not used to your charm not working?* Grace mused silently.

'Well, I'll have to pass that by the wife first before committing to it. But we both like your church building – it'll be great for the photos and all that,' he said, waving one hand dismissively. 'My wife came here as a child, you know.'

'How interesting,' Grace said in a tone that showed no interest whatsoever. Then to redress the balance she quickly went on: 'It would be good to meet your wife sometime soon – and your son.' These were the first words she'd uttered since he'd entered the office that she genuinely meant. She suddenly felt exhausted. 'Well, you know where to find us,' she said signalling the end of his visit.

'Yes ... yes I do.' He was studying her again, trying to find a weakness, a familiar foothold, something to manoeuvre with. 'Could I have the church office number, or your number?' he asked.

Grace picked up a church notice sheet and handed it to him. 'The office number is there,' she said, pointing. Sally is in the office between 9.00am and 2.00pm every weekday. We look forward to hearing from you.' *Please go now, please go now, please go now.*

'Thanks very much,' he said, turning away from her, his shoulders not as square as when he'd entered. As he walked out of the door, the secretary gave Grace a 'He is so hot!' look.

Grace made her way to the toilets and vomited as quietly as she could.

※　※　※

She was agitated for the next few days. Peter was baffled. She took a sleeping pill each night before going to bed – she didn't want to take the risk of waking in the night. She ate less and pushed herself beyond her limits on her cross trainer. When Trevor got back from holiday, she asked him to field any further enquiries for a Christening by Mr James Martin.

She went to visit her grandmother's grave on her day off. She hadn't been for a while. She took a single lily and placed it at the base of the headstone; they had been her favourite flowers. It was a sunny day with no one visiting graves nearby. She stood for a long time before she spoke.

'I miss you, Nana – who can I tell now?' She wiped her wet cheeks, one at a time with the back of her hand. 'Why can I help Chloe but not myself? How come I know just how to pray for her but not for me? I know you told me to forget the past and that God is doing a new thing. But the past has slapped me in the face ... I can't think straight ... '. Her voice trailed to a whisper as she saw movement at the edge of her vision. She looked to her right and saw an elderly gentleman slowly approaching. He wore a flat cap, and what looked like carpet slippers on his feet. Grace felt a slight tinge of resentment at the intrusion. She folded her arms and turned her body a fraction away to the left, to give herself the privacy she craved.

'Lovely day, isn't it?' he called cheerily.

She stiffened at this further intrusion, but politely turned round to respond: 'Yes, lovely.' She fished in her pocket for her sunglasses and quickly put them on to hide her red, puffy eyes. He came and stood right next to her. She couldn't believe his audacity.

'Is that your mum?' he asked bluntly.

'No, my grandmother.'

'Oh yes, I should have realised – the dates – you're much too young.' Grace made no reply. She was at a loss for words.

'Was she a believer?' he continued, unperturbed by her silence.

Grace looked startled at his language. 'Yes ... yes she was.' *Now go away!*

'Are you?'

Her head snapped round and she looked fully into his face for the first time. She was surprised to see there was no busybodyness about him. He was kindly and sort of 'twinkly' around the eyes, she thought. 'I am,' she said, eventually.

He waited.

She looked back at the grave, feeling herself softening towards him slightly, 'Actually it was Nana who prayed for me all my life and who taught me how to pray.'

Again no reply.

The constriction in her throat that had been there since meeting Mr James Martin subsided. Grace looked at the old man again. 'I'm Grace, who are you?' she asked, turning fully towards him and holding out her hand.

'Michael.' He smiled and shook it.

'Who are you here to visit?' she asked, feeling more calm than she had done for days.

'My family.'

'All of them?'

'No – not all.'

She wanted to ask more but felt it would be rude to pry. An aura of stillness surrounded him. She let it wash over her like waves over a sandcastle.

'It's good to cry.'

'Yes,' she replied simply, her defences down.

'They say there's a lake where God stores all our tears. They are precious to him, you know.'

'I like that,' she smiled and, this time, looked almost shyly at him. She noticed that his eyes were so bright, they seemed incongruous with his wrinkled skin.

'She will rise again and so will you. You're going to be okay,' he smiled. 'Your Nana is cheering you on from the finishing line.' With this, he tipped his cap at her, turned and started walking slowly away.

'Thank you,' she called after him, resisting the urge to call him back. 'Bye' she said lamely.

He raised a wrinkled, freckled hand, but didn't look back. She stood, staring after him. An insect flew into her cheek and she jumped, turning her head quickly to shoo it away.

When she looked back down the graveyard, Michael was nowhere to be seen.

※ ※ ※

All the way home in the car she felt wonderfully peaceful. She even found herself singing softly.

Upon getting home, cup of coffee in hand, she went to her desk and sat down, still thinking about Michael. Who was he? Such a lovely man.

She thought about a verse that said something about entertaining angels unawares. She looked it up – Hebrews 13:2. This sent her on a run of verses about angels. When she'd finished, she shook her head. No – it couldn't be. He was just a lovely, godly old man ... but the peace? The stillness?

Even though it was her day off, her eyes flitted to her diary that was open on one side of her desk. There was the sermon title in bold on Sunday morning's slot. She turned the gold edged pages of her Bible back to John 11 and started to read. She knew she shouldn't – that tomorrow was sermon prep day – but once she started, she couldn't stop. She read on into chapter 12. Her mind wandered over the stories, backwards and forwards. She flipped to other accounts in the gospels of the same events, jotting down some notes.

This isn't a sermon, she smiled to herself, this is just a wonderful story. Friendship, disaster, loss, grief and the impossible being possible. She had a few more hours to herself before Peter would be home from work, so she pulled her laptop towards her. She opened her writing file and began pouring all the emotion that, like mud stirred up from the bottom of a pond, had destroyed her clarity. That was until today. She felt that if she could put it in writing, she would be able to exorcise the pain.

'Lila, I have a friend for you ...'

'I divorce you. I divorce you. I divorce you.' He was writing the words as he said them matter-of-factly, the two reluctant witnesses he had brought into the house standing uncomfortably behind him. He folded the piece of parchment, straightened up and held it out to her. She looked at it helplessly. She willed her hand to reach out and take hold of it, but the useless thing wouldn't respond. With dread, she raised her eyes to his face and could see the ominous twitch by his left eye. He waited. Then suddenly he lunged at her, hitting her round the head with the note still clutched in his fist. 'Take it!' he roared.

She lay stunned on the floor, looking up at him. His nostrils were flared as he breathed hard from his exertion. He peered at her over his protruding gut, and then lifted his hand, letting the note flutter down like a wounded bird. It landed on her face. A cruel smile curled his lips as he gave her a kick. 'Now get out.' With that, he sauntered out of the house, shooing the witnesses out in front of him. Before they had even reached a polite distance, she heard him urinating on the bitter herbs she'd grown from seed and tended so carefully by their door.

Despair was like a dead weight in every muscle. Slowly she got to her feet, picked up her bundle of possessions and made her way out of the house. She'd tried to make it a home, but it had never been. It had sheltered the two of them but they had been strangers to each other.

He'd been kind at first, but after the fourth miscarriage things changed. She was his third wife. The first had died in childbirth (the baby dying with her); he had divorced the second after fifteen years of childlessness. It wasn't just the childlessness though – he had also fixed his beady eye on the lonely girl next door whose remaining parent was dying of diseased lungs.

She'd had a brother and sister, but there had been a serious falling out between them and her father. She never knew what it had been about, always being pushed out of the house by her sister when the arguments started. Her sister had sided with her brother and they had left the family home one dark day, leaving the young girl to care for her father alone. He had taken the unusual step of drawing up a legal document, using their neighbour as a witness, disinheriting her brother (and therefore sister also) and leaving the house to her. Their neighbour had watched and waited for his moment and, before her father was too ill, he had asked for her hand in marriage. He promised to care for her and signed an agreement with her father, taking ownership of her and their house. Her father passed away in the belief that his daughter would be well cared for. She was glad he didn't know the truth.

She made her way past him, out of the house. He spat on her. That was all.

She was in a daze and had no idea where she was going. If only she knew where her siblings lived, but she had not seen or heard from them in years. She wouldn't even recognise them if she saw them. Eventually, she found herself in an unfamiliar part of the city, by a well. The afternoon was drawing on and she vaguely hoped that soon some of the women would come to collect water. The sun burned down mercilessly upon her. The bruise on her forehead was spreading down to her eye. She longed to press a cool, wet cloth to it, but had nothing with which to draw water. She curled up pitifully in the lengthening shadow of the well and waited.

The next thing she knew, someone was shaking her. She opened her one good eye and saw that it was dusk. An older woman was standing over her saying, 'What are you doing here? Have you no home to go to? Where's your husband – your family?' She jerked upright remembering what had happened. Fear descended on her at the prospect of the impending night. She reached over and grabbed the woman's skirt.

'Take me home with you. I'll do anything for you – I'll cook, clean, sew – anything you like. Please don't leave me here,' she pleaded.

The older woman was looking her over impassively. 'So you have no home? No relatives who'll come looking for you?'

'No, my husband divorced me today.' She hesitated and then tried to swallow, but her throat was dry and the lie came out in a whisper: 'I have no other family.'

'No children?'

'No,' she said, hardening herself.

An understanding look crossed the older woman's face as she squatted down beside her. 'My, my, that's a good one,' she said, reaching out and gently touching the bruise. The girl winced. 'You can come home with me. I'm sure I'll find work for you to earn your keep. But let's see to this first.' She pulled off her headscarf and soaked it in her pot of water. The sensation of its coolness touching the throbbing bruise became one of the girl's treasured memories in the days and months that were to follow.

When the bruising died down and her face began to look normal again, the older woman gave her some basic chores to do. It was a shabby house in a poor area. Some of the women who lived around them were very brazen. They didn't wear headscarves and some even painted their faces. The girl began to realise what kind of place she was in and by what kind of woman she had been rescued.

'Are you a prostitute?' she dared to ask one evening as they ate their meagre meal.

The older woman laughed. 'Well thank you for thinking I could still pull it off.' She picked at her teeth with a long fingernail, tilting her head to one side. 'I used to be, but lately business has not been good.' She cupped her sagging breasts in her hands and looked down at them in mock sympathy. 'There comes a time when you just have to admit no one will pay to be with these.' She looked up at the girl and smiled. 'But they would pay to be with those,' she said, reaching over and lewdly flicking the girl's breasts, causing her to flinch.

'If you were to learn my trade, we could live much better than this,' she said, gesturing at the spartan room. 'I could teach you and I'd look after you, make sure they treated you right ... you know? We could make it work, you and I.'

The girl did not look convinced.

'It's not that bad a life. Some of the men, the regulars, can become almost like lovers. We just give them their fantasies and they give us what we need to survive. We don't have to put up with them every day, just for a short visit, and then it's over. And think – you'll be doing their poor wives a favour by sating their lust. That's one less thing those sad women will have to do.'

And so the conversation had gone on into the night. When the older woman was snoring, the girl still lay awake. How had it come to this? Her parents would turn in their graves if they knew. But it couldn't be worse than living with that beast of a husband, could it? She let hatred lock cold and hard in her chest. There was no other choice. Her jaw muscles tightened resolutely. She knew that she hadn't got it in her to dare to leave the safe-haven she'd fallen into. Anyway, there was something about the idea that appealed to her – it was something to do with power. She would be in control.

It was settled in her mind. In the morning she would start learning the oldest trade in the world.

※ ※ ※

The woman struck a deal with a previous client. Before the household steward came to inspect the girl, the old woman plundered her savings, which she kept hidden in a hole in her mattress, buying expensive perfumed oils and silks for her, and giving her prized jewellery for the girl to wear. She washed her, scraped, scrubbed and massaged her until every inch of her young body glowed smooth and sleek. She washed her hair, cut the faded ends, and brushed it until it shone, glossy black. The girl let herself enjoy the preparations. Neither woman spoke of what it was all for.

Inspection day finally arrived: the steward entered the single-roomed hovel, his crisp, white linen clothes standing in stark contrast to the uneven mud walls and earthen floor. But his cool, business-like eyes brightened when they fell on the girl sitting straight-backed, cross-legged and wrapped in red silk. She slowly rose to her feet in one agile move as the older woman had taught her. She turned, slowly unwrapping herself, until she stood naked before him, an insolent stare hiding her shame. She watched him look her over, a memory of her husband's loveless stare jarring her breathing.

'You say she's had only one owner?' he said quietly and distinctly.

'Yes – a useless husband,' the old woman spat. 'She is also apparently barren. What more could you want? Young, broken in and in no danger of pregnancy?' The girl's fists clenched. He turned, nodded slightly and smiled pragmatically at the girl, not meeting her eye.

'If what you say is true?' He raised one eyebrow questioningly towards the old woman.

'Have I ever lied to you?' she said, her wrinkles deepening on her forehead.

'If you are lying, we will soon know and there will be no mercy for you. But if you speak the truth, then she will do. How much are you asking?'

They had not talked about what they would charge – the girl had no idea what the going rate was. She could see the woman had given much thought to this matter; her face was masked ready to bargain. She glanced over at the girl, giving her the nod to cover up before she answered him. Relieved, the girl wrapped herself up in her silk. Then the haggling began.

※　※　※

The royal household called for her frequently. The old woman could have aimed no higher. She was to perform at parties held in King Herod's honour. Chuza, the King's steward, would usher her into Hasmonean Palace through the servants' entrance. He only spoke to her when it was necessary and he never touched her.

The first time was terrifying. The old woman had warned her: 'Play the part,' she'd said. 'It's not you doing it; it's a wild, fierce temptress. Maybe give her a name.'

The girl thought about it and decided to call herself Rahab after the historical prostitute who hid Israel's spies, enabling them to take the Promised Land. *Maybe this Rahab will lead me to my Promised Land?*

Surviving terror does strange things to people; it can fracture a personality. It had split the girl's in two. She presented a strong, confident harlot on the surface, skilled in the arts of erotic dance and massage with perfumed oils, but cowering in her shadow hid the vulnerable girl who had been married too young, who grieved for her family and her unborn children.

The old woman taught her how to make the oils, having turned her own hand to them when she could no longer make a living from her body. The girl was a quick learner and soon began experimenting, making her own infusions. She also discovered she was a natural at massage. She excelled in combining scent and sound: wrist and ankle bracelets jingling messages of slavery, hands deftly working each muscle group sensually and slowly.

Survival fuelled her drive to excel. But, to her chagrin, she also found herself beginning to enjoy her encounters in a perverse way. On the face of things she was independent, beautiful, young, and in demand for her skills. She and the old woman were doing very well. They moved to a bigger house at the nicer end of their road. They even had a room each and a courtyard where they grew their own herbs. But internally the vulnerable girl despised herself for what she had become. She had thought she would be in control but in reality she was not. Cravings for the comforting sensation of power overwhelmed her: the suspense, tantalising men as she danced; manipulating them into competing over her; the intoxicating sexual tension as the winner would lead her away from the crowd; the greedy craving for the next pouch of heavy coins. She had become a slave – abusing and being abused were her addictions.

I'm a disgusting thing that lives off filth at the bottom of the sea, she'd think sometimes in the middle of a loveless act. But it was as if it were coming from a detached observer. She had a recurring nightmare that she was sinking down in dark water, going deeper and deeper, not able to breathe, not able to scream. She would wake in a cold sweat.

❋ ❋ ❋

One evening, she was called to Hasmonean Palace and was instructed by Chuza to wait in an antechamber to the banqueting hall. She was beginning to wonder how much longer she would have to wait when a woman she had not seen before came in.

'Shalom,' smiled the woman.

The girl didn't know how to respond. No one ever spoke to her in a respectful manner. *She must think I'm one of the guests.* She returned the smile and hoped that 'Rahab' would play a convincing guest.

'May I sit with you for a while?' the woman asked, taking a step towards her.

The girl was uncertain, but shrugged and nodded vaguely, wrapping her flimsy silk shawl more tightly around her bare belly. She wanted to shrink away from her, but held her body still.

'My name is Lila. I'm a friend of the steward's wife,' she said as she sat down, her body turned slightly towards the girl. It was only then that the girl noticed she was pregnant. 'I have wanted to meet you for some time, but have never had the chance. What is your name?'

The girl looked at her in bewilderment. 'Rahab ... I'm Rahab.'

Why would she want to meet me?

'Rahab,' – she smiled again as if reading her mind – 'the reason I have wanted to meet you is that I have been praying for you.' She paused to let this information sink in. The girl's lips were slightly parted, her eyes wide. This was unfamiliar territory and she had no idea how to respond. An awkward silence hung between them. Lila looked away, across the room, and the girl could see her lips moving silently.

What's she doing? How does she know me?

Then turning to face her with a determined look, Lila said, 'I could be completely wrong about this, so please excuse me if I am, but several times when I have been praying for you I have seen an image of you drowning in the sea. I see you sinking down in deep water and you are terrified. I have been praying that you would be rescued. But then every time I've prayed those words, I have felt as if it is I that must come and rescue you.' She paused again, looking anxiously at her hands in her lap. She looked up questioningly into the girl's face and saw a look of shock and disbelief. She waited.

'How do you know me?' the girl asked in bewilderment.

'Joanna, the steward's wife, told me about you – just that you come and dance here for the guests of the King. I think you and I are quite alike – that's why I'm here.' Lila looked at the girl, a quizzical half smile on her lips.

'But the dream – how did you know about my dream?

'The deep water?' Lila asked.

The girl nodded her reply.

'Well, I have been following a teacher called Jesus of Nazareth. Have you heard of him?' Lila's confidence rose just by speaking his name.

'Yes, I've heard of him. They say he's a prophet of some kind? I've not heard him myself. Why would I? He wouldn't move in the circles I move in,' she looked down at her hands.

'Oh you are wrong there. He does move in your circles. He's known to eat with tax collectors and prostitutes.'

The girl was reeling. Several emotions scuttled across her features before she spoke. The last time she'd cried had been when they buried her father four years ago. She'd not shed a tear since – for any of her miscarriages, for the cruelty she'd endured from her husband or for the disaster her life had turned into. Panic rose in her throat as her eyes welled with tears. Her hand clutched at her neck.

Lila reached over and touched her arm. 'Are you all right? Can I get you a drink?' She rose quickly without waiting for an answer and crossed the room to a bronze tray that held a decanter of water and several ornamented goblets. The girl struggled fiercely to compose herself. She wanted to run, but her craving to stay and perform was still strong. She'd waited a whole week for this. She wasn't going to let this strange woman stop her now.

'I'm fine,' she said in a choked voice. She cleared her throat angrily, then said again more clearly, 'I'm fine.' She took the cup of water from Lila and drank it quickly. Lila sat down beside her again and watched her. 'It must be time for me to perform. I must go now,' said the girl. She made to move, but Lila took hold of her hand.

Why don't you care that you're defiling yourself when you touch me?

'Could I pray with you before you go?' She was smiling again and the girl couldn't cope with the warmth that was in her eyes. She obediently sat down and waited. Lila breathed deeply and closed her eyes. 'Father in heaven, please draw this daughter of yours to yourself. Please reach down and rescue her. Amen.' She opened her eyes to see the girl staring at her. 'I would love to introduce you to my teacher. Could I take you to meet him?'

'Not now, I have work to do,' the girl said stubbornly, pulling her pride and her transparent shawl more tightly around her. A bell was ringing in the distance. She stood up. 'That's my call. I'll think about what you've said. Thank you, goodbye,' she said hurriedly walked away, hips swinging, ankle bracelets jingling.

Lila felt deflated. She sat there for a long time.

※   ※   ※

'I am the good shepherd; I know my sheep and my sheep know me – just as the Father knows me and I know the Father – and I lay down my life for the sheep,' the teacher said to the crowd. Some religious leaders were arguing with him and his disciples because he had performed a miracle on the Sabbath. There was nothing like a good argument to draw attention. There were those who knew the person that had been healed, and there were others who'd witnessed the healing. News about it had spread throughout the neighbourhood because the man had been blind from birth. Excited thrill-seekers clamoured to get a good view, hoping to see another miracle. Lila was there with some other women, craning to see her teacher past the heads of angry men.

'What does he mean about laying down his life for the sheep?' Lila looked up anxiously at Joanna.

'I don't know. We'll have to ask him later,' her friend replied, standing on tiptoe as a man jostled in front of her, blocking the view. The atmosphere was getting tense. The Pharisees were getting angrier.

'Are you saying we care nothing for the flock? Who do you think you are?' one of them said, standing up as he raised his voice. 'Are we not the shepherds of Israel?' He looked round, raising his arms to his companions. There was a loud chorus of agreement. 'We work day and night to keep the people obedient to the law. We study the scriptures and follow the law! But you

– you break the law. You eat with tax collectors and prostitutes; you work on the Sabbath. It is you, not us, who doesn't care for the sheep!' he declared emphatically. Insults hailed down around the teacher.

'You're demon possessed – you're raving mad. Why should we listen to you?' The women tried to push past a shouting man, but there was no way he would let them through. He elbowed Lila in the side and she lost her balance, falling into Joanna who just managed to hold her. They retreated down an alleyway.

'Oh Father, don't let them harm him,' Lila prayed fervently as the teacher had taught her.

They waited. The women hugged each other as the noise rose to a crescendo. Then Lila looked up and saw the dancing girl standing a few feet away.

'Rahab,' she called. The girl looked over her shoulder and recognised Lila immediately. She reticently turned towards them with her head lowered. 'Peace be with you. How come you are here?' Lila asked. She reached out and pulled her in, smiling happily.

The girl raised her head uncertainly, not answering the question. 'What's going on?' she asked still looking back at the commotion.

'Jesus healed a man born blind and now the teachers of the law are angry that he did it on the Sabbath.'

'He did what? How? That's amazing. Did you see it happen?' The girl looked from one woman to the other, momentarily surprised out of her shame.

'Yes we were both there. Jesus put mud on his eyes and told him to go wash in the Pool of Siloam. When he did, he could see. He didn't know what to make of what he could see at first. It must have been such a shock for him. It's wonderful though.' Lila's face was glowing. 'It's wonderful to see you too! What are you doing here?' she reiterated her question.

'I live near here. I was on my way to the market.' The girl paused as a group of men walked past, led by a Pharisee. She knew him – he was one of her clients. She pulled her headscarf further over her face; Lila understood immediately. The crowds were beginning to disperse so the women moved out, pushing their way through to where Jesus and the disciples were.

'Come and meet the teacher. I've told him about you. Come.' Lila pulled her by the sleeve.

The girl felt uncomfortable. She stepped back from them, poised to run. But at that moment, he came into view, walking towards them. He was looking directly at her and she was rooted to the spot. She couldn't speak, emotion threatening to tear down her defences. Little beads of sweat formed on her upper lip.

As he drew closer, a wave of heat rolled through her. 'This is the girl I was telling you about,' Lila said to him. 'Rahab, this is our teacher – Jesus.'

'Her name is not Rahab,' Jesus said quietly, looking into the girl's eyes.

Lila started to correct him, but stopped herself.

'Mary,' he said. The girl's hard, beautiful face suddenly crumpled. To Lila's surprise, she fell at his feet, sobbing. Lila and Joanna knelt down beside her. Her headscarf had fallen onto her shoulders and Lila stroked her hair. Joanna had her hand on her back and was humming what sounded like a lullaby. The disciples and the other women had gathered round and were watching uncertainly.

Eventually the sobbing subsided and stillness descended upon the little group as if a portal had opened around them, connecting them to eternity. The girl lifted her head and stared with wonder into his face. 'How did you know my name?' she asked.

'We gave you that name before you were born.'

Bemused tears rolled down Mary's face. She didn't understand, 'But I am shameful,' she spluttered through mucus that was running down into her mouth. She dragged her headscarf across her upper lip and then buried her head in it.

'Forget the past. Look,' he said, reaching over to lift her chin, as he had done with Lila, 'see – I'm doing a new thing. Now leave your life of sin.' Then he placed his hand on her forehead. A jolt of power went through her and she felt an internal struggle, which subsided after a few moments. The cold hatred, the uncleanness, the filthy thoughts and compulsions all lost their grip. Her body shook and shivered for a while, like ground tremors following an earthquake.

Eventually, Jesus said: 'Joanna, Lila – stay with her.'

❊   ❊   ❊

The old woman threw her out. 'You ungrateful little whore! After all I've done for you, this is how you repay me?' She was rifling through Mary's things. 'Where's my necklace, and the ankle bracelets? Don't try and hide them from me. Give them to me now.' Her face was contorted with rage.

Mary crossed the room and lifted the rug. She felt along the floor until she came to the loose board. Her muscles were tensed for fear that the old woman would jump on her and try to grab everything she possessed.

'Ah, so that's where you hide it all,' she sneered. 'Now, give me what's mine.'

Mary handed over all the jewellery, but the money she kept. They'd already split her earnings. 'Give me the perfumed oils,' barked the old woman.

'No. I made these – they're mine.' Mary clutched the bottles to her chest.

'If it weren't for me, you would never have learned to make them. I gave you your first bottle – give them to me or you'll be sorry, you little gutter rat,' she yelled as she made to grab them.

'No!' cried Mary, moving towards the door. She couldn't give them up – making them had been the one good thing she'd done. She was much more agile than the woman and made it through the door and down to the lower level of the house, with shrieks and curses following her all the way.

'You filthy, disgusting sow! You selfish, lazy bitch! I welcomed you into my home, shared my bread with you. Get out! Get out! And never think you can come back here. You won't last a day without me, you hear – not a day! May you be struck down,' she shouted as Mary ran down the street, 'struck down with a plague!'

Mary broke into nervous laughter as she ran, the warm breeze blowing through her hair, her head scarf trailing behind her like a stream of red smoke. *I'm free – I'm free.* She ran all the way to Lila's house.

✳ ✳ ✳

Lila was finding it hard to move about these days. It was good to have an extra pair of hands around. Jair had been uncertain about having Mary live with them, but so much had changed since their encounter with Jesus. Jair finally agreed because he couldn't say no to his wife.

Jair had had every right to divorce his adulterous wife. He had stood, a broken man, for what seemed like forever in the temple that day, while Lila waited for her fate to be decided. Jair had carried her home with him, washed her wounds and tenderly held her, soothing her abused body until she finally succumbed to sleep. Yes – so much had changed. He had won her heart that day, and had given his to her.

'Another thing, Jair,' Lila was saying, taking quick breaths between sentences, 'she will help me when it's my time. And I'm going to need help after the birth with all the washing and cleaning. She will be as much a blessing to us as we will be to her,' she paused, eyes pleading.

'But she's been a prostitute – sold her body to men. What will the neighbours say if they find out? We've just moved to this neighbourhood to escape gossip in the last place! What if some of them have used her? What if she starts business up again – here, from our house? Can we trust her? Won't we become defiled?' His eyebrows were meeting above his nose in the way they always did when he became anxious.

Lila put her hand on his. 'Have you forgotten so quickly, my love? She is not so different from me. In fact, I was worse than her. I deceived, and betrayed, and stole, and hurt you – hurt you so deeply.' She couldn't help the tears that always welled up in her eyes when she thought about what she had done to him. She had grown up so much since that terrible day.

Jair looked grief stricken. 'Don't talk like that, Lila. It's all past, all forgiven. We've had a new beginning together with the teacher. This little one will be our baby – ours. I will raise it as my own. You know that.' He was stroking her cheek with the back of his forefinger.

'I love you so much,' she said, putting her hand to his face and drawing it to hers. She kissed him slowly with parted lips.

'When will Mary be back from the market?' he whispered.

She drew back from him a little and grinned. 'I think we might just have time for what you have in mind, my darling. Maybe you can bring me into labour?'

And that's just what he did.

※ ※ ※

Mary came back to find Lila squatting on the floor next to the couch. She was leaning on the edge of it, head hanging low, with Jair rubbing her back and looking frightened.

'Oh thank goodness you're here,' he said. 'Go get the midwife. Has Lila told you where she lives?' Mary nodded. She still felt awkward with Jair. She dropped the basket from her hip, scattering flour and figs across the floor. She picked up her skirts and ran as fast as she could.

In the middle of the night Lila gave birth.

Mary was overwhelmed with emotion that threatened to wrench out her innards. She thought of her four miscarriages, of the tiny things that she had not been able to sustain. They lay cold and nameless, secretly buried, under the bitter herbs she'd planted by her front door.

The midwife looked on peacefully, knowing this was another job well done.

Jair was surprised at the emotions he felt when the baby stretched out its tiny fingers and curled them round his.

Lila thought about the most precious thing in the world to her. She thought of how Jesus had been gracious to her and had taught her and Jair to be gracious to one another – to give what was not deserved, and to trust when they didn't fully understand. As she held her precious bundle, she thought of her beloved Grandmother who had first instilled faith in her. She looked at Jair and said, 'I would like to call her ... '

Jair spoke before she could, 'Anna?'

Lila cried and laughed, nodding her head.

✳ ✳ ✳

Mary was showing Lila her perfumed oils. The baby was lying asleep in Lila's lap as they sat cross-legged on the couch together.

'I didn't want to give them up. Making them has been the only good thing I've done with my life so far. Do you think I should?' She was turning one of the more beautiful alabaster jars in the palm of her hand, enjoying the cool, smooth surface and the luxuriant weight of it.

'They must be worth a fortune,' Lila marvelled. 'How many have you got?'

'Five,' she smiled. 'I want to sell a couple of them and use the money to make more. Do you know anyone I could sell through?'

'Jair would know. I can ask him. He'll be glad to know you're thinking of earning a living in a respectable manner. He was terrified you might start up your old business from our home,' Lila giggled.

Mary smiled sadly. 'Don't laugh about it. I feel ashamed enough as it is.'

Lila reached over and took her hand. 'I'm sorry ... please forgive me. I didn't mean it like that. I do know what you're going through.'

'How can you? You're a respectable, married woman with a beautiful baby girl. Your husband adores you. How could you know what I'm going through?'

There was a long pause. Mary clutched her bottle of perfume and stared miserably at the floor. The baby stirred and began mouthing for Lila's breast. She crunched up her little face and let out a high-pitched wail. Lila lifted her tunic and waited for Anna to latch on. She winced as the milk came down and then relaxed, settling herself more comfortably.

'She is not Jair's,' she said, gesturing to the half-hidden child with her free hand. 'I mean, she is now, but she wasn't.' Mary was stunned.

Lila went on. 'I committed adultery. Yes, me,' she said, looking at Mary candidly. 'Anna is the result – a bit like your perfumed oils, I suppose,' she smiled. 'How can something so precious come from something so terrible?' she mused, fondling Anna's pink hand in wonder. 'I got caught and they were going to stone me.'

She told her story, one sinner to another. They were both weeping by the time she finished.

'Anna will forever be a reminder to us that I did not get what I deserved. I got what I couldn't even imagine or hope for.'

'How has Jair forgiven you? He seems to love you so deeply – and you him?' Mary looked incredulous, wiping her face with her headscarf.

'He met with Jesus too. We have never been the same since. It was like spring coming to end an eternal winter for us.' She paused savouring the thought. 'We moved here, Jair found work and we are better off now than ever before. We only had a one-roomed house before. Now look at us – we can have you live here too!' She gestured to the stairs that led to the two bedrooms above. 'So we have never looked back. We've been following the teacher ever since.'

'What happened to Aaron?' Mary asked.

'I don't know, Mary. I keep forgiving him whenever I think of him, which unfortunately is often – Anna looks so like him. I hope he finds the forgiveness I have found. I pray for him. I pray for his wife often. I can never repay what I stole from her.'

Mary stared down at the alabaster jar in her hand. *She had got what she didn't deserve.*

She lifted the lid and raised the open neck to her nose. The heady scent brought a torrent of memories rushing through her mind.

Can anything good come from this?

❈   ❈   ❈

Jesus was going to Bethany, a small town outside Jerusalem. He'd made some friends there and asked Jair if he and his family would like to come along. They all felt privileged to be the only ones asked to accompany him.

Mary was nervous of meeting new people. She suspected they would be able to tell her previous lifestyle by some unconscious gesture or turn of phrase, or by the way she walked. So she was pensive as they made their way towards their host's home. She looked at Jesus out of the corner of her eye. He was talking to Jair about the book of Isaiah again. He was always doing this sort of thing – meeting new people, making friends. He seemed to have no fear at all of being rejected or unwelcomed by people. He was the most open, interesting and interested social person. She tried to calm her fears with the thought that, because she was with him, she would be accepted. But it wasn't really working.

As if he had become aware of her feelings, Jesus turned to her and smiled, asking, 'So, Mary, how has it been, living with these fine folk?' He gestured to Jair and Lila.

Mary was caught off guard. She pulled at her headscarf and darted a look at Lila. 'It has been wonderful, teacher. They are like family to me,' she said, blushing.

'Have you no family of your own?' he asked gently.

'None that I know of … '. Something in his expression made her go on. 'Well, I mean, I have a brother and a sister but I have not seen them for many years – since I was a young girl.'

'Why is that?'

Mary could feel the sadness and despair that had settled upon her the day they'd left making itself more comfortable round her shoulders and chest. 'I don't really know – I was too young to understand. There were many arguments between my brother and father. One day, my brother took my sister and left. I haven't seen or heard from them since.'

Jesus nodded quietly. 'Much sadness has come from that day.'

The way he said it distracted her from herself. She looked at him. He suddenly smiled broadly and his eyes sparkled with the pleasure of holding a secret. She was confused. 'Ah Mary,' he laughed, 'as long as you have the bridegroom with you, sadness cannot linger long.'

Mary wanted to tell him she still felt sad, but didn't.

They were walking between houses now, stepping over gullies and avoiding playing children. They came to a standstill outside a large house, with a high wall surrounding its courtyard. A tree generously bathed much of it in swaying shadow. Hanging branches trailed along and over the wall, dressing the cracked, baked earth in a rich pattern of green.

Jesus knocked on the wooden door that stood in the centre of the wall. It was nearing the time of rest. Perhaps their hosts were already sleeping, Mary thought. But then she heard the padding of soft leather on hard ground. She found she was holding her breath. The door opened slowly to reveal a smiling woman. She looked vaguely familiar.

'Shalom! Welcome to our home.' She spread her arms wide and bowed her head towards Jesus. As they entered, they removed their sandals and she knelt and washed their feet in a wooden bowl, drying them with a rough towel. As she did, she asked them how their journey had been and what news there was from the city.

A man came out into the courtyard, and when he greeted them, Mary felt another tingle of familiarity. She looked up at him. Something deep inside her had stirred and woken. She looked over at Jesus, whom the woman was anointing with oil in customary fashion. There was that secretive smile again. He then turned to embrace the man and, for a moment, they were lost in greeting one another. Then Jesus began introductions, starting with Jair and ending with Mary.

'This is Mary. She has been with us for the last few months. Lila and Jair have taken her into their home as she has no family that she knows of.'

Mary bowed her head and tried not to be overcome with emotion.

'And this,' Jesus said (and Mary could hear laughter in his voice), 'this is Martha, who has kindly opened her home to me and my followers this year, and her brother Lazarus.'

Mary's head shot up and her mouth hung open. She looked at Jesus, then Martha and Lazarus. Tears stung her eyes. They, in turn, were looking at her, equal astonishment forming on their faces as they watched her reaction. 'Is this our sister Mary?' Lazarus spoke first.

Jesus nodded, his eyes glistening.

Martha let out a cry and ran to Mary, flinging her arms around her. Lazarus walked hesitantly over to them. It was clear that he was not given to outbursts of emotion. He waited for Martha's angst-ridden howling to subside. Mary stood perfectly still, tears rolling silently down her cheeks. 'How has this come to be?' Lazarus asked.

Lila was rocking Anna in her arms hoping she wouldn't disturb this precious moment by demanding to be fed. Jair was standing still, lips parted and eyebrows raised in surprise. He had not expected this.

Jesus said, 'You tell them, Lila – it is because of you that Mary is with us.'

Martha lifted her head from Mary's shoulder and held her young face in her hands, wiping the tears away with her thumbs. 'I thought you looked familiar. A day has not gone by that I haven't thought of you and our father. Come out of the sun. Let us sit and hear the story.'

They ushered them unceremoniously into a large room with low couches and rich rugs on the earthen floor. Martha and Lazarus sat either side of Mary. Fear had begun to build in Mary's chest at the prospect of Lila telling her story. She looked pleadingly at Lila. As Lila read the unspoken message in her eyes she turned to Jesus and said, 'Perhaps it would be better if Mary told the part I do not know – the first part.'

Jesus smiled in agreement. 'If you're able, Mary?'

'Yes ... I am able,' Mary faltered.

Tears were running into Lazarus's beard as Mary told her brother and sister what had happened to her after they had left, and to their father. She stopped when she got to the part about the old woman finding her at the well. She cast a pleading glance at Lila again.

'He was such a stubborn fool ... ' Martha's voice trailed away as she caught Jesus' eye.

Lazarus sat quietly, stroking the blue threads in a tassel at the corner of his prayer shawl. 'We all were,' he sighed. 'I was young and arrogant. I should have been more patient, more respectful.' He looked at Jesus.

'Much sadness came from that day,' Jesus reiterated.

Mary looked forlorn. 'What happened? I never understood.'

'You were too young,' Martha whispered.

'I was also too young to be left,' Mary shot back.

Tension hung between them.

'You are right, Mary,' Lazarus admitted, shaking his head. 'We should have taken you with us. I suppose I thought he needed at least one of us to look after him and you were too young to help me with the business,' he confessed. 'He wouldn't listen to us, no matter what we did or said, he carried on smoking that evil substance.'

'What evil substance?' She looked at her brother in surprise.

'Opium. That's what the fighting was about – he said it was for pain, and at first we went along with it. After all, our mother had passed away and he grieved her deeply. But then he began squandering our wealth on it and became listless and lazy – he did no work. Our business was in jeopardy. Well, I became more and more self-righteous and angry. We were respectable members of the synagogue. I was training as a Pharisee. I gave him an ultimatum to stop or I would leave and take the business and Martha with me. He still would not listen, so I did what I said I'd do and we started again here.' He sighed deeply. 'It's only been since meeting Jesus,' he nodded and half smiled through tears at his friend, 'that I've begun to see my part in it all. Until now, I have never wanted reconciliation. I have always seen it as his fault alone.'

'But it's too late – the Eastern poison has taken him,' Martha sighed and wiped her nose with a cloth that she'd been twisting in her hands.

'I thought he died of diseased lungs,' Mary muttered. 'I never knew – I never saw him smoking.'

'Perhaps he stopped when we left, but it was too late for him, even then,' Lazarus said, his brow furrowed.

'Perhaps.' Mary felt drained of all energy, and then, in a small voice, she asked the question that had been burning the back of her throat: 'Why did you never visit? Why didn't you let me know where you were?'

Lazarus was silent. Martha could not meet her gaze.

He started shaking his head as his face crumpled. He buried it in his hands. His shoulders shook. No one spoke.

Lila interrupted the silence that hung between them. 'Mary's story is not finished yet – perhaps you need to know what happened after Mary met the old woman?' Mary lowered her head, feeling the boulder growing larger in her chest. 'Shall I tell them?' Lila asked. Mary eventually gave a single nod.

Lila told her friend's story. The look of growing horror on Martha's face said it all. A tortured expression filled Lazarus' eyes. When she'd finished there was another long silence.

Then Lazarus broke with all convention, sliding off the couch onto his knees at Mary's feet, 'I'm so sorry. My pride ... my pre-occupation with what was right ... with the business ... my lack of concern for you ... my selfish, self-righteous anger led you to this. Oh, have mercy on me ... ' he pleaded, bending down and touching her feet.

Mary instantly reached down to pull him up.

'Don't, brother ... don't do that,' she cried.

Martha did the same thing, clasping Mary's legs. 'Oh, little sister, what have we done?'

The first time they became aware of Jesus standing over them was his hands on their heads, one at a time. 'Forgive them, Father, they did not know,' he prayed quietly, resting his hands on Lazarus' and Martha's heads. Then he placed both hands on Mary's head. She felt the boulder inside her and the weight around her shoulders grow smaller and lighter.

✼ ✼ ✼

Mary, naturally, stayed in Bethany. Her siblings wanted to make up for their failures and for all that had been lost between them. Lila missed her. Even Jair conceded that he missed her too. But they were glad for her. When they saw her, she was always full of the latest discoveries she had made about her brother and sister. One thing had become apparent: Mary and Martha were very different. There had been a few stand-offs as Mary struggled to submit to her older sister's household regime. Her previous free-and-easy lifestyle was at serious odds with the very ordered and structured way in which Martha lived. Mary said she missed Lila's more relaxed approach to life, but resisted saying anything more critical.

Jesus had been staying by the River Jordan, over the hills to the east of Jerusalem, where his cousin John had first preached and baptised. Lila and Jair often called in on Mary and her family at Bethany on their return from going to listen to him teach. His following had been growing, and with it the opposition from the leaders in Jerusalem. Jair was surprised at the speed with which the opposition to Jesus had escalated among the chief priests and the teachers of the law.

On one occasion, while they were with Jesus, word came from Martha and Mary that Lazarus had been taken seriously ill, requesting that Jesus come quickly. But Jesus' response had surprised them. On receiving the news, he said, 'This sickness will not end in death. No, it is for God's glory that God's Son may be glorified through it.'

Lila knew how much he loved Lazarus, Martha and Mary, so it baffled her when he decided to stay by the Jordan for two more days. Anxiety propelled her to ask Jair if they could go to Bethany that day. The messenger would have already taken a day to get to them – she feared that, despite what Jesus said, Lazarus would not survive. She was right. By the time they got to Bethany, he had died. Mary was inconsolable. She was devastated at losing her newly found sibling and the security that reconciliation had brought. Lila had no words for her friend, but she was glad she was there. They buried him in the evening of that day.

Many from the growing community of Jesus' followers came from Jerusalem to comfort the sisters. For a few days, Bethany felt more like a city than a small town. When Jesus finally arrived, it had been four days since the burial. Mary was so desolate that she didn't move when she heard that Jesus had arrived. Martha composed herself and rose to go out to meet him. Lila went with her, supporting her by the elbow. As they approached Jesus, Lila could sense that Martha was choosing her greeting carefully, in her measured way. 'Lord, if you had been here, my brother would not have died. But I know that, even now God will give you whatever you ask.'

Jesus' smile was sad. His eyes searched Martha's, and Lila could see he was disturbed by what he found there. 'Your brother will rise again,' he said softly.

Martha looked hurt and almost angry. 'I know, he will rise again in the resurrection at the last day.'

Lila could sense the unspoken thought and almost blurted out, 'But she needs him here – now!' But she didn't.

Jesus had that fiery look in his eyes. 'I am the resurrection and the life,' his voice rose, strong and clear. 'He who believes in me will live, even though he dies, and whoever lives and believes in me will never die. Do you believe this?' he asked, holding Martha's gaze, and to Lila's surprise she could see he was willing her along, almost drawing a response from her.

Martha was silent for a moment. Then, 'Yes, Lord,' she said quietly. 'I believe that you are the Christ, the Son of God, who has come into the world.' Lila felt the tension leave Martha's body as she voiced her faith.

Jesus sighed and then there was that sad smile again. 'Where is Mary? Does she not know that I have come?"

'She knows,' was all Martha would say.

'Tell her to come to me, away from the mourners.'

Martha nodded, 'Yes, teacher.'

When Mary was told, she obediently got up and went to him. He was still just outside the village, picking his time to engage with the crowds. However, when those who had been with Mary in the house saw her leave quickly, they thought she was going to Lazarus' tomb and so they followed her. Lila and Martha watched Mary fall at Jesus' feet and, in an accusing, broken voice she cried, 'Lord, if you had been here, my brother would not have died.'

There was a fresh surge of weeping around them as the poignancy of the moment overcame the crowd. Lila choked back a sob – she was so disillusioned by his choice not to come immediately on hearing of Lazarus' illness. It didn't make sense

– she thought he loved them, thought he could have healed him.

Jesus looked hurt. He breathed deeply and Lila realised he was struggling to control his emotions. 'Where have you laid him?' he asked. Then he was weeping.

As they came to the tomb, she saw that he was still deeply moved, the tears rolling down his face and glistening in his beard. 'Take away the stone,' he commanded.

Martha stepped forward, attempting to take control of what was turning into a very emotional situation, 'But, Lord, after four days there will be a bad odour.'

'Did I not tell you that if you believed, you would see the glory of God?' He almost whispered it.

Martha was stunned. Lila could tell she'd realised this wasn't what she had initially thought it was. Lila saw her switch from fear into faith.

She turned, asking the men in the crowd to come and move the stone away from the tomb as the Lord had commanded. A hush fell across the group as the men laboured to roll the heavy stone across the uneven ground.

Then Jesus looked upwards and said, in a voice washed clear with tears: 'Father, I thank you that you have heard me. I know that you always hear me, but this is for the benefit of the people standing here, that they may believe you sent me.' Then his eyes lowered to the people: to Martha, then to Mary, to Lila and then Jair, who was standing by the stone, his chest rising and falling rapidly from the effort of moving it. Finally Jesus' gaze focused on the gaping mouth of the tomb and, in a loud voice, he commanded, 'Lazarus, come out!'

A shiny black beetle caught Lila's eye as it crawled away from the tomb. She wasn't breathing. Then she saw something moving in the shadow of the doorway. She blinked. There was something white coming into the light. She resisted the urge to scream and instead let her breath out in short bursts through pursed lips. Then he was there, standing wrapped in grave clothes, the face cloth still in place over his features. Martha trembled beside her and cried out. Mary fell sideways into Lila, who managed to catch her, even while holding Anna in the crook of her other arm. They crumpled into a heap together.

'Take off the grave clothes and let him go,' Jesus ordered, jubilantly.

Jair was the first to reach out and tentatively peel back the face cloth. He pulled it away slowly at first and then faster, throwing it on the ground with a shout. Lazarus was blinking and breathing hard. He looked bewildered. Chaos broke out. People helped Martha and Mary to their feet and led them to their brother. They were the first to embrace him … and there was no odour.

4. FEET

The extravagant woman

'Have you ever had someone close to you die?' Grace asked Chloe.

'No,' Chloe looked up from her magazine. 'I haven't succumbed to the temptation to kill Mark yet,' she laughed dryly.

'Murder, not divorce?' Grace joined in the joke.

They were sitting in a coffee shop eating orange cake and drinking cappuccinos. Their regular outings had stopped for a while during the early days after the affair, when Chloe had been too scared to venture out. But she'd been the one to suggest it today and Grace was glad to get away from the parish. She didn't want to run into James Martin again.

'I wish he'd hurl insults at me, or something, instead of being so nice. I can't bear it.'

Grace digested this information slowly as she filled her mouth with cake.

'Why do you ask? Have you?'

'Yes. My Grandmother. She died just after I became a Christian. I went to her grave on my day off last week.'

'What age were you when she died?' Chloe looked back down at her magazine absently as she turned the page. 'Ooh – that's nice,' she said, pointing at a summer outfit.

Grace tipped her head sideways to look. 'Mmmm ... ' she agreed and then went on: 'Oh, it was only a few years ago.'

'What?' Chloe forgot about fashion momentarily. 'You only became a Christian a few years ago? I thought you'd been one all your life!'

'No, not at all. But my Grandmother had prayed for me since I was born and she helped me understand what it meant when I did make the decision.'

'I guess you must miss her?' Chloe looked like focusing on Grace was taking a lot of effort, her smooth brow furrowed.

'Yes, dreadfully.' Grace felt self-conscious with the confession. 'She knew everything about me. She was my strongest reference point – do you know what I mean?' Grace leaned forward earnestly, wanting to confide in her friend.

'I do. I think Mark was mine until … ' She stopped and looked up at the ceiling, then back at Grace. 'Now I feel he doesn't know me at all … and I don't know him. Lately, it's like I'm all at sea, with no star to guide me and no lighthouse in sight.'

Grace nodded, 'That's how I feel sometimes.'

Chloe leaned her elbow on the table and cupped her chin in her hand, staring out of the window at the busy street outside. 'I guess the relationship we used to have has died. We can't resurrect it, we have to start again, and I haven't got a clue how to go about it.' Her eyes swivelled to Grace's. 'Maybe we're holding onto the corpse of the old relationship, hoping somehow to bring it to life again? Maybe we need to just bury it and grieve for it … and maybe then we might be able to start again?'

'Maybe,' Grace shrugged, fighting feelings of disappointment at Chloe's self-absorption.

'Sorry … I'm back onto me again. You must get so bored of my stuff. Goodness knows I do!' Chloe sat back into her chair again. 'So are you feeling all at sea at the minute?'

Grace pulled herself together. Chloe was only just coping with her own issues. There wasn't the room or the energy for anything else. It was her job to care for Chloe, not the other way around! 'No – not at the minute. But I'm just saying I understand how you must be feeling,' she said, smiling.

Chloe went back to her magazine. 'Doesn't that model look like an angel?' she said, pointing and angling the magazine for Grace to see. Grace just smiled and wondered, as she had done every day since her day off last week, about Michael in the graveyard.

'Have you ever thought you might have seen a real angel?' Grace asked Chloe.

'Why? Have you?' Chloe looked up.

'No ... no ... I was just wondering about that verse in Hebrews 13 that says some may have entertained angels unawares.'

'Well, if I have, they must have been very well disguised,' Chloe said smiling, then looking back to the angelic face pouting up at her from the glossy page.

'Do you think they serve us?' Grace twiddled a sugar packet between her thumb and finger.

Chloe looked up and stared out the window again, 'Ministering spirits sent to serve those who are being saved?' she quoted. 'It's a nice thought ... but I haven't noticed if they do.' She paused and flipped the magazine pages over, not really looking at the pictures. 'Maybe I'm just thick?' she laughed at herself.

Grace smiled. 'Yeah, maybe you are.'

Chloe looked offended. 'Hey, I can say that sort of thing about myself, but you're supposed to defend me, not agree!'

Grace shrugged and smirked as she went back to her orange cake. Chloe finished her magazine, while slowly sipping her cappuccino.

'That's a hideous style, don't you think?' she said, pointing to the back page, 'Or am I just getting old.'

'Do you want me to answer that?' Grace asked through her last mouthful of cake. She watched Chloe put the magazine back on the shelf and bring back the day's papers. Today wasn't about deep-and-meaningfuls. Today was about skimming the surface, shooting the breeze, enjoying wasting time together. Perhaps it was what they both needed?

'We're going on holiday together.' Chloe's voice had none of the anticipation in it that might be expected with the prospect of a holiday.

'Oh, that's nice – where?'

'Cornwall. Surfing.'

'That'll be good, won't it? The kids will love it!'

'Yes, they will.'

'When do you go?'

Chloe folded the paper closed, an anxious look in her brown eyes. 'Day after tomorrow.'

Grace reached over the table, putting her needs aside, and squeezed her hand. 'It'll be OK ... maybe you'll be able to shout at each other down by the sea, where the wind and waves can muffle the sound.'

❋   ❋   ❋

As Grace drove back home, she felt mild panic. At first, she couldn't pinpoint why, but then when she saw him walking along the high street, she knew. He didn't see her at first, as he was with his wife – she presumed – who was pushing an expensive-looking three-wheeler pram. But then, for a split second, their eyes met. Grace's pulse accelerated, as did her driving. She had to brake hard at a zebra crossing for an old lady pulling a tartan shopping bag on wheels behind her. She dragged her eyes to look in the rear-view mirror to see if he was still looking, but he was engrossed with his family in a shop window.

She stormed round to the church after leaving her car at home. She locked the heavy doors behind her, didn't switch the lights on and made her way down the aisle in the gloom. She was beside herself with a cacophony of emotions: rage, pain, terror. She paced up and down the communion rail. She finally slowed and came to a standstill in the centre, looking up to the stained glass windows above the communion table. They were beautiful, but dull today because of the dim light that shone through them from cloudy skies. She couldn't settle on any one image or on any of the texts written there.

Eventually she shouted, 'God!' and then fell on her knees. Slowly she prostrated herself until she was laying full length along the chancel. She wept uncontrollably.

When she returned home, she went straight to her desk and began writing the last part of the story from her reading of John 11–12.

❀   ❀   ❀

'Simon the leper has invited us to his house for a meal,' Martha informed Mary.

'Why's he called that? He hasn't got leprosy, otherwise we wouldn't be thinking of going, surely?' Mary looked up from scrubbing one of Lazarus' garments in a large bowl of water.

'He was ill for a time, but they say Jesus healed him. However, he doesn't talk about it. He's a Pharisee – miracles performed by Jesus don't go down very well in the circles he moves in.'

'But if it weren't for Jesus, he wouldn't be moving in those circles. He'd be an outcast. Wouldn't the miracle help them believe, especially because it's happened to one of their own? The chief priest must have verified it?'

'You would think, wouldn't you?' Martha shrugged and shook out the dripping garment that Mary passed to her. She hung it up on a rope that stretched from the doorway of the kitchen to the tree that overhung their large courtyard.

Lila and Jair had stayed since Lazarus's resurrection. Anna was sitting on Mary's lap, splashing her hands in the water, making it difficult for her to actually get the washing done. But she didn't mind. She had missed her.

'Simon's wife asked me to help serve the meal. Everyone is talking about what happened to Lazarus. They want to see him and touch him, and meet Jesus. We've never had so many invitations to meals – never had so many new friends,' she laughed. 'Will you come and help me?'

'I don't know,' Mary replied. Despite the euphoria surrounding her brother's resurrection, she still felt nervous about meeting new people, in case they recognised her from her past life. She looked up at Martha and saw the fleeting look of exasperation she had glimpsed one or two times before. She looked down at Anna quickly, 'Shall we wash another?' she asked.

Anna nodded vigorously, drooling into the water.

'So, do you think maybe Simon is a secret believer?'

Martha leaned against the doorframe, watching her sister with the child who had brought chaos to her ordered household. 'Perhaps. I've never got that impression from him or his wife, but you never know.'

Anna was getting so carried away with splashing that she was drenching herself and Mary.

'Stop that now, Anna,' scolded Martha.

'Oh, it doesn't matter, Martha, we'll dry off in no time.' But

Mary could see her sister was reaching her limit as to how much disorder she could cope with. 'I'll take her outside to dry off, while you finish this one.' She handed the last garment to Martha and gathered Anna up in her arms.

※　※　※

Mary didn't help her sister in the end. She knew Martha was cross with her, but she couldn't bring herself to do it. As the evening wore on, she became restless. Lila and Jair had retired to their room with Anna. She sat alone on her sleeping mat looking at one of the biggest bottles of her perfume. *Can anything good come from this?* The thought was never far from her mind. She stroked the smooth surface of the jar.

Her life was more complete and whole than it had ever been. She could hardly believe how Jesus had enabled reconciliation and restored her to her family. Even more incredible was what had happened to Lazarus. She smiled again at the memory of Jesus commanding him to come out of his grave. Awe and reverence swelled her chest. *But this? This will always be filthy; will never be redeemed.* She felt perplexed, so she turned to prayer, kneeling and bowing her head to the floor.

In the silence she waited. She listened to her blood whooshing in her ears, to her breathing getting slower as she settled in the presence of her Father in heaven, as Jesus had taught her. As she worshipped and waited, an image began to form in her mind. It was so sad that she began to cry. She saw herself pouring the perfumed oil on Jesus' dead body, lying listless, cold and covered in blood. Into her mind came the words, 'For you.' A shudder went through her.

For me? A sacrifice to atone for me? To redeem me? She didn't fully understand, but she wept and wept as she had never wept before. And then she knew what she wanted to do. She uncurled herself and picked up the large bottle of perfumed oil. It was the most expensive one – worth at least a good year's wages. She stood up, wrapped her shawl around her and went out of the house.

She pushed her way through the crowd that had formed round

the entrance to Simon's house. Because she was small, she was able to wriggle her way right to the doorway. She peered in, letting her eyes adjust to the gloom and then she saw that Jesus had only just entered. His back was towards her. She watched as his host approached him. Horrified, she recognised him from one of the royal parties she'd performed at. Instinctively, she pulled her headscarf down over her face. But he hadn't noticed her. She watched as he welcomed Jesus. He didn't give him any water for his feet, nor did he greet him with a kiss or anoint his head with oil, as he should have done with such an honoured guest. Mary was indignant. Why would you invite someone to your house only to insult him? Her heart was pounding. Without a moment's hesitation, she stepped in through the door and pressed herself up against the entrance wall. No one seemed to notice her and no one stopped her.

She watched as Simon led Jesus to his place at the low table. He didn't even put him in the place of honour. She saw Lazarus seated at an even lower place at the table, and wondered why Simon had invited them. Martha had thought they were to be honoured, but that was clearly not the case. Mary couldn't believe it. Her anger propelled her into the room, despite her fear that Simon would surely see her, recognise her and throw her out. Jesus saw her, recognition and welcome mingled in the smile he gave her. She felt more daring and came and stood behind him, barely holding herself together. Their host was watching her with hooded eyes. Slowly recognition crossed his face. She looked away, expecting an angry confrontation. But none came. Martha came into the room from the kitchen carrying a large, steaming bowl. When her eyes fell on Mary, she looked shocked and then embarrassed.

Mary focused on Jesus. He was the one who knew her name, who knew who she truly was. He'd cleansed her and had given her hope to be different. The vision she'd seen compelled her. A dam of repressed grief and gratitude broke. She fell, clinging to his feet and wept. She knew only too well how outrageous she was being: a woman like her touching his feet? As the tears ran in rivulets through the dust that covered them, she thought of the many men she had touched.

She pulled off her headscarf, undid her hair and let it tumble down in a glossy mass, as she had done so many times before. She heard several sharp intakes of breath around her. But Jesus didn't seem embarrassed or disturbed. She wiped his feet with her hair, whispering, 'They didn't wash your feet.' She kissed them tenderly, tasting the salt of her tears mingling with dust and sweat. The silence was a solid, tangible thing. No one moved.

She picked up the perfume bottle and passionately smashed its long neck on the edge of the table. The top rolled between goblets and platters, across the polished surface of the table, stopping accusingly in front of Simon. The scent pierced the air – a deep, rich, exotic note. This was her testimony. She tipped it up and poured it out on Jesus' feet in one fluid movement. The scent rolled in explosions like thunder round a mountain range. You could see the effect it had on those who recognised it. They were aroused, disturbed, unsettled. Simon the Pharisee regained his composure and eyed Jesus contemptuously.

If this man were a prophet, he would know who is touching him and what kind of woman she is – that she is a sinner.

'These tools of my trade, I give to you. Redeem them ... bring good out of evil,' she whispered. Sobs wracked her small shoulders as she poured the last drop of perfumed oil out onto his feet.

Jesus had not moved. He had not stopped her defiling him in this most outrageous way. He was looking at her tenderly, but with no glimmer of lust. Like the captain of a ship in a storm, he turned and looked at his host and in a calm voice, said, 'Simon, I have something to tell you.'

'Tell me, teacher,' Simon replied, sardonically.

'Two men owed money to a certain moneylender. One owed him five hundred denarii, and the other fifty. Neither of them had the money to pay him back, so he cancelled the debts of both. Now, which of them will love him more?'

Simon replied, 'I suppose the one who had the bigger debt cancelled.'

'You have judged correctly,' Jesus said.

Then he turned back to Mary and said to Simon, 'Do you see

this woman? I came into your house. You did not give me any water for my feet, but she wet my feet with her tears and wiped them with her hair. You did not give me a kiss, but this woman, from the time I entered, has not stopped kissing my feet. You did not put oil on my head, but she has poured perfume on my feet. Therefore, I tell you, her many sins have been forgiven—for she loved much. But he who has been forgiven little loves little.'

Indignation threatened to burst an artery in Simon's neck.

Then Jesus said to her, 'Your sins are forgiven.'

Chaos broke out. 'Who is this who even forgives sins?' Mary heard someone exclaim.

Jesus looked into her eyes and she knew that he loved her. He smiled and said, 'Your faith has saved you; go in peace.'

She stayed kneeling at his feet, oblivious of the chaos she'd caused and the possible embarrassment to her family. She absorbed his words, soaking up his unconditional love for her. Then eventually she crept out into the night with a full heart and an empty bottle. No one stopped her.

5. OUTCAST

The well woman

Grace felt quite vulnerable for several days after writing the last section of the story. She didn't really want to engage with anyone, but Chloe had got back from her holiday and had asked to see her, so they met in their local pub.

She reached for her glasses to check her appearance in the mirror one more time before she went out. It was an unpleasant thing to do, as she preferred the soft-focus effect. She was grateful that mid-life visual deterioration had started around the same time as her face had begun to slide. She only needed to ensure that the coarse hair, which stubbornly kept re-appearing on her chin, was spotted and successfully removed. She had sworn she would never allow facial hair to develop, unlike some of the other women she'd trained with in theological college. In her more cynical moments she'd sometimes wondered if androgyny was mandatory for women seeking ordination. However, she had agreed with the clean-faced look that many of her contemporaries espoused. She hadn't worn make-up since she'd become a Christian, not out of any puritanical theology, but because she connected it to a past that she'd rather forget.

She left the house and walked briskly down several roads to the pub. They did the best Caesar salad there, but they also fried their chips in dripping. So, if Chloe had something with chips, she would be able to have a few of them while still convincing herself that she was being healthy, eating lettuce and grilled chicken. Chloe was already seated in their favourite alcove.

'You're on time,' Chloe said, looking surprised.

'Yes, I am. Isn't it amazing?' Grace brushed aside the backhanded compliment. She pulled her chair out and sat down. 'Hope I'm not intruding on any "you time" you thought you'd have while waiting for me?' She smiled wryly.

'How did you guess?' Chloe retorted, good-naturedly. They got their drinks, ordered food and settled back into their seats.

'So how was the holiday?' Grace smiled, noting the sun-kissed glow of her friend's cheeks.

'It was pretty good, considering,' Chloe replied, spinning ice around in her glass with a straw. 'I love the sea and the weather was good. The kids loved it.' She looked up and smiled. 'Charlie didn't wet the bed once.'

'That's great.' Grace was relieved for Charlie. 'How were you and Mark?'

Chloe frowned. 'We did have a few uncomfortable moments after the kids went to bed when neither of us seemed to know what to say to each other. Thank God we brought a couple of decent DVDs.'

'Any romantic ones?'

'No!' Chloe's frown intensified. 'Thrillers.'

'Any good conversations?'

'No,' said Chloe, shaking her head. A shiny, dark lock of hair fell forward across her face. She let it hang there, partially obscuring her line of sight. 'I did a lot of thinking though,' she said, looking through her hair at Grace.

'I always think best by the sea,' Grace agreed, as her mind wandered to the holiday in Thailand that Peter and she had planned for later in the year.

'I thought a lot about my dad,' Chloe began, as the waitress arrived with their food – not a chip in sight. Grace resigned herself to healthy eating.

'What about him?' Grace asked as she crunched on a piece of lettuce. She didn't know anything about Chloe's family.

'I really loved him.' Chloe twirled a piece of pasta round and round her fork, a soft look settling on her features.

'Is he … ?' Grace stopped chewing, looking at her friend.

'No, he's still alive – lives in Dorset with a woman not much older than me. I haven't seen him for years.'

'What happened?'

'He fell in love with an eighteen year old when I was twelve. He left mum, my sister and me and rented a flat nearby so he could still come and see us. But mum wouldn't let him. She was so angry with him. She spent my teens hating him and being depressed. You can imagine how much fun puberty was for me. I missed him terribly and Mum had shut down on life. I felt like an outcast ... like an orphan.'

'That is so tough, Chloe. How did you survive?'

'I don't know that I did.' Chloe smiled sadly. 'Maybe that's why I've made such a mess now.'

'What do you mean?' Grace wiped a drop of Caesar dressing off the side of her plate with her forefinger and put it in her mouth.

'I packed a bag and secretly went to see my dad once. I wanted to live with him. But when he opened the door and saw me, his face fell. He wasn't pleased to see me. I could hear his girlfriend asking from the living room who it was. He said it was a cold-caller and came outside, pulling the door behind him. I think I felt my heart breaking then.' Her chin wobbled. 'He told me that I couldn't come in, that his girlfriend didn't want children around. He chose her over me ... ' A tear rolled down her cheek.

'Oh, Chloe, how awful. You were twelve?'

'Yeah ... ' she sniffed. 'I spent high school trying to find someone to take his place. Not good.' She looked up from her half-eaten meal, leaving her fork on the plate, curling her hair behind her ear and wiping her cheek. 'I think that's why I've loved doing youth work these last few years. I've wanted to try and give the teenagers what I never had. But look what I've done now. I've screwed it all up.'

Grace didn't know what to say. She pushed the last piece of lettuce aimlessly around her plate.

Chloe continued: 'You know, you think you've left the past behind, but it's right there in the shadows, isn't it? I've always believed that when someone becomes a Christian, the past is gone and you get to have a new life, a clean slate. But I'm not so sure about that anymore.'

Grace still didn't reply.

'What's wrong? Why aren't you saying anything?' Chloe searched Grace's face for an answer.

'Because it's a tough one.' She looked at Chloe and sighed. 'Sadly, our spirit might be willing but our flesh is, and always will be, weak.'

'You never speak about your past, Grace. You must have one?'

An anxious look skimmed across Grace's usually calm, Nordic features. 'Everyone's got a past, Chloe,' she said, shaking it off lightly.

Chloe studied Grace's face and decided not to pursue it. Instead she stuck with the subject of herself, saying, 'I'm getting there, you know. I still think about him, but not as much since you and I prayed together that day. I'd love to see him again, but I know that would do my head in.'

'And his!' Grace added.

'Yes ... ' Chloe's voice trailed away. There was a pause. The waitress came and cleared their plates away and asked if they wanted any desserts. They said they just wanted coffees.

As Chloe watched Grace, it dawned on her that Grace was very well defended. Chloe was intrigued as to what she was hiding, but knew she wasn't going to find out today.

As they emptied their cups, Chloe continued: 'I've realised I need to get some closure on the past. I don't ever want to go looking for a replacement for my dad again.'

'Is that what you were doing with Tom?' Grace ran a hand through her curls.

'Maybe ... ' Chloe shrugged.

Closure on the past – how do I get closure on the past? Grace thought, enviously. She felt emotion threatening to overwhelm her. She couldn't do this anymore. She had to go.

'That's good, Chloe. Sounds like you've done some really difficult, deep thinking.' Grace looked at her watch distractedly. 'Is that the time? Goodness, I better go!' Her smile chased the tense expression away from her features. This abrupt end left Chloe feeling slightly patronised, rejected, bewildered and even more curious.

Grace hugged and kissed her briskly on the cheek outside the pub, leaving Chloe staring after her. Grace walked home fast and, by the time she put her key in the door, she had deftly distracted herself by thinking about her sermon for Sunday. 'John 4 – the Samaritan woman at the well,' she muttered as she pushed the door open, letting it slam shut behind her.

She went to her study and sat down, kicking off her low-heeled boots irritably and flipping open her Bible. She found the passage and read it again.

She sat back and sighed deeply. 'I don't want to think about it, God.'

She looked up slowly at the picture of Peter on her desk and spoke to him this time: 'Not very different from Chloe ... or me ... this woman at the well.'

Her eyes moved to the icon her Nana had given her after their time of prayer in the old church. It hung on the wall above the picture of Peter. 'You got me,' she said to Jesus. 'Looks like I'm going to have to think ...'. He was painted in gold and blue, his gaze disconcertingly disarming.

She opened her writing file, instead of her sermon file, and her fingers began tapping on the keyboard of her laptop:

There'd been a few more run-ins with the Pharisees since the meal at Simon's house. Things had got ugly one day by the river, when some of Jesus' disciples were baptising people. Jesus himself did not baptise, but the movement of his followers had gained momentum as they had copied his cousin John, and continued to baptise. Rumour had it that Jesus' followers were gaining and baptising even more disciples than John. Passions were running high and it had actually come to blows between the Pharisees and the disciples.

Someone from within the crowd on the riverbank had yelled something about Jesus joining his cousin in Herod's dungeons and Peter, not known for his way with words, had left the person he was baptising, waded to shore and unleashed his fists on the offender. Not many found peace through the waters of baptism that day.

When the bedraggled disciples made it back to Bethany, where Jesus was staying that evening, the women had their work cut out for them, seeing to their cuts and bruises. Lila had asked Mary to fetch one of her jars of oil. She had felt wonderfully useful as she tore and folded cloth, poured oil on the makeshift bandages and handed them to Lila. Joanna and another woman called Mary worked methodically alongside Martha.

Jesus heard about what Peter had done and he smiled ruefully, shaking his head. 'It's not my way, Peter. Now we'll need to move out of Jerusalem for a while, or I will end up sharing a cell with John.' Peter's big shoulders sagged as he stared woefully at his rough hands. As Mary bandaged a deep gash on a disciple's head, she watched him out of the corner of her eye, understanding the disappointment he evidently felt with himself.

'Where will we go now, Master?' Peter raised his eyes resolutely to Jesus face.

'I think I would like to return to Galilee for a while. You could see your family again.'

Jesus looked warmly at Peter, seeming to understand something about him that the big fisherman didn't. Peter's mood lifted almost instantly.

Men are so simple, thought Mary as she watched.

Lila was sitting next to Jair who was holding a serene Anna, both arms stretched up either side of her head, eyelashes resting on round cheeks and rosebud lips parted in innocent sleep. Lila leaned over and whispered something to Jair that Mary could not quite catch. He nodded as he looked at Lila, anticipation on his face. Then they both looked down at their precious child, Lila gently touching one of her little fingers.

Mary watched them fondly. Eventually they looked up at her in unison. 'We'd like to go with Jesus,' Jair said, simply. 'Would you come too and help us with Anna?'

Lila nodded her agreement. 'What do you think?' she asked, searching Mary's eyes.

Mary looked over at Martha and wondered what her sister would make of the idea. She had been embarrassed at Mary's outrageous display of emotion at Simon the Pharisee's house. Both she and Lazarus weren't quite sure what to make of it.

Judas, one of Jesus' disciples, had been sitting next to Lazarus at Simon's table and had made the comment that it was an extravagant waste – that the perfume should have been sold and the proceeds given to the poor. Mary had noted that her brother initially had some sympathy with his thinking. After all, he was a businessman. But since his death, he had changed and had later sought her out and encouraged her in her devotion to Jesus. But Martha ... she had been ashamed – ashamed of Mary's past, so evidently displayed in her actions and distraught by her choice to so shamelessly break social convention.

Jesus had rebuked Judas and had said that they would always have the poor with them but they would not always have him. He said she'd done it in preparation for his burial. She still didn't fully understand, but it connected with the vision she'd seen earlier. No one else had understood at all.

Lazarus was willing to trust, even though he didn't understand. He'd been raised from the dead, after all, and there was no understanding that.

Despite everything, Martha still seemed to struggle with fear: fear of what other people thought and fear of losing her sister again. Mary wished she would shake it off and be free of it. She wondered if fear would inhibit her from allowing Mary to travel with Jesus and the others. As it turned out, Lazarus made the decision and Martha had no say in it. He gladly gave his permission for his youngest sister to travel with the Lord. It was the least he could do to repay her for the sufferings she'd endured.

❊　❊　❊

'Why are we going through Samaria?' Lila quietly asked Jesus. 'Wouldn't it be better to go by the road east of the Jordan Valley to Galilee?' Lila knew the route she was suggesting was longer, going through Gentile territory, but it was preferable to the shorter route they were on, heading into hated Samaritan territory.

'Why do I do anything?' Jesus replied, looking at her quizzically.

Lila, Jair and Mary were walking alongside Jesus and some of his disciples. It was amazing to the women that Jesus involved them in discussions just as he did with the men. Lila didn't reply straight away to his question but was searching his face for her answer. 'I just don't understand why we have to go through this area? These people … ' she said, her voice fading away as Jesus' facial expression changed.

'These people?' She felt the threat of a storm in his tone.

Mary willed her to stop pursuing the conversation, but Lila kept going.

'Well, they're not like us are they?' There were several grunts of agreement from the men walking on the other side of Jesus.

One of them said, 'They're descendants of Assyrians sent to colonise Israel.'

'Yes, and they've never worshipped as we do. They've always had their own idols, even sacrificing their children to them. They have their own temple on Mount Gerizim.'

Lila's face said, *What more do I need to say?*

'So, the temple in Jerusalem … ' Jesus looked over his shoulder across the hills in the general direction of Jerusalem ' … everything that's done in the name of worship there is pleasing to God?'

She knew he was referring to the terrible day they'd first met and it slowed her pace momentarily. The disciples started talking all at once. She could hear James and John vying to hold forth, as they often did. Lila skipped to get back in step with them and she tried to enter into the discussion but the others weren't listening to her. The sun was climbing higher into the sky, beating down mercilessly on their heads and Lila wondered if this was adding to the heat in the argument.

Jesus turned to Lila, ignoring the debate that was now in full flow around him, 'I do what I see my Father doing, Lila.' She wasn't sure what he meant.

They reached the small town of Sychar by midday. It was near the historic plot of ground that Jacob had given his son Joseph, and Jacob's well was there – a deep, ancient natural spring. No one had anything to draw water with, so some of them decided to go into the town to buy food and to get something to draw with. Jesus sat down in the shade of a nearby olive tree and told them to go; he wanted to rest. It was a given that the women would rest too. There was a cluster of trees a good stones-throw from the well, almost diagonally opposite to where Jesus sat. The women gathered in their shade. Lila leaned her back against one of the trees. Mary came and sat with her.

The women were unusually quiet in the fierce heat. Lila could feel herself drifting in and out of drowsiness as she fed Anna. Mary's head slowly dropped onto Lila's shoulder and jerked up again when it touched down. 'You can lean on me,' Lila murmured sleepily. Mary gratefully lowered her head onto Lila's shoulder again.

'Isn't this near where their temple used to be?'

'Yes, it is,' Lila answered.

'We're mad to be out here at this time of day,' Mary muttered.

'I know,' Lila smiled, 'but he's doing what he sees the Father doing and we're following.'

The cicadas droned in the branches above them and everything was very still. Lila watched a trail of ants wending their way under a large, arching root and disappearing with their burdens of foliage into the ground. She wondered at their ability to keep going in the heat. She could feel that Anna had dozed off, as her sucking was wobbly and intermittent. She let herself give into drowsiness.

Suddenly she became alert. From the direction of the town came a lone figure. She shimmered in the distance, becoming more solid as she drew near.

Not good to be a woman on your own ... not good to be here at this time of day either...

Lila watched her pass the tree under which Jesus was sitting. It was very near the well. She didn't appear to have seen him.

Then he spoke to her. 'Will you give me a drink?' The woman jumped and wheeled round. She seemed tensed, ready to run as she appraised him. He didn't move from his sitting position. Lila was stunned that he had spoken to her. She watched incredulously to hear the woman's response.

'You're not from around here,' she said, guardedly. 'Are you Jewish?'

Jesus nodded.

'Your accent ... ' she explained, gesturing with one hand to her mouth.

Jesus smiled slightly.

'You're a Jew and I'm a Samaritan *woman*. How can you ask me for a drink?' She set her clay pot down on the ground in front of her, letting the rope coil down around it – a barrier between them.

Lila was riveted. *Well, at least she understands.*

Jesus dropped his head to one side as if he were listening to something in the silence that hung between them. Then, in an authoritative voice, he said: 'If you knew the gift of God and who it is that asks you for a drink, you would have asked him and he would have given you living water.'

Lila suddenly realised what was going on. This was why they were here. This was what he meant about doing what he saw his Father doing. This was a divine appointment, like so many before – like her own traumatic encounter with him. How could she forget? Like Mary's encounter with him in the street – her deliverance from prostitution, her outrageous public declaration of love. How precious these stories were. She remembered one of Jesus' favourite sayings: 'I have been sent to seek and to save the lost.' It was all making sense now. The journey they'd taken was for this woman.

'Sir,' the woman said, hands on her hips, 'you have nothing to draw with and the well is deep. Where can you get this living water? Are you greater than our father Jacob, who gave us the well and drank from it himself, as did all his sons and his flocks and herds?'

You ignorant, arrogant... Lila wanted to stand up. *It's you who are the inferior race!*

Prejudice began pumping adrenalin through her blood, making her heart rate accelerate. Jesus got to his feet and purposefully walked out from under the shade of the tree into the searing midday sun towards the woman. 'Everyone who drinks of this water,' he gestured at the well behind her, 'will be thirsty again, but whoever drinks the water I give will never thirst.' He was standing in front of her now, and Lila knew the sensation the woman would feel having those eyes search hers. 'Indeed,' he paused and pressed his hand to his chest, 'the water I give will become a spring of water welling up to eternal life.' His fingers pinched together and then burst apart as his hand rose upwards from his chest.

Her shoulders had rounded slightly, her hands no longer on her hips. He'd got past her first defence. In a lowered voice, so Lila had to strain to hear, she said, 'Sir, give me this water so that I won't get thirsty and have to keep coming here to draw water.'

Why is it you come here for water at this time of day, I wonder? Lila leaned forward, realising too late that she had disturbed Anna, who started to cry. Mary lifted her head from Lila's shoulder and rubbed her face with both hands. The woman looked in their direction, perhaps realising for the first time that they were there.

'Go call your husband and come back,' Jesus said abruptly.

'I have no husband.' The woman looked back at him, the change of tack had shocked the information from her.

'You are right when you say you have no husband. The fact is, you have had five husbands and the man you now have is not your husband,' Jesus spoke matter-of-factly, like he'd read all about her life from a document. He was looking at her intently, 'What you have said is quite true.'

The woman took a step back from him and leaned up against the low wall of the well. Lila and Mary looked at each other in amazement at the skill with which this man, whom they had come to admire so deeply, could pierce to the very core of a person. 'So that's why she's here alone, at this time of day ... How does he do that?' whispered Lila.

Mary shook her head.

After a long pause, in which Lila imagined the woman trying to gather her wits about her, she said: 'Sir, I can see that you are a prophet.' She paused and then raised another defence. 'Our fathers worshipped on this mountain, but you Jews claim that the place where we must worship is in Jerusalem.'

'What's she doing?' Mary asked Lila.

'It's like wrestling with a snake!' Lila replied. 'First the racial barriers, then the moral, and now the religious ... she is very well defended!'

'But she's met her match today, I think,' Mary smiled, now wide awake, a thrill running through her as she watched their Master at work.

'Believe me, woman, a time is coming when you will worship the Father neither on this mountain, nor in Jerusalem. You Samaritans worship what you do not know; we worship what we do know, for salvation is from the Jews.' He hit the wall of the well with his hand to emphasise each word of his last phrase. He was a masterful communicator. The women held their breath.

'Yet, a time is coming, and has now come, when the true worshippers will worship the Father in spirit and truth, for they are the worshippers the Father seeks.' His voice had taken a tone he might have used with a frightened child. 'God is spirit, and his worshippers must worship in spirit and truth,' he said gently. Lila could see the woman's body leaning towards him slightly.

This is your moment … don't waste it … listen to him.

'I know that the Messiah is coming. When he comes, he will explain everything to us.' The yearning in her voice was unmistakable.

'I who speak to you am he,' Jesus declared.

A bird chirruped in the tree above them. Lila looked up, celebrating silently with it.

Just then, the men returned. Lila could see from their expressions that they were surprised to see him deep in conversation with a Samaritan woman, but they walked past him, saying nothing. When she abruptly left her water jar with Jesus and ran towards the town, several of the disciples walked over to him. Lila knew their curiosity would be killing them.

'Come and eat something, rabbi,' James said respectfully, motioning towards the whole group now gathered under the trees. But Jesus' attention was somewhere else – his face was lifted up towards the sky, an exultant expression playing on his features. Lila watched him, longing to be party to his thoughts. She felt irritated by the men and their pre-occupation with food, which seemed to belittle the holy moment that had just occurred. Another disciple insisted he have something to eat, pulling at his sleeve.

Jesus lowered his face in a profoundly patient manner and opened his eyes. He looked affectionately at the disciple who was demanding he eat and said, 'I have food to eat that you know nothing about.' The disciple looked baffled and turned with a quizzical look on his face to James and John. Jesus began to walk over towards the group who were eating bread and raisins and the men followed him slowly.

'Could someone have brought him food?' James asked John. John shrugged his shoulders in answer. They sat down near Lila and Mary. James turned to them and asked, 'Did that woman give him some food?'

'I don't think so,' Mary replied.

'My food is to do the will of him who sent me and to finish his work,' he leaned forward animatedly, raising one hand and pointing heavenward. Every eye focused on him now. 'Do you not say, "Four months more and then the harvest?" I tell you, open your eyes and look at the fields!' He stretched wide his arms, almost knocking John's bread out of his hand as he raised it to his mouth. He turned and apologetically touched John's arm. John smiled back and bit into his bread, just happy to be sitting so close to him. 'They are ripe to harvest the crop for eternal life.'

'What happened while we were gone?' James asked Jair who was on the other side of Lila. 'He was so tired when we left, but now look at him.'

'Well, I don't think it's over yet,' Jair said hesitantly. 'He had an incredible conversation with that woman and I think she'll be back shortly.'

'She left her water jar. I did wonder about that. Do you think we could use it while she's gone?' James asked. 'We couldn't find anything in the town to draw water with.'

'I'm sure she wouldn't mind,' Jair replied. They both rose, leaving their food. People came out to them, one by one, to cup their hands to their mouths as they poured the cool, crystal clear water. Mary came with Lila so they could take turns holding Anna.

'What did Jesus mean about the harvest? Does he want us to work in the fields when we get to Galilee? I thought harvest wasn't for another couple of months?' Mary wiped water off her chin with the back of her hand.

Lila was looking past her towards the town, 'I think you'll get your answer in a moment.' Mary turned to follow her line of sight, fixed on a crowd of people shimmering in the distance, a small dust cloud rising in their wake. As they drew nearer, all the disciples rose to their feet defensively. Jesus came out to the well and gestured to them with his hands to sit down again. All but Peter, James and John obeyed; they stood behind him protectively.

The woman led the crowd. She came striding up to Jesus, shouting, 'This is the man.' The crowd of Samaritans gathered round him noisily. Peter pushed his sleeves up above his elbows, lowering his head as he squared off his shoulders, ready for a fight. Jesus turned to him, shaking his head sternly. All the others left the shade of the trees, straining curiously to see what was happening. Lila and Mary were right there in the centre of it all, as they had been the last to get a drink.

'This is the man I told you about,' shouted the woman in her coarse voice. 'He told me everything I ever did.'

'And there's a lot to tell,' sniggered someone in the crowd. Laughter broke out.

'Yes … so? As if you have all lived perfect lives.' The woman rounded on them aggressively. She turned back to Jesus, a softer expression on her face. 'You told me everything I ever did. You got through all my defences. You made me feel like I wasn't an outcast for the first time in my life. You explained things to me; things I've always longed to understand. Tell them what you told me.'

She turned bossily, making the townsfolk sit down in the wet earth around the well, slapping a few heads that initially resisted her demands. *She really is rough,* Mary smiled to herself, *rougher than me.* She flicked a look at Jesus and saw he was enjoying himself immensely. Peter, James and John looked more relaxed, but still stayed standing as Jesus began to speak to them.

As the sun was getting lower in the sky, the woman stood up and urged Jesus to stay with her. 'Your followers can stay too. We'll put them up in our homes, won't we? Who wants the privilege of a prophet's blessing?' she asked the crowd. Several hands shot up immediately, others rose more slowly, not fully convinced of the blessing she referred to. 'Come on, come on. Let's show these Jews some real Samaritan hospitality.' And before they knew it, she had them organised.

It was two days later before they could continue their journey to Galilee. The woman had harassed and cajoled more and more people from the town to listen to Jesus. Because of an outcast like her, many believed in him. The word 'Messiah' spread like wildfire through the town.

One old woman leaned over to Lila at the end of the second day and said in a cracked voice, 'We have heard for ourselves and know that this man really is the Saviour of the world.'

'Yes, I believe he is,' Lila replied simply, pressing her hand to her chest, thinking of her own memories of profound divine encounter. It was, she thought, like he'd said – a spring of living water bubbling silently inside her.

6. MERCY

The audacious woman

'You know how they say it gets darkest before the dawn. Well, it must be nearly dawn,' Chloe laughed hollowly on the phone. Anxiety tingled up Grace's spine as she listened. 'There was me thinking it was all about me getting myself sorted out. But this week, in our marriage counselling session, Mark told me he's addicted to pornography. He said he'd always looked at it since his early teens, like most blokes – which justifies it of course, doesn't it?' she asked angrily, not wanting an answer. 'He said he lost control over it when he bought his palm top last year.'

'Oh Chloe ... I'm so sorry to hear that.' Grace thought her response sounded lame.

Chloe went on, not seeming to mind, 'It's all making sense now: the distance that's formed between us; the feeling I'd get when we had sex – like it didn't really matter if I was there or not. He had no interest in me as a person – no wonder there wasn't any intimacy between us. I feel like I don't even know him at all.'

'How did you feel in the session when he said it?' Grace asked.

'I felt betrayed – sickened – angry. I'd been feeling so guilty for hurting him, so ashamed of being deceptive and unfaithful to him, when all along he'd been no better.'

'Did you say that to him?'

'Yes, I did. But as I said it, I remembered our prayer time on the floor. I remembered your story of Lila. I stopped ranting at Mark then.' She paused and Grace enjoyed a fleeting moment of satisfaction. 'He needs as much healing and forgiveness as me, doesn't he? This thing is so much bigger than

I can cope with. To be honest, I feel really overwhelmed.'

'What did he say after that?' Grace asked.

'He said it wasn't about whether or not I was there when we were having sex. He said it was more about him feeling so terrible about himself that he was incapable of relating to me on any meaningful level. He said finding out about my affair was the wake-up call he'd needed. He blamed himself for driving me into someone else's arms. He's told his prayer cell and has been praying regularly with them ever since. He's made his palm top and computer accountable to them. He's also booked himself into a retreat house that one of his mates has recommended. He wants to know if I'll go with him.'

Chloe didn't tell Grace how desolate she was feeling. It was too frightening an emotion to speak of; she felt as fragile as bone china. Maybe if she went on retreat with Mark she would begin to feel better?

'You still there?' Grace asked.

'Yes ... sorry. I know this is gonna sound really hypocritical, but somehow secretly masturbating over porn on the internet seems so pubescent – so dehumanising. At least an affair is with another person – it's about connecting with someone, even if it is someone who belongs to someone else. The only good feeling I have towards Mark right now is that I feel sorry for him – I don't know if I'll ever be able to love him again.' The confusion in her voice was palpable.

'Chloe, how do you know that making a connection with you was it for Tom? Maybe it was it for you, but for him it might have been more about something akin to what Mark's been doing? Or just a bolster to his ego?' Grace was aware that she was speaking too quickly, hurrying because what she was saying would hurt her friend.

Chloe retorted, 'He wanted me. He wanted me.' Her voice rose. 'That's what drew me – that's what I was craving ... and don't you see ... now I know why I'm in the mess I'm in. Mark didn't want me. He just wanted the next fix of sex. It wasn't me that interested him any more.'

'Chloe, you can't blame Mark for your adultery.'

Silence.

'Look, all I'm saying is, Mark and Tom may not be so different. Maybe they both had similar needs, but self-medicated in different ways?'

'Like what?'

'Needs like, oh, I don't know, maybe to feel powerful through illicit sex?'

'Oh, please spare me the psycho-babble. Tom's nothing like Mark,' Chloe snapped. 'You sound like our marriage counsellor.'

'Do I really? What did she say?' Grace struggled to keep annoyance out of her voice.

'She was saying that a lot of people – men and women – women? Can you believe that? I find it very hard to believe. I don't know any women who watch porn – do you?

'Maybe the women you know don't talk about it?'

'Well, do you watch it?'

'No.' Grace felt an old pang of shame as she said it.

'I didn't think you would. Anyway, what was I saying? Oh yes – she said there are people getting hooked on porn these days because it's so in your face – so easily accessible. She said she thought a lot of people succumb to it because of abuse, neglect and loneliness in their childhood. Well, I was getting pretty angry by this stage and I said that it also happened to appeal to the darker side of our nature. I said it allows undisciplined men to relate to women as sex objects and not as people.'

'What did the counsellor say to that?'

'Oh, she was nodding her head, agreeing with me – I couldn't even have a good argument with her! She said, for men who fear rejection and believe themselves to be unworthy of love, getting their needs met without having to relate to someone is a very appealing option.'

'Very isolating too,' Grace said sadly.

'Yeah, I hadn't seen it that way before. But then I thought, wait a minute, Mark's Mum was very supportive and loving, so that couldn't be the reason for it with him, could it? And then all of a sudden, Mark started getting all choked up and said that when his Dad died, he was about ten and his mum went into a depression for a couple of years. He said he knew she did the best she could, but he felt very alienated from her – it was like she was there in body, doing all the right things, but she was emotionally absent. Being an only child, he'd felt really lonely.'

'Well, that's quite something for him to say.'

'I suppose so. But then, listen to this, he said he'd found a stash of his dad's old porn magazines while his mum was at the funeral directors. He was looking for something – anything – as a keepsake of his dad. Some keepsake! He's been hooked ever since. The counsellor was nodding her head in that annoying counsellor-type-way again and said that it could be that Mark had begun to believe back then that maybe there would never be anyone in the world that would care about him. Mark was openly crying by this stage. I was so shocked – I've never seen him do that before,' Chloe paused for a long time on the other end of the line. Grace waited.

'Anyway,' she said in a heavier, tired voice, her anger spent, 'the counsellor went on to say that, later in life, even though he was happily married to me, Mark may have struggled with feelings of isolation. Mark was just sitting there, staring at the floor. She said that, if left unchecked, those painful feelings could lead to addictive behaviour. What easier addiction than the immediate and secret gratification of porn?'

'Bit like us with Galaxy chocolate?' Grace laughed dryly.

'Yep,' Chloe sighed, 'I suppose so. I was lonely as a kid too, you know. I wanted to be wanted then, same as I do now ... but no one was interested, not really. Maybe Mark and I were attracted to each other's pain? Maybe we subliminally wanted to heal each other?'

'Maybe ... of course, Mark being drop-dead gorgeous had nothing to do with it for you?' Grace smiled.

'Well, that helped.' Grace could hear the reciprocal smile in Chloe's voice. 'But why does someone else come along who wants me like I've always dreamed of being wanted, when I'm married? Why wasn't he around when I was free and available?'

'Maybe he wouldn't have been attracted to you back then? Maybe part of his wanting you was because you were forbidden fruit?'

'I don't know ... maybe ... ' she sighed.

Grace was feeling drained and so wound up the conversation, 'It sounds like you've got a good counsellor there. She's helped you both open up quite a lot, hasn't she?' Chloe 'ummed' in agreement. 'Hang in there, babe. I know it's tough, but it'll be worth it in the end.'

'Thanks for listening to me venting. I don't know what I'd do without you.'

'You're so welcome – love you,' Grace said, smiling.

'Love you too,' Chloe said warmly. 'Would you guys have the kids for us if I decide to go with Mark on retreat?'

'Sure – when is it again?'

'Next weekend.'

'Okay. I'll check with Peter. I'd better go now and finish my sermon prep.'

'Oh sorry – you should have said. I wouldn't have gone on so long.'

'It's fine, Chloe. It's sort of on the same subject.'

'You're preaching about pornography?'

'No,' she laughed, 'mercy.'

Chloe hadn't understood what mercy had to do with pornography. All Grace would say was she'd have to come on Sunday if she wanted to find out.

After Grace put the phone down, she stared at her sermon notes for a long time. Before Chloe had rung, she'd been thinking about the ability to step into someone else's shoes and see with their eyes, feel with their feelings and think with their thoughts. Jesus had stepped into human shoes – he'd had mercy. He'd come to call humanity to do the same. Would Chloe and Mark be able to do that on retreat next weekend? She turned to Mark 7, one of the set readings for Sunday. As she read it again, her creativity kicked in. She opened her laptop and went to her 'story' folder.

'I know I shouldn't ... I really should stick with the sermon ... but ... ' strong images of Lila, Jair and Mary were irresistibly forming in her mind. She began to write:

The wind blew in gusts through the sun-drenched seaside town. It rattled wooden chimes hanging from rickety, weather-beaten doorposts. Mary had missed the sea since leaving Galilee. So had Lila. They had stayed in Galilee for a while, meeting Peter's family and some of the other disciples' families as well. But Jesus had wanted to go to Tyre on the Mediterranean coast and so they had followed.

The women had both been excited by the prospect of glimpsing the vast sea they'd only heard tales about. They walked with Anna, tottering now between them, clinging to their fingers. Time had gone so quickly. It was hard to believe she would soon be able to walk on her own. With each gust, Anna looked shocked as wisps of her hair whipped her fat little cheeks. The smell of the sea that each blast of wind brought was making Lila feel nauseous.

'Are we nearly there?' Lila called out.

The men were about fifty yards in front of them. Jair stopped in mid conversation turning to see where his wife was, shading his eyes with one hand. 'It's not much further, Lila. Do you want me to carry Anna on my shoulders?'

'That would be good,' she shouted back as another burst of wind blasted into her face, ripping her voice away. She reached out for the wall next to her and steadied herself. Mary bent down and picked Anna up, kissing her. They leaned against the wall and waited for Jair. The other women who'd been walking behind slowed to a stop around them.

'Are you all right?' Mary asked Lila.

'I'm feeling slightly sick. I think it's the smell of the sea.' Lila tried to smile as she clutched her stomach. She reached over to Anna and stroked her hair, trying to distract everyone's attention from herself. 'I'm fine. It's this little one we need to be worried about. She's missed her afternoon nap.'

'Hello, my little dumpling!' Jair reached the group and immediately Anna's face lit up.

'Dada!' she sang out, reaching her chubby hands towards him. Mary nearly lost hold of her as she wriggled towards her father.

'Ah ... my darling. You've been such a good girl. You've missed your sleep and I haven't heard you cry once.' He buried his bearded face in her neck, sending her into squeals and giggles. Mary watched wistfully.

'How much further have we to go?' Lila asked him, looking anxious.

'If memory serves, it's about three streets down there on the left,' he pointed down the sloping street past the other men. 'We may even get a glimpse of the sea from there,' he smiled at her encouragingly. 'I'm sure my brother's family will be preparing food for us as we speak.'

With that, Lila vomited into the gutter.

When they eventually reached the third turning, they were

rewarded with a glimpse of blue expanse shimmering between the rooftops. 'Look, Lila, there's the sea,' Jair called over his shoulder.

Lila couldn't have cared less.

※　※　※

'I'll get her some yoghurt. That should calm her stomach down,' Mary whispered to Jair as they withdrew from the darkened room where Lila and Anna lay.

'Get some dates as well – I want to give them as a gift to my brothers' wife.'

The women followed the road down to the sea front. The market was just coming to life again as the afternoon shadows lengthened. The wind had died down, leaving the town basking in balmy sunshine, stretched out along the coast like a sleek cat. The sea was casting its spell on them. Like little girls, they ran down to the beach, squeezing between the fishing boats, shopping lists momentarily forgotten. Mary was the first to undo her sandals and stick her feet into the clear, effervescent waves. She splashed the other women, who, in turn, splashed her back. There was a lot of squealing and laughter. She didn't want to go back to the errand; she wanted to keep on playing. She'd had so little childhood, controlling the little girl within her was a struggle. The waves were calling her out to play. But eventually they sat on the beach, dried their feet and put their sandals back on.

They slowly made their way among the stalls, led by the older Mary Magdalene. The younger Mary begrudgingly looked for yoghurt. She found a woman selling it in small clay pots.

'You're not from around here, are you?' the woman asked as she wrapped the pot in muslin.

Mary shook her head, 'Jerusalem, but we've been by Lake Galilee.'

'I can't remember the last time I played in the waves.' The woman sounded older than she looked. 'Not many people from here get that excited about the sea.' She smiled as she handed Mary the curds. 'I'm from Greece originally, but I've lived here all my life.'

'Do you speak Greek?' Mary was remembering the Greek nobles that she'd entertained at Herod's palace. Her face flushed slightly at the memory.

'Oh yes, my mother made me speak it at home all the time. I spoke it to my daughter ... until last year,' a shadow crossed her pleasant features.

'Why did you stop last year?' Mary asked, rummaging in her pouch for coins to pay for the yoghurt.

'Ah!' The woman looked away and spat into the dirt. 'A bad thing happened.' She looked back up at Mary: 'The gods were angry,' she said with a fatalistic shrug.

Mary's curiosity got the better of her. 'What do you mean?'

'You don't want to know.' The woman took the coins from her and nodded as if that was the end of the matter.

'But I do want to know,' Mary said earnestly, her unhappiness at having to leave the waves behind forgotten.

The woman eyed her for a moment as if weighing her up. Then she leaned forward and said in a low voice, 'An unclean spirit torments my daughter. No one can help her. I've tried everything.'

At that moment the others came up behind Mary. She asked, 'When did it start?'

The woman hesitated, looking uncertainly at them, but something in their faces must have assured her because she drew in a deep breath and said slowly, 'It was at the New Year festival. I wanted good luck for my daughter, you see, so I took her to the priest of Molech.' Mary flinched at the name of the Canaanite god. 'Oh don't worry. It's not like that. We're good people, you see?' She looked earnestly at the three of them. 'You Jews think we're ignorant and depraved, but we don't sacrifice our children any more – we are civilized now – well, most of us. I've heard tales of it still going on in secret – but it's forbidden.' She scratched her head and pulled her shawl higher up on her head. Mary had composed her features, hiding her distaste.

'Go on,' she said, encouragingly.

'I took her to the priest and had to wait nearly all day – there were so many children with their anxious mothers all hoping for a blessed year. Each child passes through fire – a purification, a dedication – you see?' The women didn't see. 'The priest took her into his room to prepare her. I waited nervously outside. I don't know what he did, but I knew I was not to enter with her. When she came out, Anat stepped between the flames; she had a strange look on her face. I thought she glowed with an unearthly light.' The woman's voice quivered. 'I fell on my face in gratitude to the deity for his blessing on Anat. But then I heard her scream. When I looked up, the priest had grabbed her and she was kicking and screaming. She bit him and he dropped her. Then she went limp – as if she were dead. I carried her home and she has been like that ever since: sometimes crazy, sometimes as if she were dead.'

Mary reached out and took hold of the woman's hand. 'I'm so sorry this has happened to you. I'm so sorry for your daughter.' Surprised by her touch, the woman's eyes brimmed with tears. Then, 'I have known something of the torment your daughter is going through.'

The woman looked at her through narrowed eyes. 'Have you heard of Jesus of Nazareth?' Mary asked.

Mary's identification clearly touched the woman and her tone softened further, 'Is he the one who's been travelling around Galilee? We've heard stories of miracles from there.' The woman was looking intently at Mary.

'Yes, that's him. We're here with him now. I know he could help your daughter,' Mary said.

The woman wasted no time. As soon as she heard this, she called to her neighbour to mind her stall and followed the women. When they got to the house, Jesus was sitting in the courtyard teaching a crowd of people. Jair's brother had gathered all his Jewish neighbours together. He was a wealthy man and his property was the largest in the street, so there was plenty of room. His servants were taking advantage of the last of the daylight and were in the process of lighting lanterns hanging from a tree at the centre of the courtyard. A servant brought Jesus a cup of water and as he paused to drink, the Greek woman urgently pushed her way towards him and fell at his feet. Mary was just behind her.

'Please help me, Master – my daughter is plagued by an unclean spirit. Have mercy. I've heard that you have authority over such things. This girl told me you could help me.' she gestured to Mary. Jesus looked at Mary's eager face and then looked back down at the woman at his feet.

With a tinge of something that felt to Mary like long-suffering, he said, 'First let the children eat all they want, for it is not right to take the children's bread and toss it to their dogs.'

Mary was shocked. She hadn't expected this response. There was a general murmur of agreement from the Jewish people around Jesus. An old man with a long silver ringlets and a flowing beard spoke up, 'This is a wise proverb, rabbi. It is as it should be. Even this woman must know it to be true.' Mary flinched, not fully understanding what was going on. She looked at Jesus again and saw that he was trying not to smile. She was even more confused.

'Yes, Lord,' replied the Greek woman with good humour, 'but even the dogs under the table eat the children's crumbs.'

There were a few intakes of breath and then some laughter at the woman's audacity. Jesus looked delighted, clapped his hands and laughed, 'For such a reply, you may go; the demon has left your daughter.' He then bent down and helped her to her feet.

'Thank you,' she said, holding his hand to her forehead. 'Thank you for your mercy, Master.' Letting go of his hand she backed out through the crowd of onlookers. Some pushed her, showing their irritation at a 'dog eating the children's bread'. Mary struggled through after her. Jesus called John and sent him after the women. Together they made their way behind the Greek woman, who had broken into a run down the road, into the growing gloom of nightfall.

'Wait,' called Mary.

The woman looked over her shoulder and shouted something. 'What?' Mary shouted back.

The woman slowed to a brisk walk as she turned her head and yelled, 'I can't wait any longer! I've waited too long already!'

They caught up with her and together wound their way through the crowded alleyways and bustling streets of Tyre. When they came to her door, they were all breathless. Mary leaned her back up against the wall of the house.

John recovered regular breathing first. 'Not bad for girls.' An affectionate grin split his boyish face. Mary grimaced at him. 'It's not too dark for me to see you,' he said.

'I know,' she retorted.

'Are you ok?' Mary asked the woman who was standing next to her and staring blankly at her front door.

'What if nothing's changed?' her eyes flicked to Mary and then back to the door.

'Believe me. If he said it was so, then it is so. I know – he did this for me.' Mary pushed herself off the wall and came alongside the woman. 'What's your name?'

'Sophia.'

'Wisdom.' She put her hand on her shoulder. 'Well, Sophia, you cannot be wiser than to put your trust in Jesus. We believe he is the longed-for Messiah. He has come to save his people from their sins. And today, he has extended his power to you, a Gentile. You are highly favoured. In a moment, you will see little Anat as you knew her before. Mark this day in your heart for this is the day that salvation has entered your home.'

With that, Sophia pushed the door of her house open and called, 'Ma? Ma? Are you here? Is Anat all right?' Laughter floated down from above them. 'Ma? Ma?' A door opened and two pairs of feet could be heard on the wooden stairs, one heavy and slow and the other light and quick.

'Mama … it's me. Mama … where have you been?' A little girl of about eight ran down the stairs and threw herself into her mother's arms.

'Anat! My darling!' Sophia sobbed into her daughter's hair. Mary and John looked on in wonder.

Sophia pulled back from her daughter and held her at arm's length. 'Let me see you.' She searched Anat's little face in the lamplight. The child obediently stood still, her oval face tilted upwards. 'It's gone. It's really gone,' she whispered.

'Yes, it has. I felt sick and then shook and then I … I was

changed,' replied Anat. 'I sat up and grandma looked shocked. She saw me shaking, didn't you, grandma?'

'I did. I was dozing in my chair beside Anat when suddenly her body began to quake violently. It woke me up!' said the old woman, who had slowly made her way down the rickety stairs. 'It was a very strange thing. I can't explain it. But when I realised she was herself again, I cried and cried, eh Anat? You've come back to us.' The old woman affectionately tousled her granddaughter's hair.

'Who are they?' Anat asked in a lowered voice as she stared at the strangers over her mother's shoulder.

Sophia stood up from her kneeling position in front of her daughter and turned to her new friends, wiping her eyes, 'These are the people who made it possible for you to be set free. I met them in the market place and they told me about a man called Jesus who they follow. They believe he is the Jewish Messiah – a holy man.' Anat's arms were around her mother's waist, her head resting on her bosom. Sophia was stroking her hair and her grandmother had her arm round her as well. 'It was this Jesus that I went to see and asked him to cast the unclean spirit out of you.' She looked down into her daughter's eyes, 'Even though I'm not Jewish, I thought it was worth asking him. Oh, Anat! Ma!' she looked from one to the other, 'You must meet him. There is something about him. It made me want to be Jewish,' she laughed. The old woman shot her an incredulous look.

Mary came over to them and John came closer. 'There is something about him,' Mary spoke quietly. 'He has told us that if we know him, then we know what God is like. He speaks of God as his father and he's taught us to pray, calling God our father too. He says that he and his father are one. He heals people of terrible sicknesses and diseases and, oh ... you should see how he treats sinners – I mean – outcasts, like me. He steps into our shoes – I've never known mercy like this before. He has changed my life.'

'And mine,' said John, solemnly.

'When can I meet him?' Anat's voice piped up from the centre of the huddle.

'You could come tomorrow and see him before we leave? Come

early though, because we will want to start our journey before the sun gets too high in the sky,' said John. He looked at Mary, 'We must go now. It's getting late.'

As they made their way to the door, Sophia touched Mary on the arm. 'Thank you,' she said, smiling gratefully.

Mary nodded and then reached over and stroked Anat's cheek. 'See you tomorrow.' She smiled as she stepped into the dark.

※　※　※

Lila was feeling no better. She had not been able to keep anything down. The yoghurt had been a welcome coolness sinking down her throat into her stomach, but a short while later it came up again. 'What is wrong with me?' she wailed to Jair, who was holding Anna upside down and tickling her tummy.

'I don't know, my love,' he turned Anna up the right way and sat her in his lap. She reached up and tried to grab his beard, but he ducked his head out of range and tickled her, sending her into giggles again.

'Do you have to make such a noise?' Lila asked reproachfully, burying her face in her hands. 'The last time I felt like this was when I was pregnant with you,' she said, sliding her hands down her face and looked pointedly at Anna, who took this as an invitation and launched herself out of Jair's lap and into a crawl across the thin mattress they were sitting on. She grabbed Lila's hair to pull herself up and then planted her mouth on Lila's, drooling shamelessly into it.

'Mama,' Anna said proudly.

Lila just managed to hand Anna back to Jair before she lunged, retching into the bowl at the foot of the mattress again. Anna began to cry.

Jair looked stunned. Revelation was dawning in his eyes as he soothed Anna's rejection. 'I know this is impossible ... but do you think you might be pregnant again?'

Lila, sat back from the bowl of bile, pulling her long, wavy hair away from her face. She went very still, staring at her husband.

'Mama!' wailed Anna. Jair let her go to Lila.

'I'm sorry, Anna.' Lila picked her up and hugged her. 'Mummy's just not very well right now. Mummy loves you sweetie. I'm so sorry.' Anna stopped crying and stuck her thumb in her mouth, resting her head on Lila's shoulder contentedly.

Lila knew it was true. 'I think I am ... am I?' she put one hand down onto her pelvis, not taking her eyes off Jair. 'Do you think I am?'

'I do.' He paused, a slow smile began cracking his serious features. 'That seer did say that one day a powerful stranger would bring the curse to an end.' He suddenly leapt up. 'I must go and speak with Jesus. Do you think he's asleep yet? It's not that late, is it? I'll go now ... I'll be back soon ... '. He was a ball of nervous energy. He took one step over to Lila, hugged her and then was gone.

She stayed very still, enjoying the sensation of Anna's contented weight on her chest. A deep surge of emotion welled up in her until it slowly came up her throat and into her mouth. For a moment she thought she was going to vomit again, but instead she found herself singing a wordless song. Anna listened quietly.

❊　❊　❊

The morning brought a fresh surge of vomiting for Lila, a thrill of excitement for Jair and a new tooth for Anna.

'That explains the dribbling, doesn't it?' she said, rubbing her fingertip over the new, white protrusion in Anna's upper gum. 'Poor love.' She smiled into Anna's round face.

Jair lifted Anna onto his lap and gave her a dried fig to chew on. 'You'll soon have a brother or sister to play with – who'd have thought it?' he beamed. Lila was watching them both. Stealthily, like a mosquito, an uncomfortable thought bit her. *If I am pregnant, will he love his own child more than Anna?* She ignored it. But mosquito bites swell and itch for days to come.

They had all gathered in the courtyard to say their farewells. Jesus was sitting under the tree in the centre of the courtyard, surrounded by a hoard of giggling children. 'Where did they all come from?' Lila asked Jair.

'They're the servants' children,' Jair replied. 'Usually they're kept out of the way. I hope Jesus doesn't mind?' His eyebrows had drawn together above his nose.

'Look at him, Jair. Does he look like he minds?' Lila retorted irritably. Jair looked mildly taken aback by her tone but said nothing. She was holding Anna on her hip, who had begun to strain towards the group of children, holding out her arms and shouting, 'Bup ... bup!'

Lila squatted down and let Anna stand on her plump little feet. Anna had a firm grip of one of Lila's fingers as she launched into a lurching stagger towards Jesus. When she got to the outer circle of laughing children, she banged on their backs with her free hand, shouting 'Bup! Bup!' They turned and obediently made room for her until she'd climbed and crawled over them to Jesus' knees, happily leaving her mother behind. Lila moved back to stand beside Jair where she could survey the scene. Jesus picked Anna up onto his lap, never breaking the pace of the story he was telling. When he got to the punch line, the children let out loud cheers of raucous laughter. Anna joined in, pulling at his beard and clapping her hands.

As Jesus was laughing with the children, he looked straight at Lila for a split second. It was like an arrow fired across the space between them, hitting its mark in her heart. She smiled uncertainly back at him. She somehow knew he was addressing the fearful thought that had quickly become a barrier between her and Jair.

Mary emerged from the house as the Greek woman arrived with her daughter and mother. Excitedly, she ran to open the gates. 'You came. I'm so glad you came,' she exclaimed.

'How could we not come?' Sophia responded.

'Where is he?' Anat asked impatiently, tugging at her mother's skirts as she came through the gate.

'Don't be rude, Anat,' her grandmother scolded, looking uncomfortable in unfamiliar surroundings.

'But I don't want to miss him,' Anat replied helplessly.

'You haven't missed him, Anat. He's just over there – with all the children. Under the tree – see?' Mary had crouched down to reassure the little girl.

Anat followed the line of Mary's pointing finger and watched the man and the children in the bright morning sunshine, enjoying each other's company.

'Do you want me to take you over to him?' Mary asked.

Anat looked up at her mother, then at Mary and back again to her mother.

Sophia smiled encouragingly, 'That would be good, wouldn't it Anat? We'd all like to go over to him.' With this reassurance, the child took Mary's hand and crossed the courtyard towards Jesus, followed by her family.

Jesus watched them approach, and Lila thought she saw a tear glint at the corner of his eye, or perhaps it was just reflected sunlight. He stood up, hoisting Anna onto his hip, and stretched out his right arm in welcome. 'You came back,' he said, smiling expansively. The children were all leaning their heads back and squinting up at the new arrivals.

'I wanted Anat to meet the one who set her free. I wanted my mother,' she paused and pulled her mother by the sleeve so that she couldn't hide behind her, 'I wanted my mother to meet you also. We can never thank you enough for what you've done for Anat.'

Jesus picked his way between the children and came to stand beside Sophia. 'Believe in me,' he said simply as he looked her in the eye.

'I do,' Sophia responded.

'Then follow me,' he replied. Without waiting for her answer, he dropped down to his knees to be at eye level with her daughter. Anna let out a squeal of delight and clutched at his tunic with the free-fall. Jesus studied Anat's oval face for a moment. He looked up at Sophia and asked, 'May I bless her?'

Sophia's face crumpled. 'That's what I was seeking when she became tormented.'

'I know,' replied Jesus.

'The priest was a bad man,' Anat whispered. Sophia caught her breath in her throat, exchanging an anguished glance with her mother.

'I know,' said Jesus. 'May I take it for you?' he was looking at Anat, showed her the palm of his hand as he raised it slowly to place upon her head. She nodded as they exchanged a little smile.

Anna followed suit, reaching out and patting her hair with a chubby hand and making cooing noises.

Sophia and her mother cried quietly as Mary put her arms round both their shoulders.

When Jesus finished praying, he stood up and called, 'Jair! Come and take your daughter. I think she needs to be changed.'

Jair hurried over, smiling apologetically at Jesus as he relieved him of his damp child. 'Sorry about that, rabbi.'

'Think nothing of it,' Jesus replied. Then, in a loud voice, he addressed everyone gathered in the courtyard – Jair's relatives and servants, the neighbours, his disciples and the women – 'Things that cause people to sin are bound to come, but woe to that person through whom they come. It would be better for him to be thrown into the sea,' (he gestured to the glistening blue beyond the flat roof of the house), 'with a millstone tied round his neck than for him to cause one of these little ones to sin. So watch yourselves.'

A stunned silence followed.

Jair and Lila exchanged glances. Sophia and her mother wept. Mary had her eyes serenely fixed on Jesus. She thought of her little ones buried under bitter herbs.

It was Anat who broke the silence. 'Where are you going?' she asked Jesus.

Jesus looked down at her, smiling softly. 'I'm on my way to Jerusalem.'

'Can we go with you?'

7. LIFE

The girl and the woman who got their lives back

Grace stared at her computer screen for a long time. She couldn't stop the pain in her chest. Usually she could, but this time it wouldn't obey. Mercy ... mercy ... she wrestled with the concept. She read over Jesus' words again. It would be better for him to be thrown into the sea with a millstone tied round his neck than for him to cause one of these little ones to sin. She was gripping the edge of her desk so hard that her knuckles had gone white. A sob broke from her lips, opening a floodgate that had been kept securely locked for years. Panicked, she struggled to regain control of her emotions, but it was too late. She had dreaded this moment for so long, thinking that if she came undone, she would never be able to put herself back together again. The first huge wave of pain subsided. She fell to her knees beside her desk sobbing, 'Oh, God ... oh, God, please help me.'

A second wave submerged her, a turbulent current of grief, shame and rage. There was no way of stopping the torrent of gut wrenching sobs that were pouring out of her mouth. She gave up fighting and rolled with each subsequent wave as they hit her.

Eventually she calmed down enough to sit up. Her eyes were so swollen she could hardly see. She wanted to crawl into bed and hide, but then it occurred to her that Peter would be home soon. Her heart lifted momentarily at the thought of him. She looked at her watch and realised how long she had been crying. He would be home any minute. She resolved that this time she would tell him everything.

He wouldn't reject her, not now, not after all these years together?

Even if he did, she knew she had to tell him. She hadn't the strength to carry this secret any longer.

She stood up slowly, holding onto her desk for support. She made her way to the bathroom and looked at her reflection in the mirror. 'Not so beautiful now,' she jeered at herself as she turned on the cold tap. She splashed water on her face, cupping it over her eyes to bring down the swelling. She was drying her face when she heard Peter's footsteps on the gravel drive.

Peter was shocked at his wife's appearance. She was normally composed and calm, her features the epitome of beauty. She clung to him once he shut the front door and he held her, stroking her hair as she cried helplessly on his shoulder. He asked her what was wrong several times but didn't get a reply for a while. Eventually she pulled away from him and he asked her if she'd like a drink, maybe a whisky? She'd nodded wordlessly and followed him into the kitchen like a lost child. Peter was becoming more and more alarmed. In their twelve years of marriage, he'd never seen her in this state before.

After he'd poured their drinks, he sat down at the kitchen table and beckoned her to come and sit on his lap. She declined, sitting down opposite him instead. Worry lines creased his forehead. He searched her eyes, waiting for her to speak.

After a few sips of her drink she lifted her eyes to his and took a deep breath. 'I have to tell you something that I haven't told you before – I haven't told anyone but my grandmother.' Peter waited silently, stroking her hand that lay limply on the table between them. 'I haven't even wanted to think about it, because I hate myself so much for it. I guess you could say I've lived a double life, in a way.' She paused, searching his eyes to see if he was ready for what she was about to say.

'Remember how I was at dad's funeral?' She pulled her hand away from his and folded it into the other on her lap. Peter nodded. 'You were so kind to me. I couldn't bring myself to tell you then – but I should have.' She looked lost. Peter resisted the desire to reach for her. She had gone deathly pale. He knew he had to let her do this, no matter how painful it was.

'It's my writing that's brought it up to the surface. It's what's been going on with Chloe too. I can't go on any more without you knowing.' She rubbed her forehead agitatedly. Peter crushed his impatience and waited. 'I don't know where to start,' she said, looking at him helplessly.

'Start anywhere, sweetheart. I don't mind,' he said, smiling.

Grace took a deep breath and stared hard at her hands. 'You know how everyone said how close dad and I were? That I was his princess? He'd always wanted a girl. My brothers all knew it, everyone knew it.' Peter nodded.

'It wasn't always as it should have been.'

Peter felt sick.

'He'd touch me sometimes … '. Her voice had dropped to a whisper. 'He used to take pictures of me. I loved the attention he gave me, even though I didn't like the way he touched me. I trusted him. But one day mum found a pile of the photos and I heard them rowing. She said some terrible things. That's when I realised. I was about thirteen,' she stared vacantly away from Peter.

'That was it – I couldn't stand to be near him after that. He'd been my idol: my wonderful father, respectable judge, pillar of the community. He'd wanted me to follow in his footsteps and study law. I rejected him completely after that. We had some terrible rows through sixth form. When I went to Cambridge I cut myself off completely from my family. None of them ever knew why, except dad maybe. I instructed the university not to accept any of his cheques. I returned every cheque he sent me.

'I was working two jobs while studying to pay my own way. You know me – so stubborn.' Peter smiled in agreement, but Grace didn't smile back. 'One of my Chelsea friends used to tell me I should do modelling. My mum had been a model and I thought – why not? It beat cleaning up after people. She introduced me to the agency she worked for,' her voice dropped again so that Peter had to lean forward to hear her, 'and they took me straight away. After a while they asked me if I'd like to meet one of their partner companies that ran a high spec escort agency. It was a lot more money and it seemed like a natural progression to me back then. I had become pretty hard and calculating, thinking I was this great independent woman.' She lifted her haunted eyes to Peters. 'Looking back now, I realise my boundaries were already broken. I was easy pickings.' She paused and shook her head, 'It's incredible how you can convince yourself.'

He was processing what she was saying – no emotion showed on his face at first. Confused, he said, 'I don't understand … ?'

Grace shifted in her seat. 'Nowhere did it say in writing that sex was part of the deal. Men paid for beautiful women to accompany them to business functions or to the theatre. But the unspoken understanding was that more times than not, that's where it would end up, if we were willing.'

Peter's face had drained of all colour. He stared at his wife.

'They were mostly foreign – businessmen, sheiks, diplomats. It was all very discreet and tasteful. No one at Cambridge ever knew what I did on the weekends. I did it for about two years. I'd earned enough money by then to see me through my degree and Masters.

Peter looked like he didn't know what to say but was about to speak anyway. Grace held up her hand to stop him. 'There's more,' she said, floating on an undulating current of despair. Now Peter looked like he was falling off a cliff.

'The reason I stopped wasn't that I'd earned enough money or that I realised the error of my ways. I got pregnant.' Her voice sounded very far away to her.

'I always made my clients use protection,' her voice became even more distant, 'but one wouldn't listen – he forced me to have unprotected sex.' She was silent for a time, staring into space.

'I had an abortion and got an infection that left me the way I am now.' Hearing herself confess it was shocking. Her heart was pounding. She wasn't sure who was more traumatised – her or Peter. They stared silently at each other.

Fear was creeping up Grace's throat, constricting her breathing as she gazed at her husband. The voice of her well-educated-journalist-and-priest self was telling her that he was in shock and that she needed to give him time to digest what he'd heard. But the child in her wanted him to take her in his arms and hold her.

'Did you report it to the police?' Peter asked.

Grace smiled a sad little smile, 'No. It was a risk of the job. It was my choice, my fault. They wouldn't have done anything about it.'

'But that man is out there, free to do it again. Don't you think you should report him, for the sake of any other victims?'

'I know. I've seen him recently.'

'What? Where?' Peter's voice was full of alarm.

'He came into the parish office to book a Christening service for his son,' she said flatly.

'Oh my God!' Peter breathed. Then another thought hit him: 'Did he recognise you?'

'No. Hooker turned priest? No ... I used to straighten and dye my hair back then and I wore colour contacts too.'

He looked slightly reassured, and then worried again, 'What are you going to do?' he asked, the enormity of the situation exploding in his brain.

'Well, I asked Trevor to take the Christening ... and I've been thinking a lot. I need to get closure on the past somehow. I guess my writing's been helping me.'

'But what about him? Aren't you going to report him to the police? You still can, you know.'

'And risk my past life leaking out? The press would love that, wouldn't they? I can see it on the front page of every paper. No, Peter, I'd never work again in any church in the country.'

Peter's eyes were watery. He slowly wiped them with the heel of his hand and then reached over and took her hands in his. He held them firmly on the table between them as he got control of his emotions. At last he said, 'I've waited so long for this. After Helen died, I never thought I'd love again; never thought I'd want someone to love me again. But then you came along,' he smiled brokenly at her. Grace stared at his hands.

'You know, I've always known there was something between you and me. I thought you were withholding something of yourself from me because you loved the "big man upstairs" more than me. I tried to resign myself to it, but I guess secretly I was hoping it was something else. I couldn't compete with him, could I?' He squeezed her hand. 'Come here,' he said, pulling her towards him. She came and sat on his lap. She rested her head on his shoulder, exhausted.

※　※　※

How will my past be healed? The little girl inside me? How do children heal? Grace wondered. People said they were resilient and robust, but she knew better. She'd carried wounds within herself and covered them over, layer upon layer, for many years. The trouble was that the pain had resolutely clawed its way through to the surface.

Chloe's children were furiously growing layers over their wounds.

On the first night of the weekend that Chloe and Mark were away on retreat, Grace was tucking the youngest into bed. He lay very still, straight as a poker, arms rigidly at his sides. She read him a story and they said his special prayer together, but Grace saw no sign of him relaxing. *What does he need? What do I say to a five year old that will make any sense of what his mummy and daddy have done to his world?*

'Well, Charlie, I think I'd better go see what your brother and sister are up to.' Grace patted his hand as she began to stand up.

'Don't go,' he whispered.

Grace sat back down again. 'Okay,' she said. 'Are you worried about anything?' *Of course he's worried, you idiot.*

Then in a choked voice he said, 'Will mummy come back?'

Grace's throat constricted, 'Of course she will! She's coming back day after tomorrow with daddy, honey. She couldn't stay away from you for very long. I bet she's missing you right now.' Grace squeezed his hand. 'What made you think she might not come back?'

Tears rolled into his dark hair. He let out a sob. 'Ollie told me that when your mum likes someone else, she doesn't come back. That's what happened to his mum.' He pulled his hand away from Grace's and buried his fists into his eyes.

'Oh, Charlie, sweetheart.' Grace reached out and stroked his forehead. 'Mummy isn't leaving you ... or daddy. She loves you very much.' *Help!* She waited for inspiration. 'Mummy and daddy have gone away to spend some special time together, asking God to help them fix their mistakes. You see?'

Charlie curled up into a ball, burying his head against her leg. She wrapped her arms round his little body. Eventually his sobs subsided. She pulled away from him a little and ran her fingers through his damp hair. He wiped his nose on his pyjama sleeve, leaving a long silver trail across images of Bart Simpson. 'Shall we pray for mummy and daddy?' Grace asked. Charlie nodded exhaustedly.

'Dear God,' Grace whispered, 'help mummy and daddy love each other. Help them fix their mistakes. And please help Charlie know he is very, very loved by both of them and that he is safe in your hands.' Grace paused wondering if that was enough, and then, 'Amen.'

She opened her eyes to see Charlie's face relaxing. She stayed until he was fast asleep.

Later, as she sat on the sofa with her laptop and her Bible open beside her, she turned to prayer.

Heal my pain, Lord, so I can help these little ones heal too. Show me the lies that have been sown into my mind and reveal your truth to me.

She thought of the passage from Luke 8 she had been reading. She wondered what it had been like for Jairus' daughter to be dead and then to come back to life. Part of her had been dead since she was thirteen. It felt like Jesus was saying to her, 'Little girl, get up.'

Grace opened her 'story' file in her documents and began to write:

She hadn't left her daughter's side for three days. She'd watched helplessly as the fever had relentlessly raged through her child's body, mocking her with moments of remission, only to return with a fiercer vengeance. She'd been praying incessantly, swaying backwards and forwards with the agony of the inevitable.

She was reciting a psalm in a whispery voice as she rocked: 'I waited patiently for the Lord; he turned to me and heard my cry. He lifted me out of the slimy pit, out of the mud and mire; he set my feet on a rock and gave me a firm place to stand. He put a new song ...', her eyes filled with tears again as her throat constricted, ' ... in my mouth.' Her mouth opened wide in a silent howl.

With tremendous effort, she pulled herself back from the brink, reached over and soaked the cloth she held in her hand in a bowl of water beside the bed. She wrung it out and placed it on her daughter's forehead, resolutely continuing her recitation of the psalm, hoping the ritual would hold her together: '... A hymn of praise to our God. Many will see and fear and put their trust in the Lord. Blessed is the person who makes the Lord their trust, who does not look to the proud, to those who turn aside to false gods. Many, O Lord my God, are the wonders you have done. The things you planned for us, no one can recount to you; were I to speak of them, they would be too many to declare.'

Her mind went blank.

She stared at her daughter's pallid face. Her eyes focused on her lips. They were cracked and dry. She dipped her finger into the water and then held it under the child's nose. She felt a very slight cooling sensation as frail breath touched damp skin.

She returned to her rocking, knowing she had missed out a whole chunk of the psalm, but was incapable of locating it in her mind. 'Be pleased, O Lord, to save me; O Lord, come quick to help me … '. A swell of terror overwhelmed her and she howled hoarsely, burying her head in her hands. It slowly washed through her, pulling at her like a strong current, her limbs heavy, her chest aching. Saliva thickened in her mouth, making her words stick together in clumps. 'I am poor and needy,' she wept. 'May the Lord think of me. You are my help and my deliverer; O my God, do not delay.'

She lifted her head and looked at her daughter again. There was no change. She reached for the cloth and repeated the ritual. Tenderly, she wiped the child's arms and hands, chest, neck and face. She watched the moisture evaporate instantly on hot skin. She replaced the cloth on her forehead, bent down and gently kissed her on those parchment-like lips. *Let me take this for you … let it be mine, not yours.* She held her in her arms and rocked her.

Jairus came into the darkened room. He closed the door behind him and leaned up against it as his eyes adjusted to the gloom. The dull pain in his chest grew stronger. With an effort, he pushed himself off the door and moved silently to stand beside his wife, resting his left hand on her shoulder. *How could so much life and joy be swallowed up in so much pain?* He traced his daughter's profile, remembering how her smile could make his heart skip a beat; how she had brought so much laughter and love into their lives when they had begun to think that such a privilege would never be theirs.

'I've finished arrangements for the Sabbath. The attendant will see to everything else at synagogue,' he spoke softly. She nodded, not looking up. How like him to speak of the mundane at a time like this. Her skin felt irritated where his hand rested. She wanted to shrug it off, but didn't.

Instead, she asked, 'Are the servants back from the well yet?'

'No.' There was a long silence as they watched their child's shallow breathing.

'I need the cooler water. This,' she pointed at the bowl, 'is now lukewarm.'

'I know,' he frowned, hating his helplessness to protect or provide.

He could hear the murmur of the mourners who had been gathering all day under the tree that shaded the front of their home. He worried that she could hear them too. He'd ordered them to be quiet. But the women couldn't help themselves any more than vultures could help cawing.

'I'll go and see if they've returned yet.' *At least that's something I can do*, he thought as he turned to go. She nodded – relieved he was leaving.

Outside, the professional mourners were glad to see him to talk money. He repressed his revulsion of them under a well-constructed calm. Many years of leading the synagogue had taught him never to show his emotions to the crowd. He allowed one of them to broker the deal, appearing to bargain, bringing her to the figure he had settled on in his own mind. Not so low that it would look as if his daughter were of no value to him, but not so high as to give too much ground to them.

He walked through them to the edge of the hill that marked the boundary of his property. He could see for miles, but the view didn't please him today. He was searching the slopes for figures laden with water jars. Suddenly they appeared about a hundred metres down in front of him, from behind some bushes. His heart lifted. 'What's taken you so long?' he called.

'It's the teacher, Jesus,' they shouted together. 'He's here, he's coming here.' They crossed the space between them quicker than Jairus thought possible. Breathless, his maid began explaining who Jesus was.

'I know who he is,' Jairus interrupted her mid flow. 'I've heard the stories just as you have.'

She hardly paused for breath. She'd heard the news while gathering water at the well. She was so sorry they were late, but they'd met one of Jesus' followers – a woman with a new baby, so tiny – only six weeks old. She'd just come out of seclusion. Anyway, Jesus and his disciples had gone across the lake to the region of the Gerasenes while a small group of women had remained in town to look after the mother and child.

Jairus was losing his patience. The maid must have noticed because she suddenly ended in a rush, 'She said she was sure Jesus would heal your daughter.'

'Take the water to your mistress immediately. She has been waiting long enough for it,' He said curtly. As she gathered up her water jars, looking deflated, Jairus felt convicted. He rallied, 'Forgive me.' He inclined his head stiffly and she responded with an accepting nod. 'Where did you say I could find this Jesus?'

※ ※ ※

He was running – not something that befitted the dignity of his office – and running down hill at that. He slipped on the dirt track a few times. Once, he fell, cutting the palm of his hand on a rock. The blood quickly congealed in the heat – a sticky mess. He held his hand above his head to slow the bleeding. With his other hand he held his robes so as not to trip over them. He made his way down through the fringe of the town and was relieved to reach the even surface of the streets. People stopped and stared as he hurried past. Why would the synagogue ruler be so undignified? Women marvelled at glimpsing his legs as he ran past. Some were curious enough to follow him right down to the harbour.

A crowd had already gathered there and the talk was of the miracle worker. Jairus shaded his eyes with his wounded hand, scanning the horizon. He wiped his forehead and daubed at the sweat running in rivulets down his neck with his sleeve. His heart refused to slow its pace, his stomach was as tight as a drum. He made his way through the crowd, like Moses parting the Red Sea.

He came to the water's edge and stood next to a young family. A toddler was sitting on the wet sand, squealing with delight as each wave washed over her chubby feet and legs. Her father squatted behind her, celebrating each wave with her. The mother looked on with a newborn in her arms. They didn't seem as needy as the rest of the crowd. Perhaps this was the woman that his servant met at the well?

As he waited, he focused on the waves lapping gently over the child, trying to calm himself. Being unable to do so, he eventually looked up again and saw the boat they'd all been waiting for bearing down upon them. The noise level was rising around him as people began calling out their requests: 'My wife is crippled, please come and heal her'; 'My child is oppressed by an unclean spirit. Will you come?'; 'I am blind. Have mercy on me, Son of David.' And so on, and so on. *No one ever expects such things from the rabbis. What authority does this man have?* he wondered.

As men got out of the boat and waded through the shallows to the shore, the crowd became frenzied. Jairus had never seen anything like it before. He saw the father grab up his child and swing her onto his shoulder. With his free hand he held his wife's hand. Despite the urgency of his mission, Jairus was surprised at this public intimacy. Then the father let go of his wife's hand and waded out into the water to greet the man that Jairus thought must be Jesus. Jairus was disappointed – he was rather ordinary. The father embraced him. Jesus looked up and laughed with the little girl, clasping her hand in his. His face lit up even more when he saw the mother standing on the shore with her precious bundle. It was as if no one else were on the beach but them. Jesus came over to her, took the little baby in his arms, kissed his head and looked into the mother's eyes with such tenderness. She was crying. Her husband was beaming.

Jairus could wait no longer. He pushed into their personal space and fell at Jesus feet.

'Forgive me, rabbi,' he shouted above the noise of the crowd, throwing any remaining dignity aside. 'Please would you come to my house. My only daughter is dying. You are our only hope. Please would you come.' He was holding Jesus feet, his nose touching the sand. He hardly dared look up.

He heard the woman say, 'This must be the man I heard about today. He is a good man, the ruler of the synagogue here. His twelve-year-old daughter has had a fever for days. It was I who told his servants that you would be coming this way today.'

Jairus felt a hand on his shoulder. 'Come, show me the way to your home.' He looked up into eyes that were somehow familiar. He battled a surge of emotion. 'Come, brother. Let's go quickly. There is still time,' Jesus said as he smiled. Jairus got to his feet, self-consciously dusting the sand off his nose and knees. Jesus held onto his shoulder as the crowd crushed around him. Jairus led them through the clamour.

They'd hardly got off the beach when suddenly Jesus gripped Jairus's shoulder hard and stopped.

'Who touched me?' he asked.

There was a moment of confusion. People looked around, shaking their heads in bewilderment. Jairus was looking at Jesus' face, wondering why he was doing this, when he knew they had so little time. One of his disciples, a big, weathered seaman said, 'Master, the people are crowding and pressing against you.' Jairus willed Jesus' to listen and move on.

But Jesus said, 'Someone touched me; I know that power has gone out from me.' He was slowly scanning the crowd as if time had stood still. Then a woman crawled out from the thicket of shabby legs on her hands and knees, trembling and quivering like a leaf caught in a strong wind. She fell prostrate at his feet. Silence descended from the centre out to the edge of the crowd as everyone strained to hear.

Pressure was building in Jairus's chest. He wanted to kick the woman's pathetic body out of the way, but when she eventually got up, sitting back on her knees, his body involuntarily jerked in horror. He recognised her dusty features. He hadn't seen her for a very long time but the years of seclusion had done little to age her. Memories of her laughing with his wife flashed across his mind. She had been a good friend, praying faithfully for them to conceive a child; never giving up hope when everyone else had. The birth of their daughter had heralded a life change of equal magnitude for her as it had for them.

She had begun haemorrhaging in their year of joy and had

never stopped. Custom damned her unclean, along with anyone she touched or even on whom her shadow fell. After several expensive treatments, her husband eventually built a small room for her adjacent to their home. She could do nothing but watch from her one window as he brought in another woman to fulfil his needs and raise their three young sons.

Jairus's wife had been her only visitor, coming during her own monthly uncleanness. This woman had never even seen the child she had laboured for in prayer. Jairus' eyes filled with tears as he looked at her now. What courage had it taken for her to come out today? She had defiled a rabbi – this great teacher – this prophet – just by touching his garments in the hope that he would heal her. How many others had she defiled in the crush of humanity around her? Surely they would stone her for this? He held his breath, waiting for her to speak.

'I touched you, Lord. I thought, if I can just touch the tassel of his prayer shawl then I will be healed, I will be made holy again and restored to my people,' she paused, swallowing hard. 'I have been bleeding for twelve years and no one has been able to help me.' A collective gasp went up from the crowd. She began to cry. 'I have spent my days crying out to God to restore me. When I overheard my sons talking of your arrival in our town, I knew that God had sent you to me. The moment I touched the tassel on your prayer shawl I felt in my body that I had been healed,' she sobbed. All eyes were now on Jesus. How would he respond? Jairus' tears continued to run down his cheeks. This encounter had set an internal process in motion that he was powerless to stop. He watched as the woman with the baby came and knelt down beside his wife's friend. She put her arm around her shoulders reassuringly. Several people tried to pull her away. How precious that first touch must have been.

Then Jesus broke the silence. 'Daughter,' – *not woman? A rabbi calling her a daughter of Israel – there is no higher accolade – calling an unclean woman 'clean',* Jairus thought, amazed – 'your faith has healed you. Go in peace.'

Who does she believe him to be? Jairus wondered. And then the question turned in towards himself. *Who do I believe him to be?*

Why do I think he can heal my daughter? But just then he heard a commotion behind him. He turned round to see one of his servants pushing his way through to them. The young lad was sweating and out of breath as he came to stand next to Jairus, his chest heaving and his head bowed with the effort of composing himself. Jairus felt something like a heavy stone sink in his guts. When he raised his head, Jairus read the agony in his eyes. 'Your daughter is dead,' he said slowly. 'Don't bother the teacher anymore.' His voice failed him and broke.

Unbidden, a primal wail of despair rose in Jairus' throat. It forced itself out of his mouth like a demon. Jesus reached over and gripped his shoulder, 'Don't be afraid; just believe, and she will be healed.'

He fixed him with a steely stare and held his gaze. Jairus stared back in desolation. *How? She's dead – how can she be healed?*

The two women had risen to their feet. 'Jairus?' the healed woman reached out her hand hesitantly. Jesus saw her compassion and took hold of her hand, drawing it to Jairus' wounded hand. He put it into his, palm against palm. The healing was complete. She was now fully restored into her community, touched by the synagogue ruler. Jairus stared stupidly at their clasped hands, still in a state of shock.

'Come. Let's go to your daughter,' Jesus said. Jairus turned, slowly letting go of the woman's hand. As he did, the sticky scab that had formed over the deep gash caught and peeled off. He looked, expecting to see fresh bleeding, but all he saw was the smooth surface of his palm.

※　※　※

'I've never seen her,' the woman said to Lila as they walked behind Jesus.

'The daughter?' Lila asked.

'Yes. I prayed for her to be conceived. Her mother is my only friend. I've been in seclusion ever since she was born. I heard the news of her illness and these last few days I have been praying for her life.'

'I suppose you had nothing else to do with your time but pray,' Lila said, smiling.

'I was bitter at first,' she sighed. 'When my husband brought in his lover to look after my boys, I wanted to die. But slowly, with each new day, God melted my heart. I have spent these twelve years learning to love – to forgive, to listen, to pray.'

'What will you do now?' Lila looked at her sadly.

'I will love my husband again – if he will have me – and I will love my sons.' She looked invigorated, holding her skirts in her hands as they climbed the hill, surrounded by the excited crowd.

'What about his lover?' Lila asked between breaths, as she struggled to keep up.

'I've forgiven her. My boys love her – if she stays, then so be it. But I've often wondered why he hasn't married her. He could have divorced me and married her.' She stopped in the shade of a tree to allow Lila the chance to recover. She looked down at her new friend, 'I have entrusted it into God's hands. He has healed me and restored me,' she laughed, 'so I will trust him for what's to come.'

Lila shifted the weight of her son on her chest and adjusted her shawl to shade his downy head from the sun. 'Lila.' It was Jair's voice calling from behind them. Lila turned round, squinting against the dazzling sea that lay below them in the distance. She searched until she lighted on Anna's curly hair bouncing above the heads of the crowd. Her face broke into a smile as she waved.

She turned and looked directly at the woman. 'My husband forgave me.'

The woman looked puzzled at first and then understanding dawned in her eyes. Jair reached them and Anna was shouting, 'Mama, Mama!' reaching her arms out, unbalancing Jair.

'Do you want to take Anna for a while? She's been asking for you.' Jair hoisted his daughter down off his shoulder. Anna lunged at Lila's legs and clung to them, all the while shouting, 'Mama, Mama,' as if this was a reunion concluding a long separation. Lila wobbled a bit with the impact but Jair steadied her. He gently took his son in his arms, looking down at him with pleasure. Lila bent and lifted Anna into her arms, kissing her on both cheeks.

'Hello, my lovely, how are you?'

'Baba Ooah,' Anna turned round, reaching for her brother.

'Yes, he's fine. He'll need feeding soon, but Joshua is fine.' She ran her fingers through Anna's hair, tugging gently at a knot.

'Anna is a beautiful name. I've always liked that name. It means grace doesn't it?' The woman asked, watching them intently.

'Yes. We called her that after my grandmother ... and also because I got what I did not deserve,' Lila said, smiling at Anna and then at the woman. The woman's eyes opened slightly wider and then welled with tears as she looked at Lila and then at Jair. They smiled back at her and then looked affectionately at each other.

'Jesus has done this for us,' Jair gestured to Anna and Joshua. 'He has given us life in all its fullness and we will follow him wherever he goes. Come on. We'd better keep going. I want to be there when that little girl gets off her deathbed.' Jair started to walk, beckoning Lila with a jerk of his head. The women moved out from the shade.

'I want to go ahead and meet my friend ... I hope you don't mind?' the woman asked apologetically.

'Oh no – you go! What a day this is for both of you. We'll see you in a while ... Shalom sister,' Lila said, smiling.

'Shalom.' The woman waved as she turned with huge energy to climb the rest of the hill before them.

❋ ❋ ❋

Waves of sound drifted down towards them, rising and falling in a melancholic, wordless, tuneless cacophony. It washed over them in increasingly strong waves as they neared the top of the hill. Lila's nerves couldn't take the strain of it.

'I hate that sound,' she said to Jair.

'It is very hopeless, isn't it?' he responded.

'They made a sound like that for my father. I was expected to join in, but couldn't. I felt neither sorrow nor loss for him. I didn't even really know him. That's worse, isn't it? Indifference?' She looked at him for an answer. 'I wish I'd had some emotion for him; even hatred would have been better than nothing?'

Jair reached for her hand and squeezed it. He didn't hold it for long because both their hands were damp with sweat. He didn't say anything – it was enough. He'd heard her and understood. Suddenly they'd reached the top of the hill. Lila had carried Anna for the last bit of the climb and now put her down.

Anna staggered over to some wild flowers and began picking them. There was what appeared to be an argument going on outside the house that stood shaded by a sycamore tree. Lila fondly remembered the tree that had guarded their first home. She shepherded Anna towards it. Jesus was standing at the door surrounded by mourners. They were jeering at something he'd just said.

'Not dead? She's as dead as she's ever going to be!' one toothless woman cackled to another within earshot of Lila.

Having subdued the mourners, Jesus turned and went into the house, followed by Jairus and a woman that Lila presumed must be his wife. Three of Jesus' disciples went in after them. The door was shut. The mourners sat fiddling with their shawls or inspecting their fingernails. A low hum of muttered conversation replaced the earlier fracas. Jair and Lila found the woman who'd been healed sitting near the door and sat down beside her. Jair handed Joshua to Lila as he had begun to cry hungrily. Lila deftly put him to her breast under her shawl. She winced as her milk came down and then settled herself against the wall of the house. Anna handed her a crumpled bunch of flowers.

'They're lovely, darling. Thank you so much.' She hugged her daughter with her free arm. Anna then started lifting up her mother's shawl.

'Ooaah?' she asked. Lila playfully pulled the shawl down, out of her hands.

'Yes, Joshua is fine. He'll be out in a little while and then you can see him.' Anna looked like she wasn't sure, but Jair distracted her with a piece of bread from the pouch on his hip.

'Can I have some, Jair?' Lila asked. 'Would you like some too?' she turned to her new friend.

'Yes please. I haven't eaten since dawn.' Jair passed Lila some bread and she broke it in half and passed it on. 'This is my first shared meal in twelve years,' she said, looking like she was going to cry, but then she started to laugh softly. 'Praise be!' she exclaimed, stuffing a piece of bread into her mouth and grinning widely at Lila and Jair.

'Did you see your friend – the girl's mother?' Lila asked.

'I did,' she swallowed and brushed a crumb from her lower lip. 'She was sitting here wailing with them, heaping dust on her head. It was awful to see. When she realised it was me, she was totally bewildered. She wasn't sure what to make of my presence. When I told her Jesus had healed me and that I was no longer unclean, I could see her struggle to believe it. When I hugged her she gasped and then staring at me, realisation dawned in her eyes. I would never have touched her if I had been unclean. I would never do that to anyone – she knew me. I could see she was putting two and two together. "If he could do this for you, could he raise my child from the dead?" she whispered. I didn't know the answer to that. Jesus told everyone that the child wasn't dead, but asleep. But she knew her child was dead. She'd been there when there was no breath, when the body started to cool. She was staring at him uncertainly. I told her to trust him – to do whatever he said.'

❅ ❅ ❅

She was floating in what felt like warm water.

Weightless.

What a relief from the aching and heaviness.

It was as if she had been trapped in thick, hot blankets and had now been released. Everywhere she looked, she saw light. Not just ordinary light, but shimmering, undulating, kaleidoscopic light. How long had she been here? She didn't know, or care. Where was she? She had no idea, but she liked it. The light flickered round her fingers as she moved them. It felt like it was playing with her. It was then that she realised she could see through her fingers. She was more intrigued than shocked. She held her hand up in front of her face. It was milky and translucent. She realised she too was full of light, slightly different from what she was floating in, but still glowing softly and undulating with the light around her.

Then she felt a voice reverberate through her. Everything responded to it. The light rippled, sparkled and crackled, tingling the surface of her. It made her laugh. Then she saw something in the distance. What was it? As she looked she realised she was travelling at speed towards it or it towards her, she wasn't sure which. It was her house – she recognised the tree. Why were so many people gathered outside? She had no time to wait for an answer. She flew past a woman outside the front door who was glowing with the same light she was in. She could see into the house like she could see into her body. She saw her mother and father – she noticed one of her father's hands was glowing too – and she saw four other men in her room. Why were they all there? One of them was full of light – even brighter than her light. Did her light originate from his? It felt like the light she was in was returning to its source. Feelings of warmth and attraction towards him flooded her and somehow she knew that it was his voice she had felt calling her.

She saw her body lying on her bed. She seemed to slow down and hover over herself, studying her own face but feeling somehow that it wasn't hers. Before she could ponder this further she felt a heavy weight pulling at her. She tried to struggle against it, but then looked at the shining man. Something about his gaze reassured her so she stopped fighting it.

She felt herself become very heavy. Everything went dark.

The next thing she knew, someone was taking hold of her hand. It felt like a breeze was blowing through that hand into hers. It travelled up her arm and across her chest and down into her stomach, up her neck and head until she took in a huge gasp of air. Her eyes flew open with the force of it. It hurt! She saw her mother and father's tear-stained faces leaning over her, behind another unfamiliar face. She focused on him in bewilderment.

She was certain he'd told her to get up. She wasn't quite sure how she knew that, but she liked him and she wanted to obey him. His grip on her hand strengthened as she tensed her stomach muscles. It really hurt. Her face contorted with the pain. She was in a sitting position now, her legs sliding heavily to the edge of the bed, then over the side, her knees bending stiffly, her feet touching the rough, earthen floor. Then, leaning forward she pushed herself off the bed and slowly stood up. Her mother was sobbing hysterically while her father stared open-mouthed.

'Give her something to eat,' said the shining man.

One of the other men left the room immediately and returned shortly with some bread. The shining man smiled at her, broke the bread, giving thanks for it and handed her a piece. She looked at it and then slowly lifted it to her mouth. Her eyes rose to meet his as he took a bite of bread simultaneously. She began chewing. It was dry – she had no saliva in her mouth. Her mother must have sensed this because she shakily handed her a cup of water. She drank deeply. A silken silence wove itself between them.

It was torn by a cracked, dry voice – her voice: 'Who are you?'

※ ※ ※

Grace looked at the time on her computer screen. It was 3:00am but she was wide awake. She stretched her legs and arched her back, running her hands through her hair. She lay back against Chloe's sofa and closed her eyes, her mind full of images of the shining man.

'Little girl, get up.' The words echoed through her mind. Then again and again until they seemed to permeate every part of her being. The memory of standing outside her parent's bedroom door when she was thirteen, listening to them arguing about her, came sharply into focus. She could smell the roses her mum had cut that morning from their garden and arranged in a bowl on the hall table that stood next to their door. She could hear her mum's voice rising and falling with one accusation after another. She felt the horrible twisting in her stomach as she understood for the first time why her daddy had shown her so much attention. She felt herself retching and saw herself running to the toilet to vomit. Then she lay on the floor by the toilet for ages feeling heavy, numb, dead.

'It's her fault,' came the familiar, cruel words. 'She's a little whore.'

Grace involuntarily jerked her knees up to her chest. 'Jesus, where were you then – when I needed you? If you'd helped me, I would never have made the choices I made later on,' she cried.

As she waited, she became aware of a light growing brighter in her memory. She saw herself raising her head off the bathroom floor and looking around her. The light was getting so bright she had to shield her eyes as she sat up. Then she saw the shining man standing there beside her thirteen-year-old self, and he was saying, 'Little girl, get up.'

Jesus took her by the hand and led her back to her parent's bedroom, past the pale pink roses. He opened the door and ushered her in. She saw her father, his head hanging, crying over photographs scattered across their bed. Her mother was standing with her back to the door, gripping the bed frame. Grace felt safe with Jesus holding her hand. She trusted that he would know what to do. He led her round the bed until she stood in front of her father and could now see her mother's angry, beautiful face. They were both utterly broken people. Grace had never thought of them like that before. She felt sorry for them as she watched them.

She found herself turning to Jesus and asking, 'Can you help them?'

He looked down at her with great compassion and kindness and asked, 'Can *you* help them?'

A rush of emotion caught in her throat, 'Yes ... I want to forgive them. I want to show them mercy. I'm so sorry for withholding it from them for so long – they're so broken.'

Jesus smiled at her. Then he lifted his arms, stretching them out, a pained look crossing his features. She was reminded of how it must have been for him on the cross. As she watched all the pictures on the bed started to move towards Jesus like leaves caught by a wind. They rose into the air in a swirl and rushed to him, disappearing among the folds of his robe. Empowered, she moved towards her father first.

'I forgive you,' she said to him, though he didn't respond. 'You don't owe me anything anymore. Jesus has paid your debt to me.' She began to cry with the wonder of the truth.

'I forgive you,' she said as she turned to her mother, whose face was suspended in an angry shout. 'I know you didn't mean me to hear. Jesus has taken your judgement of me. I won't live under it anymore.'

She felt huge relief and a deep surge of love for them. She noticed that Jesus seemed bigger and that the three of them seemed closer to him, his arms encompassing them.

Then, suddenly the image changed and she was in the stranglehold of James Martin. She panicked and cried out. She felt as if she was being pushed out of her body. She realised that she was looking at the memory from a different angle. The torment had always been that she remembered it only from looking up at him helplessly, unable to stop him or free herself. Now she found she was looking down on herself from somewhere on the ceiling. Instead of seeing herself alone, being raped, she saw Christ filling her body with his presence. He was taking her place. He was entering into her suffering with her. For the first time in her whole life she did not feel alone. 'You are with me,' she cried out the revelation.

She heard him say, 'Father, forgive him – he doesn't know the full extent of what he is doing.'

She found herself praying too: 'Father, I forgive him. If Christ in me forgives him, then I forgive him.'

As the image faded, she felt Jesus say, 'Little girl ... you are growing up.' In the stillness that followed, Grace felt whole.

Slowly, she became aware of being on Chloe and Mark's living room sofa again. She didn't know if she had been asleep and dreaming or whether it had been a waking dream. Dawn light was streaking through the window where the curtains didn't quite meet. The light fell in a long shaft across the room, landing on her open Bible.

8. BETTER

Sisters

When Chloe and Mark returned from retreat, the children went crazy. Grace had never seen them so excited. There was a frenzy about it all that belied what, at a cursory glance, looked like a happy family. The 'For Sale' sign had gone up on their house that morning, which had probably added to the already strong undercurrent of uncertainty among them.

When Grace hugged Chloe, she wanted to somehow pass on some of the joy she felt that morning, but she noticed that, despite her pleasure at seeing her children again, Chloe's eyes were still sad and distant. Grace gave her a reassuring look that said – *don't worry, you'll get there in the end.* Grace prayed silently as she went to put the kettle on in the kitchen, listening to three voices vying for their parents' attention. She heard a fight break out between the two older ones:

'I want to tell them.'

'But I started telling them first.'

'It's not fair, just because you're the oldest.'

Thump! Scream! Thudding of feet up the stairs. Doors slamming.

Chloe came into the kitchen holding Charlie on her hip. He was too big really to be carried, but Grace could see the comfort they were both giving each other. Chloe looked wearily at Grace and rolled her eyes. 'Mark's gone after them. Melany shouldn't hit Josh like that, should she Charlie?' She looked at her son, who was leaning his head on her shoulder. He lifted it momentarily and shook it, his big eyes wide with the injustice of it all.

'Do you want England's answer to all life's traumas?' Grace smiled ruefully, holding up the teapot.

'No, I want a strong coffee please – strong and black.' She sat down settling Charlie on her lap and stroking his hair.

'Since when have you had it strong and black?' Grace looked up in surprise.

'Since the last while.' She waved absently with her free hand. 'I need the caffeine hit.'

Mark came into the kitchen, followed by two very sullen children who took their stand either side of their mother looking more like clothes hanging on a line than energetic offspring. They said their sorries begrudgingly and Chloe wrapped her arms around them both. 'Now why don't you all tell us the story – you've each got a sentence at a time, Okay?' Chloe injected a sense of fun into her voice and soon the kids were playing the game and telling their story, competing for the longest sentence. The mood lifted and they were the happy family again. Mark slumped down into a chair across the table from Grace and gratefully received his cup of coffee.

Grace watched Chloe and Mark's body language as the children settled down around the kitchen table, eating chocolate-chip cookies they had made over the weekend and chattering airily. It wasn't looking good. There was a space around Mark and Chloe, an opposing magnetic field. Every time they came near each other, or their hands nearly touched reaching for something, there was a subtle propulsion in the opposite direction.

They finished their coffees and there was no obvious reason for Grace to hang around any longer. 'I better make a move,' she said, collecting the cups and dumping them in the sink.

She turned and caught a pleading look in Chloe's eyes, but she didn't respond. Whatever was going on, they needed to sort it out between themselves somehow. Grace felt guilty, but wanted to get home and tell Peter about what had happened to her in the small hours before dawn. Her resolve strengthened as she leaned down, gave Chloe and Charlie a hug and then moved to Mark. He awkwardly stood to say goodbye and thanked her, holding her at arm's length and then leaning in, giving her something between an air kiss and a bloke's 'three slaps on the back' hug. She felt so sorry for him – he was all at sea. She wanted to tell him that he was a good guy and that it was all going to be okay, but she didn't. She just squeezed his arm hard.

※　※　※

'The Archdeacon's coming to see us.' Chloe's voice sounded panicked down the phone. 'I tried to put him off, but he's coming, today of all days. The movers are arriving in an hour and the place is a mess. Would you be able to come over? I don't think I can face him; I know he sees me as the evil whore.'

'Why's he doing that? Surely he knows that we're looking after you guys? What reason did he give?' Grace asked in alarm.

'He just said he'd heard we were moving and he wanted to have a pastoral visit with us before we go.' Anxiety made her voice sound higher than normal.

'What time's he coming?'

'In half an hour – can you make it over?'

Grace looked at the pile of clothes on the floor beside the washing machine and tried to re-adjust her day in her head. *I can stick a wash on now and should be able to do the cleaning when I get back – I just won't dust. I should still be able to get to St Paul's by 1:00pm.* She looked at her diary where she'd scrawled down the baptism visit she was doing at another church, which had no clergy, and then at the clock knowing full well how bad she was at measuring the time it took to do anything. *If the worst comes to the worst I'll clean tomorrow afternoon,* she thought. She hated moving her weekly date with the vacuum cleaner. It was the one thing in her life that gave her an instant result for her labour. She loved the ten minutes after she'd completely cleaned the house.

She shoved a load into the washing machine, pushed the door shut with her knee as she poured washing powder into the slot and turned it on. She grabbed her half-eaten piece of toast, her bag, her diary and phone and headed for the door, trying to sling her bag over her shoulder while still eating. Oops – keys. She'd nearly let the door slam behind her. The last time she'd locked herself out had really screwed up her day. She got the keys and successfully exited the house at last. No wonder so many women suffer from IBS; she was trying to remember if she'd even gone to the toilet that morning.

The freedom and happiness she had felt in the dawn light, sitting on Chloe's sofa had not left her all week. There was a spring in her step as she got to Chloe's just in time to see the Archdeacon parking up.

'Hello, Colin,' she said, smiling politely.

'Hello, hello,' he said, looking slightly perturbed by her presence, but smiling brightly through it. He was a stocky little man, full of restless energy that shouted 'bishop', but he'd been stuck with 'archdeacon' and it didn't look likely, at this stage in his life, that he'd ever fulfil the aspiration.

'Chloe asked me to come over for your visit. I hope that's all right with you?'

'Of course,' he beamed, 'that's totally understandable,' but his eyes looked baffled. 'We – I mean the bishop and I – are very grateful for your pastoral care of Chloe and Mark. Thank you so much for all you've done.' Grace nodded and smiled in response. As they walked up the drive, he asked how things were going with her curacy.

'Very well thank you, Colin.' She didn't want to tell him any more – she didn't believe he was really interested, knowing he disagreed with the ordination of women to the priesthood. She was an anathema to him. She felt some of her joy drain away.

They waited for Chloe to answer the doorbell in an awkward silence. 'Hi Colin,' Chloe said in that nervous, high voice as she ushered them into a hallway piled high with boxes. 'You'll have to excuse the mess ... do you want a cup of coffee or tea?' She led them into the kitchen, which looked like a bomb had hit it. It took a moment before Grace realised that Mark was sitting at the table, surrounded by piles of crockery wrapped in paper.

'Hello, Mark.' Colin infused the greeting with sympathy as he shook his hand meaningfully. 'Coffee would be great,' he said. There was a minute shift in his tone as he answered Chloe. They moved things off chairs and sat down with Mark while Chloe made the drinks. Every line of her frame was tense.

They'd all got their mugs in their hands and Chloe sat down beside Mark, opposite Grace. Grace noticed that one more button was done up on Chloe's shirt than before. Colin cleared his throat and asked, 'So, how are you both?'

How do you think they are? Grace resisted looking heavenward. She could hear Peter's voice in her head: *You can be so ungracious sometimes!*

'Well ... we're a bit stressed,' Mark said, spreading his hands indicating the mess around him.

'Yes, I can see that.' Colin's tone was pleasant but officious. 'I'm sorry about visiting today, of all days. But I wouldn't be doing my job if I hadn't caught you before you left.' he gave Mark a self-satisfied smile. The preamble over, he launched in: 'I want you to know that disciplinary measures are in process.' He looked politely at Chloe, who immediately averted her eyes. 'I also wanted you to know that the church has three interviewees lined up for the youth worker's job, which is good news.' His eyes sparkled with administrative pleasure, 'and things seem to be getting back to some semblance of normality.' Then he looked at Grace, 'I'm sure you know all this already, Grace, but I didn't know you were going to be here and I wanted to make sure Chloe knew that the good work she'd begun will soon be carried on.' He didn't wait for her to answer before going on, 'You've been meeting with the young people at the church, haven't you?'

'Yes – yes I have.' Grace realised his eyes had dropped to her chest and she quickly moved her hand to cover whatever he could see.

'So it seems all the bases are covered.' His tongue flicked his lips as he raised his eyebrows and looked away to Mark and then Chloe. 'Do you know what church you might be attending after you move?'

Now there's a loaded question, Grace couldn't help smiling.

'We're actually going to stay at this church,' Mark said, looking to Grace for support. 'We'll probably keep going here, even though it's a bit of a drive from the new house.'

Chloe was fiddling with her wedding ring. There was a pause as Colin digested this information. *So they're not moving out of your area ... oh dear, poor you ... the problem isn't going away*, Grace crowed silently.

'I thought you might want to go somewhere further away where people don't know you or your ... um ... history.' Colin's eyebrows had pulled together, deepening the furrow that started at the top of his nose and continued into his Brill-creamed, corrugated hairline.

Chloe looked up at this, fire in her eyes. *Good girl – you go for it*, Grace cheered in her head.

'Why would we want to do that?' Chloe asked. Colin was taken aback. She looked at Grace and then said in a less fierce tone, 'We need to be with people who really know us and love us, and who will help us through this mess.'

'I see,' replied Colin, not seeing at all.

'Admittedly, we haven't been to any services since … ' Mark faltered. 'But so many people have been to see us and are praying for us. We got married here. Many of these people made a vow to help us keep our vows. When we do go back to church services, we won't have to put on a good front. We know we're loved here, don't we?' Mark gingerly put his arm round the back of Chloe's chair and looked at her.

'We do,' her eyes lifted momentarily to meet his, then down again.

'Well … ' Colin straightened his shoulders as he inhaled deeply. 'I want to assure you of my prayers for you in this difficult time.' He was looking solely at Mark. 'God can do immeasurably more than we could ever ask or imagine,' he quoted. 'It wouldn't be what I would recommend, but if you're sure?' Mark nodded.

Colin looked frustrated. It was not the tidy end to the matter he had envisaged. However, his business was done for now and he quickly lost his focus, making polite conversation about moving house and the stresses that entailed. He drank his coffee down to the dregs and then rose to leave.

As Grace walked down the drive with him to their respective cars, he shook his head and confided, 'I've had women throw themselves at me like that, you know, over the years. I'm just so glad my wife has been able to see them coming and warn me against them.'

'Really?' Grace quickly changed her facial expression to one of pastoral concern, 'I mean, really?'

He flicked an uncertain glance her way and decided to continue. 'Yes. I think powerful men can be very attractive to women.' He'd stopped at the gate and was searching her face for any hint of that being true for her.

'A bit like David and Bathsheba?' Grace asked, trying to downplay the sarcasm in her voice as she rummaged for her keys in her bag. She looked up quizzically and saw that she'd thrown him. *Oops, I've come across too strongly. Say something funny.* 'That Bathsheba – she really shouldn't have been bathing on her roof terrace in full view of the palace. What was she thinking? Poor David didn't stand a chance!' Colin looked like he was on more familiar ground.

'There's nothing new under the sun, is there? History repeats itself again and again and still we don't seem to learn,' he sighed, in a way contrived to seem long-suffering. Grace joined him in his wise shaking of the head.

But then she couldn't help it; she just couldn't let it go. She was overcome with an urge she knew she'd regret as she opened her big, fat mouth: 'You know, Colin, I am attracted to powerful men – but only those who have whatever power has been given them under control. That's why I'm so attracted to Jesus: he was meek – he had all the power in the universe and yet he chose to use it to serve us, to give his life up for us. Now that's an attractive, powerful man! Did you ever think that maybe that's what Chloe was hoping for? That's certainly what all us women – no, not just us women – the whole human race are hoping for.'

Grace had run out of urge and she suddenly felt self-conscious as Colin cleared his throat: 'I'm not sure what I did to deserve that?' He looked affronted as he unnecessarily straightened his dog collar.

Grace flustered around in her bag with her keys again, 'Don't mind me, Colin – sorry, just venting.' She tried to smile, but her lips weren't working – they were tensed and quivering. 'Rest assured we'll do our best to help Chloe and Mark through this.' With an effort, Grace made her voice light again. 'Don't know what the outcome will be, but we'll do our best.' She forced her lips to obey this time, curving them into a bright smile as she unlocked her car, wanting to get away as fast as she could.

'Yes, I'm sure you have what's best in mind for them both.' His voice was clipped and intensely polite. 'My regards to your husband,' he said, bowing his head stiffly and walking to his car as she slammed her door shut.

'Something that rhymes with banker is what comes to mind right now!' she muttered under her breath and started the car. Overcome with remorse for her rash outburst she started praying as she drove away, remembering that she needed to bless and not curse. 'Sorry, oh I'm so sorry for being so rude... bless him ... bless his wife ... may he realise how lucky he is to have her.'

❋   ❋   ❋

A few days later the girls had arranged to surprise Chloe by turning up at her new house. They came bearing three cooked meals, flowers and a couple of bottles of champagne. Tears welled up in Chloe's eyes when she saw them all crowding in on the doorstep. There were boxes still around, but the living room and kitchen looked like they'd pretty much been sorted. They sat down round the kitchen table, all talking at once, as Chloe tried to remember where she'd put the champagne glasses. Mo was bubbly as ever chatting about the move she'd made a couple of years ago. Val was cheerfully engaged in conversation with two of the others and Grace was leaning back, observing.

'Where are Mark and the kids?' Mo asked.

'Oh, Mark took them bowling so I could unpack more boxes upstairs. It's easier when they're not around,' she explained as she gently placed the crystal glasses down on the table.

'How are they coping with the change of schools and everything?' Mo asked.

'Oh, it's early days yet. They've had a few new friends over to the house already, so that's a good sign. Watch this space.' She smiled a sad little smile.

She popped the champagne cork and everyone cheered as they held their glasses up to catch the overflow of bubbles. 'Well, here's to new beginnings,' Val said.

'And here's to you, girl.' Grace smiled and raised her glass before taking a sip.

'Ah – this is the first time I've sat down all day.' Chloe sighed as she closed her eyes, raised her shoulders tightly up to her ears and then relaxed them, leaning her head to one side and then the other. Her eyes opened slowly like someone already very drunk. 'I'm exhausted.'

'I know the feeling,' said Mo. 'Moving is one of the most stressful things you can do, so they say. It took me a month to stop chewing my fingers after I moved.' She stretched out her stubby fingers that still looked like they got chewed when not adorned with fake nails. She giggled at the evidence and admitted, 'I still do, actually.'

'Are you sleeping all right?' Val asked Chloe.

'No, not really ... must be all the lovin' that's keeping me awake,' she said, smiling ruefully.

'Really?' Mo asked, incredulously. 'I mean, after what's happened,' she paused realising she'd gone where angels fear to tread, '... I thought that would be off the table for a while?'

Chloe gave her a mock glare. 'No – I'm being sarcastic! We did at first

– like that could solve everything,' she looked disgusted at the thought, 'but we've stopped, 'cause it can't. I'm even scared he'll touch me now. I just lie very still and hope he won't come near. I guess he knows, even though I've not said anything. I just lie there, hour after endless hour listening to him breathing, waiting for sleep to come. And then the day starts all over again.' She took a big swig from her glass.

'Sounds like you're shutting down,' Val assessed, and Grace nodded in agreement. 'You've lost your job, your reputation, your lover, your marriage, your home – all at once. It's not surprising you feel like you do.' She patted Chloe's hand maternally.

'When you put it like that, why don't I just end it all now?' Chloe looked bleakly into her empty glass.

'Is that how you feel?' Val asked quietly.

Chloe pursed her lips tightly and reached for the bottle. She filled her glass and then topped up everyone else's.

'We've all probably felt like that at one time or another,' Grace said as she looked at the other women for back up. She longed to tell Chloe about her own past, but professionalism kept her secret.

'When Mike broke up with me, I felt like that,' Mo said, 'that's why I moved – just to have something to do. You know, Chloe, I was on anti-depressants for two years as I sorted my life out. I used to wonder if I'd ever feel any different, or whether I was just going to have to live with the bleakness forever. But it did change slowly – rest, Prozac, counselling and prayer got me through in the end. It's early days for you.'

Chloe looked up from studying the tiny pillars of bubbles rising in her glass. 'I guess I thought it would all be better by now ... but it seems to be getting worse.' Her chin wobbled. They all reached out to her as a tear made its way out of her eye.

'Hey, Chloe, remember what you said to me – it's always darkest before the dawn. Hang in there. We're with you all the way.' Grace squeezed her hand.

'Yeah we are. I think you're amazing, how you've kept going – selling your house, moving, sorting out new schools for the kids and even going to church. You're doing so great,' Mo said, smiling encouragingly.

Chloe wiped her cheek with the back of her hand and sniffed, 'But I don't think I love Mark any more. I don't even know if I want to. We've ruined what we had. I've tried and I know he's tried, but we just can't recapture it. It's frightening. There's just this big empty space between us – this no man's land.' She paused, trying to compose herself. 'And then there's this other empty space,' she pointed to her chest 'that just aches all the time.' She broke down with a sob.

'Oh love,' Val whispered, rubbing her back.

Mo looked very focused suddenly. She gripped Chloe's hands across the table and said, 'Chloe – we believe in resurrection, don't we?' Chloe's sobs slowed down as she raised her head and looked at Mo through sticky eyelashes. 'Don't you think a new love could rise out of the ashes of the old for you and Mark? Maybe you've been trying too hard to hold on to the old. Maybe the old love wasn't as good as what's coming? You only loved the bits you allowed each other to see before. Now maybe you will love each other knowing everything – the good, the bad and the ugly. Maybe you need to let go of the old and start praying for the new to come.' She took in a deep breath, 'This is what the Lord says to you, "Forget the former things; do not dwell on the past. See, I am doing a new thing! Now it springs up; do you not perceive it? I am making a way in the desert and streams in the wasteland."' Mo paused – she seemed to be listening or thinking, waiting for more, 'I, even I am he who blots out your transgressions, for my own sake, and remembers your sins no more.'

A hush followed. Chloe had gone very still, eyes shut, lips parted, hands limp on the table. Then in a whisper she began to pray, 'Oh God, help me want to love Mark. I've got nothing. You'll have to do it – like you've said. And please heal the ache in my fickle heart for what's not mine.'

Grace smiled and raised her glass as Chloe opened her moist eyes. 'Well said.'

'That was Isaiah 43, wasn't it?' Val asked.

'I don't know,' said Mo. 'I know it's in the Bible somewhere,' she laughed.

Chloe abruptly stood up. 'Need to wash my face. Shall I get another bottle while I'm up?' she looked round at them through piggy eyes.

When Chloe had gone, Val leaned in and whispered, 'I think she needs to go see her doctor – get something to help her through the next six months or so. Don't you?' There were several nods around the table.

'Well, we've got the prayer covered and she hasn't got a job, so she can rest … ' Mo trailed off as she thought. 'I could recommend my counsellor to her? I know she's been for marriage counselling with Mark, but maybe some one-to-one counselling would help now?' Mo raised her eyebrows.

Chloe returned, bottle in hand. 'You talking about me, girls?' Her voice sounded a little more positive than before.

'Yes, we were actually.' Grace smiled affectionately at her. 'We were saying that … ' Grace deferred to Mo.

'I think you might need to see your doctor. They might give you something just to give your brain a rest, you know, for six months or so? Do you think you might do that?' Mo reached over and touched Chloe's hand, running her finger along a greeny-blue vein.

'Aren't they for wimps? Shouldn't God be enough for me?' Chloe looked anxious.

'Don't you think God was involved in the invention of them, like he was involved with the discovery of penicillin? They'll help you rest; help you get your head together, restore the feel-good chemical in your brain. It's better to admit you need help – it's fear that keeps us going, worrying about what others might think of us if we were to ask for help. Believe me, I know.' Mo looked certain.

Chloe pondered Mo's advice, 'I don't know … '.

'Hey, you can't be worrying about what people might think, can you?' Mo laughed, slapping the table.

'Mmmph!' Chloe grudgingly let a smile form on her lips, 'No, I can't get any lower, can I?'

'The only way is up from here.' Grace smiled, raising her glass and pointing to the ceiling.

Mo joined her, holding her champagne glass like a microphone. They leaned against each other's shoulders, heads touching, eyes scrunched shut, champagne glasses pressed to lips, arms spread wide, singing at the top of their lungs some half-remembered eighties song about holding on.

Suddenly the front door opened and the kids came tumbling in.

'I won, I won!' Charlie shouted.

Melany had her fingers in her ears shouting, 'You can't sing!'

Mark stood behind them surveying the scene, 'So, a lot of unpacking got done then?' he said, smiling. He'd not seen Chloe laughing for months. Even though the tell-tale signs of tears were evident on her face and the unpacking hadn't got done, it was better to come home to this.

�֍ �֍ ✖

'I've been on them for three weeks now and I have noticed a difference. My mind isn't running down the same spiralling tracks as much. But I kind of feel a bit blank. It's better than feeling like I did before though. This last week I've been sleeping a bit better too.' Grace listened to Chloe's voice on the phone, trying to put her finger on the thing that was absent in it. She realised that it was less edgy, less agitated.

'That's good. I am so glad you've done that Chloe. You will feel even better in a month or so.' Grace smiled, thinking of her friend's striking face.

'Yeah. I've had two sessions with Mo's counsellor too. It was weird, 'cause she didn't really say much, she just got me going and I talked and talked. When she called time it was such a shock. I didn't want to stop. When I came out the second time, I just sat in the car and sobbed my heart out. It felt so releasing. Like a really good massage – does that sound weird?'

'No, it sounds good – I might go myself,' Grace laughed.

'Well, I don't know why I've never done it before – it's amazing. I think I really thought anti-depressants and counselling were for weak, needy people ... well ... maybe they are ... I've just realised I'm one of them ... and it's not so bad.'

'It's when we're weak, that we are strong, isn't it? God's power is revealed when we admit how weak we are and how much we need all the help he's made available to us.' Grace was doodling on her sermon notes for Wednesday's midweek communion service. She realised she was drawing a single rose bud again, like she often did.

'Sounds like good material for a sermon,' Chloe said.

Grace laughed, 'You guessed it – you caught me in the middle of preparing one.'

'What's it on?' Chloe seemed to really want to know. Grace wondered if her love for ministry was still there, buried underneath the rubble.

'Oh, it's based on Luke 10 – Martha and Mary. I've just been thinking about why resting and sitting still is so hard for us to do. We're always in a rush somewhere, doing something – especially us women. We're constantly juggling about ten things at once, trying to live the dream. We were on holiday last year in Spain and they don't seem to have a problem at all with sitting still and resting. Maybe it's the heat?' Grace wondered, her mind going off on a tangent.

'Yeah, but it would have been hot in Israel too and Martha was running round like a headless chicken, wasn't she? So it must be more to do with personal ambitions or personality types, or cultural expectations or roles in society, don't you think?' Chloe asked.

Grace put the finishing touches to her doodle, 'Uhuh ... hey, it sounds like you'd be better at this than me. Are you free to preach this Wednesday?'

'Very funny,' Chloe quipped. 'I might be learning all about "rest", but I don't think I'll be doing anything in the public eye again for a very long time ... if ever.'

'Never say never,' Grace said. There was silence on the other end of the line. 'Chloe?'

'Yep.'

'Thought I'd lost you there.'

'You did ... around "you free to preach this Wednesday?"'

'Well, since you're not – I'd better crack on and finish it.'

But as usual, Grace had her story file open as well as the sermon document she was working on. She clicked on her writing folder to where she'd last left off. As she read over the end of 'Life', she couldn't resist a new chapter:

They had slowly been making their way back towards Jerusalem over the last few months. A sense of foreboding pestered Lila like a fly she couldn't catch and kill. She'd begun to have nightmares. She didn't know if it was due to maternal anxiety, now that she was mother of two precious children, or whether it was something to do with the transient lifestyle they had been living. But the dreams were growing in intensity and she was beginning to fear sleep. She would often wake, soaked in sweat, her heart hammering in her ribcage, a prisoner demanding release. She'd lie still, waiting for her body to calm down, trying to remember what it was that sent terror coursing through her nervous system. But always it slipped out of reach, a sinking Leviathan under the opaque surface of her subconscious. She'd tried to explain it to Jair but, being one who could sleep through both their children's squalling, he hadn't empathised.

'I have nightmares too,' Mary responded immediately when Lila finally shared it with her. They were walking up towards Bethany.

'What are yours about?' Lila asked.

Mary's mouth twisted to one side, her eyebrows lowered over her dark eyes. 'I don't have the one I used to have about drowning – that stopped after I met Jesus. But I do have others. There's one that frightens me the most.'

'Go on,' Lila looked at her, shifting Joshua's weight on her hip. He was getting so heavy these days.

'Well, it started coming to me when I lived with the old woman. It stopped for a while after I came to live with you, but recently it's returned. It starts out with me watering the herbs I planted outside my front door. It doesn't look like my old house, but I know it is. It's warm and the sunshine is bright around me – I begin dancing like I used to at the palace. I feel aroused and powerful as the wind blows the leaves of my herbs – they make a rustling noise. Suddenly a dark shadow falls over my herbs and I try to turn to see what's blocking the sun, but my body is paralysed. I can't move, no matter how hard I try, and then suddenly I'm falling into the herbs, but it's now become a black hole. I fall and fall, trying to scream, but no sound comes out. Then I wake up.'

'That's awful,' Lila frowned.

'It doesn't sound like much, does it? But it terrifies me.'

After they'd walked in silence for several paces, Lila said: 'I don't know what to say to comfort you ... but it does sound like it's about things that aren't resolved in your past. What do you think?' she leaned in to try and make eye contact with Mary.

'I just wish it would go away.' Mary rubbed her left eye angrily. 'It belongs in the past – why won't it stay there?'

'I don't know,' Lila said helplessly. An oily uneasiness was slithering in her guts as she'd listened to Mary's description of her dream. If only she could remember hers.

'Life is so good now. I mean – I'm happy, happier than I've ever been. I have my brother and sister and a home, and I love helping you look after Anna and Joshua. I love travelling – meeting so many interesting people, being with Jesus and seeing him heal the sick and set people free. I know I'm loved by true friends.' She looked searchingly at Lila. 'Will I always have to carry the past with me?' she asked, anguish burning in her eyes.

Again, they walked in silence. Lila lifted her arm off Mary's shoulders to move Joshua onto her other hip. 'Let me carry him for a while,' Mary said apologetically reaching over to Joshua. Lila gladly relinquished her chubby bundle, who was happily sucking his thumb. 'Come here, Shua,' she smiled, calling him the nickname his sister had given him. He smiled back immediately, gurgling behind his thumb.

'Thank you – he is getting so heavy. I won't be able to carry him on long walks much longer. Jair says he'll soon have to make a cart for him to sit in.' Lila arched her back and winced.

'That sounds like a good idea. Why didn't he think of it before for Anna?' Mary said bouncing Joshua on her hip. He chuckled.

'Maybe she didn't get so big so quickly? Maybe we were so enthralled with her being our first little miracle that we didn't want to put her down? I don't know … '

'Maybe your dream is from your past too?' Mary cut in abruptly. 'Maybe coming back to Jerusalem is stirring up all the old stuff for us both?' she looked at Lila, a frown creasing her flawless forehead.

'Maybe … ' There was the slithering again in the pit of her stomach. They walked on in thoughtful silence, broken only by their footsteps and Joshua's contented slurping sounds. She had not spent much time – any time – dwelling on her affair with Aaron, or on the traumatic day that had changed her life forever. Like a bird let out of a net, her mind had flown from it as fast and as far away as possible. She had focused on Jair: on their reconciliation; on the baby growing in her womb and the wonder of giving birth to her first child; on Jesus' teachings; on the new friends she had made among his followers; on travelling, and on the miracles and healings she had witnessed. Then, just when she thought her cup could not get any fuller, yet another unbelievable blessing had been poured into her life. Conceiving Joshua had sent her reeling yet again at the extravagance of God to someone as unworthy as her. No, she had not thought about the past much. Maybe Mary was right? Maybe returning to Jerusalem was bringing it all back with a vengeance.

❋   ❋   ❋

Jesus was teaching in Martha and Mary's courtyard. Men were crammed in where they could; some were sitting on the high wall and even a few were in a tree that overhung it. He had been teaching most of the afternoon, having arrived in the morning and the sun was beginning to drop behind the tree, casting leafy shadows onto the heads of the men who sat engrossed.

It had been a wonderful homecoming, Martha and Lazarus had been so pleased to see Mary again. But when Mary sat right at Jesus' feet while he taught, Martha became sullen and quiet. Women were meant to be in the background, either preparing food or washing clothes, or playing with children, if they wanted to listen to his teachings.

However, Mary was oblivious. She also seemed impervious to pressure from the men. Embarrassment, guilt, insults, domination or manipulation had no effect on her. Lila watched, giggling from the kitchen door, as several men had tried and failed. Mary Magdalene, who was leaning up against the wall nearby smiled too.

Martha was busy behind them in the kitchen, preparing the evening meal. Lazarus had bought a whole lamb from the market and it was sizzling on a spit. It had taken Martha a good part of the morning to build up a big enough fire before she could place the lamb over it. The kitchen was unbearably hot. Lila had taken it in turns with her to fan the fire and keep it stoked.

The other part of the morning, Martha had spent kneading a large amount of dough. A big, bottomless earthen jar stood to one side, ready to become a bread oven when placed over the fire. Next to where Martha stood, turning the spit, was a pile of vegetables in a basket waiting to be peeled and cut. As the day had worn on, Lila couldn't help but be aware of the tension that was building in the kitchen around their host. Nothing was said, but the atmosphere was heavy with the threat of an emotional thunderstorm. She did her best to please her, but every time she was distracted by laughter outside, she could feel the tension mounting.

Lila wasn't that much use anyway, because she had Joshua on her hip or at her breast. Anna ran in and out of the kitchen between Lila and Jair, who had taken a seat at the back to be nearby. At one point, she'd knocked the basket of vegetables over, sending them tumbling across the uneven, earthen floor. Martha had said nothing but she didn't need to – her face said it all. Lila had stayed out of the kitchen for a while after that.

'I don't know why you're bothering,' Mary Magdalene said to her.

'I feel bad for her. She has so much to do and her sister isn't helping her at all,' Lila said.

'Of course she's not. Why would you want to be in a stuffy kitchen when you can be listening to the Messiah?' Mary's eyes gleamed.

'It just seems a bit unfair – there are so many people to feed and Martha's only trying to be a good hostess.'

'Haven't we always had enough to eat wherever we've gone? We're not fussy – we'll eat stale bread and sleep on hard ground if it means we can be with him.' She nodded in the direction of Jesus who was laughing about something with those nearest him. 'You're too worried about what people think of you, you know.' Mary's eyes bored into her.

Lila was stunned. She felt hurt, then angry. She opened her mouth but wasn't sure what she wanted to say in return.

Mary saw her advantage and pressed her point: 'You spent so long on the outside trying to get in that, now you're in, you want to use your freedom to please people? You're better than that, Lila. I know you were traumatised when they dragged you through Jerusalem to your death. There can't be many experiences of rejection worse than that. But he saved you so you could be free – have life in all its fullness, not so you could go back to hobbling along in shackles of fear. Don't you want to be a free woman? Aren't you tired of the old ways? I know I am.'

Martha must have been listening. Suddenly she stormed out through the kitchen door, glaring at Lila and Mary Magdalene. Then she began pushing her way through the seated men towards Jesus.

'Oh dear,' whispered Lila, 'here it comes.'

She got to Jesus and hesitated a moment. Her sister was staring up at her in amazed bewilderment, along with everyone else. As Martha looked down into her sibling's upturned face, sparks of anger lit her eyes. Lila cringed. Martha looked at Jesus and, in a tattletale voice, said, 'Lord, don't you care that my sister has left me to do the work by myself? Tell her to help me.' Her fists were balled tightly at her sides, her body rigid with indignation.

Jesus was looking affectionately at Martha as she spoke. *How does he do that? It's like being affectionate towards an angry cat,* Lila thought. Then he looked down at Mary with the same expression. Her head was down with one hand shielding her face. He returned his timeless gaze to Martha's infuriated features.

'Martha, Martha,' he answered her. 'You are worried and upset about many things.' Concern and kindness were written across his face. Martha's body relaxed a little as her feelings were acknowledged. She stopped glaring at her younger sister and focused on him. Now that he really had her attention, he smiled at her. Her lips twitched as a reciprocal smile tried to break through her scowl. He beckoned her to sit down beside Mary – a few men begrudgingly shuffled out of the way. The sisters were now facing each other. It looked like the storm might pass.

'You've been worried and upset about many things,' Jesus repeated, 'but only one thing is needed.' He looked from Martha to Mary. 'Mary has chosen what is better, and it will not be taken away from her.' Mary's head had slowly lifted until she was gazing devotedly into his face.

'Why does he give so much time to these women?' Lila heard one man mutter to another. A baffled shrug was the only reply. 'The woman's right! Her sister should have been helping her. At this rate, we're never going to eat.'

Mary Magdalene rolled her eyes at Lila. 'Come on, let's cut

up those vegetables for Martha.' When they entered the kitchen, they were both surprised to see Jair deftly peeling and chopping. If the men outside could have seen Jair, they would have been more uncomfortable with what he was doing than with what Mary was doing. A rush of affection swelled Lila's chest as her husband looked up and smiled his crooked smile at her.

�֍ ✖ ✖

Jair was kissing her behind her ear as he ran his hand lightly down her neck. A thrill ran through her torso. Her lips found his mouth as she reached her hands around his lower back, feeling the shape of his muscles with her fingertips. But suddenly it was Aaron pressing into her; taking, not giving, forcing her submission. Harsh light flashed around them, blinding her. Then he was gone. Rough hands grabbed her and began dragging her down the road by her hair; her legs weren't working properly; her head was throbbing and she saw drops of blood falling in the dirt in front of her feet. She felt sheer terror as they took her up a hill. She was finding it hard to breathe, hard to walk, her body was in raw pain. They threw her in front of a crowd and everything went into slow motion as she hurtled through space. She woke as she landed on hard stone paving, sweating profusely.

So that was the dream.

Her heart beat loudly in her ears. Her breathing sawed in her throat. She pressed her hand into the sweat on her belly and the loose chemise she wore was saturated in a second. Then the tears came. When they had run dry she lay still listening to Jair, Anna and Joshua sleeping: heavy breathing, verging on snoring from Jair; a sighing – almost singing – from Anna and light, shallow breaths from Joshua. Slowly calm settled in her, like a still clear day when it's possible to see forever.

A bubble of pain and grief had come up from somewhere within her, ripping through the surface of her mind. It had to come out – it had to be expressed. She remembered something Jesus had said to Peter a few days before. He'd asked Jesus how many times he should forgive and had wondered whether seven times was too many? Jesus had said seventy times seven – infinity, forever, never stop, keep forgiving until it's all done.

She made herself picture Aaron's beguilingly handsome face in her mind and slowly, deliberately, she acknowledged how much he had hurt her that day. She had trusted him; she had thought what they had shared had been mutual – how foolish she had been; she had believed he would defend her. She'd looked for him among the leering men that swarmed around her – that's how deceived she'd been. It had meant nothing to him.

She forgave him again.

She hovered over the still surface of her deep, absorbing the calm into every fibre of her being. Then Joshua began to cry. She had been looking forward to cutting this night feed out of his routine, but tonight holding him was a great comfort.

※　※　※

It seemed they were to stay in Bethany for some time. As the days wore on, Jesus didn't speak of the next destination. Everyone settled into routines that had otherwise been impossible while travelling. Jair went into Jerusalem and made contact with those he'd worked with before. He visited their old neighbours and enquired about the house. On returning, he suggested to Lila that, if Jesus was taking an extended rest from travelling, maybe they should consider returning home. They spoke with Jesus and he encouraged them to do so. Travelling out daily to Bethany to be with the rest of the community would not be too onerous a task.

On their return home, Lila went to the market to buy food, leaving Joshua with Jair. She took Anna with her, excited to share the thrill of the big city with her. They were enjoying their adventure so much that Lila only realised that she had wandered much farther than she should, when her breasts started leaking milk. Looking at the shadows she realised the time and that she would be late back to feed Joshua. 'Come, Anna, let's go home. Shua will be wailing with hunger! Shall I carry you so we can hurry back?' Anna shook her curly head. Even though she was only two-and-a-half, she was very determined.

'I can walk fast, Mummy,' Anna said importantly.

They rounded a corner as Lila was looking at Anna, her heart fit to burst with maternal love. She wasn't looking where she was going. 'I'm so sorry,' she said as she bumped into someone. Realising it was a man, she bowed her head slightly and pulled her headscarf forward demurely. She raised her eyes to see if her apology had been accepted. A tremor ran through her, setting every nerve on edge. She involuntarily stepped backwards. It was Aaron.

They both stood frozen, staring at each other. Emotion flashed through his eyes. Her own emotions thundered and echoed across mountains of pain, conflicting and confusing. She realised she was holding Anna's hand very tightly. It took a huge effort to force herself to loosen her grip. She pulled Anna behind her skirts protectively. Anna looked up at her mother bewildered by the energy that ricocheted between her and this stranger. It seemed like an eternity, but it must have only been moments that they stood, an island in the human river of the marketplace.

'Shalom, Lila,' Aaron eventually said in that deep voice which had once held so much allure for her.

'Shalom,' she replied quietly. She realised the calm from the other night was still there, inside her, bedrock underneath the initial shock. It really might be Shalom – peace – she thought.

'I've often wondered if we would meet again.' He was smiling now. 'The last time we saw each other was so very unfortunate,' he paused. She wondered at his choice of words to describe one of the most horrific experiences of her life. 'I've hoped for a more pleasant opportunity to present itself ... and here it is, God given, when least expected.' He spread his hands magnanimously.

Something was niggling in Lila's mind but nervousness momentarily blocked her ability to remember it. Suddenly maternal instinct kicked in and she began to shake. Anna felt it and clung more tightly to her mothers' skirts. 'Mummy, I want to go home,' she cried plaintively.

'What? Who is this?' He looked down in surprise.

The fierce tigress instinct rising in Lila's chest made its way to her vocal chords in the form of a low growl. She quickly repressed it and fought to control her features. 'This is my daughter,' she said, forcing a casual tone. She watched him like a hawk, trying to predict his next move.

'Well, shalom, little one. Have you got a name?' He bent forward, interest sparking in his eyes. *Don't tell him your name, my love,* Lila pleaded silently. Anna didn't reply. 'You must be in your second or third year, am I right?' he continued in a soft tone, which he obviously reserved for children. He raised his eyes questioningly to Lila's face.

Horror twisted Lila's stomach into a knot. 'It is no concern of yours what age she is,' she snapped, regretting it immediately. Aaron's eyes brightened even more.

'I thought you couldn't ... '. He left the sentence hanging. She didn't reply and averted her gaze. 'What interesting eyes she has ... ' his voice trailed off as he studied Anna's face. Dread pulled at the knot in her stomach. There was no mistaking it: Anna had her father's eyes.

All the fight went out of Lila and the urge for flight took hold. 'We need to go,' she said too quickly.

'Don't.' He reached out to grab her arm, but Lila pulled away from him, dragging Anna with her, her little feet barely touching the ground. Aaron didn't block their way and didn't follow them. He just stood staring at their retreating figures, a wondering smile playing around his lips.

Lila's legs held out until they reached the end of their street. Poor little Anna ran to keep up with her, tears streaming down her face. When they turned into their street, Lila's knees buckled and she fell, her parcels tumbling from the basket on her hip. Anna began wailing as she ran to pick one then another off the ground. As it happened, Jair was sitting on the front step of their home with Joshua in his lap. When he heard Anna's cry, he raised his head and saw Lila lying in the road. He leapt up and ran with the baby grasped in his arms.

'Lila – what's wrong? What happened?' he cried, kneeling down beside her in the road.

'A man – in the market,' Anna sobbed.

'Here, Anna, give those to me – let's put them in the basket. Don't cry, sweetheart. Come ... come here.' Anna curled up beside her father and buried her face in his chest. 'There, there, it's all going to be all right.' He rubbed Anna's back gently. 'Lila, what happened?'

Slowly Lila raised her head, her face covered in dust down one side. She looked pleadingly into Jair's eyes, unable to speak. 'Anna, let's help Mummy get up and get the food into the house, shall we? Mummy will be better when she's had a drink of water. Would you like a drink too?' He looked down into Anna's innocent face and stroked her hair. Anna nodded. Joshua reached out and grabbed his sister's hair. 'No, Shua, don't do that.' Jair loosened his grip before Anna could start crying again.

They somehow managed to get into the house fully intact without having drawn a crowd. Lila collapsed gratefully onto the couch. Anna crawled up beside her mother and began gently patting her hand. Lila started crying.

Jair went to get water, carrying Joshua with him, though he was beginning to grizzle for his feed. 'Wait 'til Mummy's had a drink Shua – then she will feed you,' he soothed, a worried frown creasing his forehead.

'Did someone molest you or hurt you?' he asked.

Lila shook her head as she drank the water.

'What happened?' Jair sat down beside her. Joshua reached for his mother and Lila lifted her arms weakly to take him. 'Are you sure?' he asked. Lila nodded and managed to make an 'mmmm' sound. Joshua mouthed for Lila's breast, despite Lila's efforts to just hug him. She pulled herself up against the back of the couch and let her son under her tunic. She let her head fall back against the wall. Anna lay her head down on Lila's lap and stuck her thumb in her mouth.

Jair hadn't taken his eyes off Lila's face, waiting for an answer. Finally Lila opened her eyes and looked at her husband. 'I met Aaron,' she said flatly.

'Oh,' Jair breathed.

'Shall we leave?' Lila worried.

'Lila, he won't want Anna – he already has four children, maybe more now. He's not going to be interested in another, especially a girl,' Jair said, holding her hand, stroking it tenderly.

'But shall we go somewhere else?' It was as if she hadn't heard him.

'Look at me, my love.' He put one finger under her chin and raised her head. She held his gaze for a moment and then looked away. 'There is nothing he can do. Anna is ours and always will be.'

'You didn't see his face when he realised ... he will not let this rest until ... until, I don't know.' She could feel herself detaching and drifting up to the ceiling.

'Let's go and talk to Jesus about this, if it's worrying you so much. I'm sure he will be able to calm your mind better than I can.'

She looked up, 'Can we go now?'

'But we've only just arrived,' he replied, knowing it was no use using this logic as an argument.

�֎ ✖ ✖

His face wore a look of concern as he listened to Lila. 'What should we do?' she asked, when the story was told.

'What has your husband said?' he asked, quietly looking at Jair.

Lila shook her head and stared at the floor. The men exchanged a heartfelt look. 'Lila,' he said, his voice still quiet but firm. 'Trust him, he's a good man.'

Lila looked at Jesus and then at Jair, 'I know he is,' she said, half smiling, 'I'm just frightened.'

'Anna will always be his – a reminder of the mercy and grace you have both known.' Jesus smiled, his skin crinkling round his dark, sad eyes. 'After I have suffered and died, these blessings you have known will be poured out in full for all people,' he paused, 'but the darkness will become very dark before I rise again.' He had been talking like this for some time now. It was clear by Lila and Jair's faces that they didn't know what he meant, but he carried on: 'Anna will be a reminder in the darkest moments of the sweetness you have known,' he smiled at Jair, 'so be at peace.'

'What do you mean you will have to suffer and die? What do you mean you will rise again? I don't understand,' she said, frustration furrowing her brow. He didn't reply so she went on, 'I've had this sense of foreboding.' Lila was studying him intently. 'I've felt it since we began journeying back to Jerusalem. Has it something to do with what you are saying?' she asked.

Jesus searched her eyes as she spoke but still didn't answer her questions. After a moment's silence he said, 'Let's pray together.' He rose to his feet, lifting his hands up in customary style. They stood with him, holding their hands palms up. By now, they were used to his mysterious ways and didn't press him for answers. Jesus closed his eyes and raised his head heavenward, 'Abba, Father ... ' he prayed. No rabbi they'd ever heard prayed this way – he knew who he was speaking with. 'Your will be done here on earth as it is in heaven ...' He then placed his hands on Jair's and Lila's heads. 'Be at peace' he said authoritatively. Warmth rolled down through her head, neck and shoulders into the rest of her torso. It glowed in her belly. The residual effects of trauma and fear melted away. 'For your glory's sake, Father. Amen.'

Lila opened her eyes and surprised herself by smiling at Jesus and then at Jair who hugged her. 'You must not sin in your anger, but be very courageous,' Jesus said, reaching over and gripping Jair's shoulder, staring into his eyes disconcertingly. 'Remember – the Father will show Himself strong on behalf of those who are weak.' Jair's face grew very serious as he tried to understand. Lila felt the weight of his words rest upon her husband like a cloak. She wondered what it could mean. Jair was not an angry man.

As they were leaving, Mary came out to say goodbye to them. The moon had risen and the stars hung large and luminous in the inky sky above them. She hugged Lila close for a while. 'I'm so sorry that happened to you today. I wish I'd been with you.'

Lila eventually drew back from her and kissed her cheek. 'Thank you, Mary. I'm better for having been with Jesus. The only sadness I feel now is because he keeps speaking of his death.'

'Yes – I know. I keep thinking about what he said to me when I anointed him – that I was preparing him for his burial,' Mary replied.

'He is leading us in directions we would not naturally want to go,' Jair said. 'Sitting at his feet, you have begun to explore the deep things of God, Mary. Perhaps you experienced prophetic insight?'

'But Jesus isn't going to die,' Lila said, incredulously. 'He's younger than us, he's healthy and full of vitality – he heals the sick, for goodness sake – he's not going to die.' She was frowning and shaking her head.

'He has spoken of it too often, my love.' Jair gently stroked her arm. 'Something is coming that we do not and will not understand, or he wouldn't be warning us now. You two wouldn't be having forebodings, as others are. We must be alert and ready for whatever is to come, like it or not.'

Lila felt confused. She thought her dream had been about forgiving Aaron, or forewarning her of their accidental meeting, but somehow listening to Jair, she sensed that there were further layers of meaning.

9. UNTIE

The crippled woman

'... and a woman was there who had been crippled by a spirit for eighteen years. She was bent over and could not straighten up at all. When Jesus saw her, he called her forward and said to her, "Woman, you are set free from your infirmity." Then he put his hands on her, and immediately she straightened up and praised God.'

Charlie was scribbling on a piece of paper as he knelt, leaning on the wooden pew, listening to the reading. Josh and Melany had gone to their youth groups, but Charlie had refused to leave his mum. Grace was amazed that they were there at all. It must have been such a hard thing for Chloe to do. It was the third time they'd been to church since the affair and Grace was acutely aware of how vulnerable Chloe must be feeling, sitting in the congregation, as she stood up to preach.

'How many of us have been twisted out of shape by things in our lives – fears, insecurities, unforgiven or unhealed hurts and addictions? We put on a good front, especially here in church, but the truth is, behind the façade we're not much different than this woman we've read about today. The only difference is that her infirmity was clear for all to see. Most of ours are really well hidden. But they still limit us, deform us and cause us, and those around us much pain and suffering.'

Charlie must have been listening, because he climbed up on the pew and grabbed his mum's head to whisper into her ear, loud enough for everyone in the pews around him to hear: 'What's a "diction"?'

A few giggles escaped those sitting nearby. Chloe whispered back, 'It's something you can't help yourself doing. It makes you sad in the end.'

'Like picking my nose?' he asked, forgetting to whisper.

'Shh!' Chloe smiled as she gently pushed him down into a sitting position.

Grace laughed with everyone else and said to Charlie,'Yes, I guess picking your nose is one of those things we don't want anyone to see us doing. I'll have to take your word on it being an addiction. Thank you, Charlie.'

Charlie went red and put his head down, earnestly colouring in a big yellow sun on his drawing. Chloe rubbed his back and ran her fingers through his hair. As Grace looked at them she saw that Mark had tears in his eyes. Her sermon was nearly over.

'Listen to what Jesus had to say to those who were indignant about healing taking place in their weekly worship service: "Doesn't each of you on the Sabbath untie his ox or donkey from the stall and lead it out to give it water? Then should not this woman, a daughter of Abraham, whom Satan has kept bound for eighteen long years, be set free on the Sabbath day from what bound her?"

'You see, church should be the place where it's okay to be real about the things that are wrong in our lives. This should be the place where we get free from the things that tie us up in knots. Jesus is here by His Holy Spirit today – the one who is anointed to proclaim freedom for the prisoners and recovery of sight for the blind, to release the oppressed and proclaim that this is the time of God's favour.'

Grace let silence hang for a moment, to let people process what she had been saying.

Then, as she closed her Bible, she said: 'If you want to start getting free from anything that's twisted you out of shape, then come forward today and we,' she flicked a look at her two male colleagues sitting robed behind her in their prayer stalls, 'will be here to pray with you. The musicians are going to continue leading us in worship,' she said, looking back at the band leader who had panic written across his face, 'but if you need to go and get your kids, then please feel free to go. There's coffee and tea available, but if you want to stay and do business with God, then please stay. Let's stand and sing our last hymn together.'

Grace knew this was not the way services normally ended at St Matt's. She knew that Trevor, who was holding the reins in the absence of a vicar, would be uncomfortable with this change in style. She had been breaking with the conservative evangelical tradition of the church more and more openly and it had caused some tension in leadership meetings. But Grace was tired of toeing the party line. Why hadn't cerebral sermons, thorough exegesis, long-winded, theologically correct prayers and singing with gusto deterred Tom and Chloe from adultery? Why hadn't they helped heal the damage that had subsequently followed? She herself had found very little healing for her own past in church services. Theological college had never taught her of the recent, wonderfully strange ways God had been working. She was determined to let Him do what he wanted to do, no matter how odd it might be. She wanted Mark and Chloe, and everyone who had been so damaged by recent events, to experience what she had begun to experience through encountering Jesus' healing presence. She wanted St Matt's to be a place where people really would find Him and life in all its fullness.

'Do I need to get prayer, mum?' Charlie asked.

'No, love, you're fine ... just fine.' Chloe leaned down and kissed him. Then she looked at Grace. She turned to Mark and he nodded his head, unable to speak. Val was sitting behind them and she asked if they'd like her to take Charlie. They gratefully nodded their heads.

'Come on Charlie, let's go get some biscuits – maybe they have doughnuts today?' Charlie looked uncertainly at Chloe.

'I'll be over in a minute, love,' she assured him. 'We just need to spend a bit of time here ... ' her voice petered out, uncertain of what else to say to her son.

Charlie's face lit up with an epiphany – 'Do you pick your nose too, Mum?'

✲   ✲   ✲

Chloe knelt at the communion rail next to Mark.

I'm here, waiting for you.

Please help me.

I miss the intensity – the passion.

Can't get him out of my head. Especially when Mark and I try to make love. These last few nights I keep seeing him – smelling him.

How can I? Even after months of counselling, soul searching, prayer and time together on retreat. I've crossed a line – do I have to pay the price of a hollow marriage ... live with these consequences forever?

Grace had laid her hands on Chloe's head and was gently praying under her breath. Trevor was praying for Mark – Chloe could hear him reciting one of the psalms: 'Even the darkness will not be dark to you; the night will shine like the day, for darkness is as light to you.' She could hear Mark breathing deeply.

How is it ever going to be good again? Help me love Mark …

Chloe opened one eye to look at Mark and she saw out of her peripheral vision that several others had joined them at the rail. The musicians were playing a little too loudly for her liking. She felt irritated by Grace's hand on her head.

That compassionate, sweaty palm will plaster my hair to my forehead. Bet she's never even had a lustful thought in that Christian, 'how can I help you' head of hers.

O God – help me!

She was crying, her whole body tensing up with frustration.

Oh, what the hell … whatever …

She let out held breath as she smiled through her tears thinking of Charlie picking his nose.

※　※　※

Bishop Duncan was having his early morning cup of green tea. It was Monday and the sun poured through the large arching window, cascading across the smooth surface of his leather topped desk. It didn't quite reach the pile of papers that awaited his attention that day, and until it did, he permitted himself the pleasure of sitting still and staring out the window. He should have been a monk – he'd always known it. More and more these days his mind circled round that thought. But Wendy had tirelessly chased him and in the end she had won him over, heart, body and soul. His mother was over the moon – she'd always wanted grandchildren; she'd only been able to have him. Well – he'd done his duty. He'd given her four beauties to dote upon. His eyes scanned the photos neatly lining the far edge of his desk. A swell of affection rose in his chest. Yes – marriage and family had been good. He was grateful that Wendy had not given up on him. But there was little room for stillness and contemplation in this life of his.

The light had caught him unawares – it had now fully embraced the pile of papers. Bishop Duncan frowned, but obediently roused himself, downed the last of his tea, gently placing his cup and saucer to one side and slid the papers in front of him. His attentive secretary had heard the clink of china and briskly entered his office to remove the empty cup, knowing how much he hated clutter of any kind. They exchanged wordless, familiar smiles and she left knowing he would not want to be disturbed for at least another hour.

He placed his half-rimmed spectacles on his hooked nose and lifted the first document.

Ah! Bloody egos and libidos.

He lay the document down and leaned back into the comforting smell of his old leather chair. The Archdeacon was recommending that the Revd Thomas Winter be given six months leave of absence. The diocesan head of pastoral care was meeting with him regularly, and he and his wife were going for couples counselling. Colin's long-term suggestion was that said vicar be offered a country parish, while having regular meetings with the head of pastoral care for at least a year.

After careful investigation, it was Colin's considered opinion that the fault lay with the woman in question and not with said vicar. He had met with both of them separately and it was quite clear to him that this was an open and shut case. Like Adam, the vicar had been deceived by the temptress. Pastoral sensitivity was needed to ensure that Revd Winter's ministry was restored and that he and his wife made a good recovery. The woman in question and her husband seemed to be doing well under the pastoral care of Revd Grace Hutchinson. Colin complimented Bishop Duncan on choosing her for the task, although he alluded to anxiety over her possible feminist inclinations.

The disciplinary list is looking more and more like my Christmas card list every year. Bishop Duncan ran his hand carefully over the top of his thinning hair as he cast his mind back to last Christmas. *Tom must have come to one of our dinners?* He waited until his mind located the names with the faces. *Ah yes – confident chap, pastoral, people-person, man's man, conservative, pretty wife, from a solid evangelical stable. Obviously not had much training in self-knowledge. Yes ... he'd never left the diocese; did his curacy here ... was an associate minister here – this was his first title post. No trouble like this before? Well, no record of it. Was a high flyer in a big insurance company before theological training ... been married for fifteen years ... three children.*

Bishop Duncan went still. He closed his eyes and lifted his face heavenwards and waited.

It would be best to follow Colin's recommendation, although he doubted Colin's opinion regarding where the fault lay. Knowing Colin, he'd probably had many near misses with his own egocentric, wandering eye. Bishop Duncan suspected that Colin's wife had become his secretary so as to guard him more closely.

※ ※ ※

No one saw Tom leave the vicarage. It was 2.00am when he drove away. The removals company would come later that morning to gut the vicarage. A most unhappy interregnum lay ahead, during which the parish council would re-invent their parish profile and decide what sort of vicar they would next like to attract to the job, as well as worrying about the pending interviews for a new youth worker.

Chloe lay awake in her new house wondering if his body was yearning for hers like hers was for his.

Charlie was dreaming that his mummy was running down a dark alleyway away from him. He was chasing after her. He called out but no sound came from his mouth. His legs felt like they were wading through thick mud.

He woke up, screaming, 'Mummy!' He was clammy with sweet sweat.

Chloe guiltily jerked out of fantasy and ran to Charlie's room.

'It's okay, darling. I'm here. Mummy's here.' She sat beside Charlie, who clung to her sobbing.

'Don't leave me, mummy. Don't go,' he blurted into her chest.

'I'm not going anywhere, my darling. I'll never leave you,' she said, stroking his damp hair until he calmed down.

The dark heaviness, which so far had been held at bay, surged over her Prozac barricade and swamped Chloe's chest. She gave into it: loss, despair and longing gnawed around the edges of the gaping wound in her soul. She'd let him in; they had been bound to one another until discovery had torn him from her, taking chunks of her soul with the tangled roots of passion and desire. She thought of a line from the film *Notting Hill* – '*It's as if I've taken love heroin and now I can't ever have it again.*'

'I can't ever have it again,' she whispered as she lay down beside her son.

'I can't ever have it again,' she repeated in dazed agony. Her mind drifted to other lines from the film, *'It's like I've opened Pandora's box … .' and then Spike says, 'I knew a girl at school called Pandora … never got to see her box, though.'* She smiled wanly thinking of the hapless Welshman smirking as he said that line. Tears soaked into her son's pillow. The time ticked past on his Bart Simpson clock and slowly, mercifully she drifted into exhausted sleep.

�֎ ✖ ✖

In her curate's house near the church, Grace was sitting up in bed beside a snoring Peter. She was writing furiously, reflecting on the aftermath of Sunday's service. She loved how people had responded and come for prayer. They had been there until 1.00pm praying for folk. Her colleagues had been amazed at the effect of their feeble prayers; people had wept openly, some stayed kneeling at the communion rail lost in worship; others sat in pews singing softly, without anyone leading them. Everyone had been buzzing afterwards at the sense of the presence of God in the service. Trevor had said he thought he was going to fall over at one point. He had gone home to read up on the history of revivals.

Grace was thinking about the crippled woman in her sermon. She was thinking of freedom, of cutting the ties that bind. She closed her journal and reached for her laptop on her bedside table. She could almost smell Mary's perfumed oils. She began to write:

❀ ❀ ❀

Mary deftly drove her thumb into the knot between Lila's shoulder blades. The fragrance of the oil washed in waves over them both as she worked Lila's muscles. She'd come to stay for a few days.

'You are so good at this,' Lila groaned into her pillow. 'Thank you very much. Joshua is becoming such a little fatty – walking with him on my hip to Bethany today must have done this.'

'And carrying Anna too at times. I saw you with them both,' Mary scolded.

'She gets so jealous if she thinks he's getting more attention than her.'

'Oh, Lila, you know better than to give in to that – where was Jair anyway?' Mary was digging in under her shoulder blades.

'Ow!' Lila cried involuntarily.

'Sorry. Too hard?'

'Mmmmmm,' Lila replied.

'You're probably tense from your encounter the other day too, don't you think?' Mary hazarded.

'I think you could be right,' Lila mumbled into her pillow.

'So where was Jair yesterday?' Mary persisted.

'He got caught up in a big discussion. He knew you were there to help me,' Lila said, defending him.

Mary felt a stab of guilt, 'Well, I was with you some of the time.' She moved her fingers in a running motion down either side of Lila's spine repeatedly.

Lila didn't reply. Mary worked on in silence, losing herself to the skill of intuitive massage.

When she had finished she covered Lila with a shawl and left her to doze.

She came out into Lila's sun-drenched back yard and stretched. The woman across the alley, a hunchback, was leaning on her low wall watching the world go by, her head at its usual awkward angle. Mary had tried not to stare the first time she'd met her, and she still found it hard. The curvature of her spine cruelly twisted and arched her torso so that her head hung down at the level of her stomach. But she was a warm and gracious woman none the less, and had become friendly with Lila and Mary. I wonder if I could straighten her back out, Mary mused as she waved and then stretched again. Jair was sitting in the shade playing with the children. To one side were a pair of half-made sandals. His tools were resting on top of them.

She loved to watch him work, usually by lamplight, when the children were asleep. She had admired his flexibility when they had been travelling. He'd given up the security of work in Jerusalem to follow Jesus. She loved the way he'd provided for his family; the way he'd had an implicit trust that they were doing the right thing, meandering across the country with the motley group of people that followed Jesus. His old work partners had gladly welcomed him back on his return to the city and it was good to see him settling into a routine again.

Of course, she had contributed to her friends' income too, for having her live with them. She had sold two of her bottles of perfumed oil. She had two left. Instead of using some of the money to make more, as she had first thought, she had given it all to Jair to do with as he pleased. Lila and Jair had been overwhelmed. They'd never seen so much money at one time in all their lives. Together they had sat by flickering candlelight, talking into the night. They'd agreed together to give half of it to fund Jesus and his disciples as they travelled.

'Mary!' Anna saw her and shouted with delight. 'Come see! Daddy is letting Joshua eat ants.'

'Shh, Anna. Don't say it so loud, or mummy will hear,' Jair chuckled.

'Don't tell mummy or she'll get cross with daddy,' Anna whispered conspiratorially, her chubby finger dramatically pressed to her lips.

Mary sat down beside Joshua who was totally focused on trying to pick up ants and get them into his mouth before they escaped. He wasn't having much success. Anna plonked herself into Mary's lap. 'You smell lov-e-ly,' she said drawing out the new, grown-up word she had recently learned as she picked up one of Mary's hands and held it to her nose.

'She's been massaging Mummy,' Jair said.

'Massage me,' Anna demanded.

'Would you be all right for a bit if I work on these sandals? I need to finish them today. The man is coming to pick them up this evening. He only gave them to me to fix yesterday.' Jair looked pleadingly at Mary.

'That's fine, Jair. I'll just massage this young lady and keep an eye on the ant king. Are you going to stay here to work?'

'Yes.' He picked up the sandals and his tools and placed them in front of him.

Mary began gently massaging Anna's tiny shoulders.

'Mmmmmm,' Anna mimicked her mother. Mary stifled a laugh as Jair cocked one eyebrow and shook his head.

※　※　※

'So, where were you?' Lila asked as they washed the baby's clothes.

Mary looked surprised. 'I was walking with everyone else,' she gestured vaguely.

'Yes, but who in particular?' Lila pursued it like a hunting dog with a scent.

Mary squirmed. There was no way out. She felt she was a little girl who'd been found out doing something she shouldn't. 'I'm a grown woman. I can talk to whoever I like. Everyone at Bethany is a follower of Jesus. We're like an extended family, aren't we?' She glared petulantly at Lila, viciously scrubbing the cloth in her hand.

'If you're not ashamed of who you were with, then why are you being so defensive?' Lila hid her anxiety behind hooded eyes and a mild tone as she tightly wrung out a cloth.

'Don't be so patronising, Lila. You're not my mother and anyway who are you to judge me?' It was a slap in the face. Both women knew it. Mary stood up, turned on her heel uncertainly and stormed out of the room, dripping soapy water as she went. Lila was left reeling, still holding a wet cloth in mid-air.

So this is the thanks I get for sharing my home with you – you little tramp. Wait 'til I tell Jair and Lazarus. Lila was seething. She threw the washing down and went in search of Jair. He was putting the finishing touches to the sandals while the children slept beside him in the shade of the tree in their back yard. 'Did you see Mary go through here?' she demanded, struggling to keep her voice down.

Jair looked up from his work in surprise. 'Yes. She stormed past without so much as a word. Why?' He was already regretting his question.

'She has been flirting with that man again. You know the one I mean.' She folded her wet arms across her chest emphatically.

'You mean the wealthy one?' He wanted to be sure he got it right before wading in any deeper.

'Yes, the one who's always bragging about how much he gives to the poor. It's the way he looks at her. I've seen him when he's thought no one's watching. I think he probably saw her perform before ... you know ... in her old life, maybe at the palace? Anyway, I swear, Jair, he's up to no good and she's falling for him. Surely she should know better by now? And she insulted me.' Her hand went to her cheek as she was suddenly overwhelmed with emotion.

Jair motioned for her to come and sit with him. She flopped down beside him and he put his arm around her shoulders as she leaned her head on his. 'You have really grown to love her, haven't you?'

Lila nodded, wiping away a tear. 'She reminds me of me. I had no one looking out for me. Yes, I had parents but they didn't care about me. I'm so glad that you did – that you paid the dowry – that you wanted me. What would my life have been like if Aaron had got me?' she lifted her head and looked into his eyes.

They hadn't spoken of him since the incident in the market. There was a long pause and then she said, 'He looks at her like Aaron used to look at me.' She scribbled in the dirt with her finger and suddenly remembered Jesus fingers writing in the dust. Emotion caught her off-guard again and tears rolled down her face. She whispered, 'Forgive me for calling her a tramp. I'm so sorry.'

'What, my love?' Jair leaned in to try to hear her.

'Nothing,' She replied. 'Will you speak to her? She'll listen to you. We must also speak with Lazarus and Martha.'

'I'll try with Mary, but it's really Lazarus' place to do that.' He smiled uncertainly.

※　※　※

Mary hadn't come back until long after dark. Lila lay asleep with a child in each arm, but Jair was waiting for her in the backyard. Mary's heart sank when she saw him.

'Where have you been?' he asked quietly.

'I'm sorry, Jair. I lost track of time.' She stood still, her head hanging.

'Where have you been?' he repeated calmly.

'I was with some of Jesus' disciples. They invited me to have a meal with them.' She raised her head a little.

'Were you the only woman there?' he asked.

There was a long pause, then, 'Yes'.

'Was Jesus there?'

Another pause. 'No.'

'Mary. Come sit down with me. Let's talk about this.'

She pensively obeyed. The stars twinkled over their heads. The moon shot dancing shafts of light through the swaying branches of the tree onto Jair's features.

He spoke slowly, measuring each thought carefully. He knew if he put a word wrong, she would stop listening to him. 'It's been good having you as part of our family over these last two years, even though you have your own family now. You are like a sister to Lila and me. The children adore you and you've been so incredibly generous with what is yours. We hope we have been a blessing to you too?'

'Yes, you have, Jair.' Her voice was subdued.

Silence hung between them as they both absorbed the meaning of what had been said and unsaid.

'Aaron was a good friend of mine, you know.' Mary's head jerked up in surprise. She hadn't expected him to speak of him. 'Yes. We grew up together. I was always in his shadow. I can remember wanting to be like him. He was so confident and purposeful. I knew he'd go far – which he has. He's a Pharisee now – I think he's on the Sanhedrin, a respected member of the religious ruling party. When he teaches in the synagogue, people listen.'

As fascinated as she was, Mary was beginning to wonder where this was leading. Jair didn't seem to notice. He went on: 'Even when he was secretly coupling with my wife, I was hanging on his every word in synagogue. He would often make his way to speak with me afterwards and I always felt privileged that someone of such stature wanted my opinion on his teaching,' he sighed. 'Now I know he was simply enjoying my ignorance, revelling in the power he had over me – stealing from under my nose.'

Mary didn't know what to say. She felt awkward. 'Jair, I don't know why you're telling me this.'

Then he turned to her and looked her full in the face. 'Mary, this man you are interested in – he is the same sort of man. He is playing with you and will use you and then spit you out. Lila can see this. She is only trying to protect you because she loves you.'

'But he's following Jesus with us. He's friendly with Jesus' disciples.' Her jaw muscles tightened.

'Yes,' he agreed, 'but for how long? I guarantee you he has ulterior motives. I don't know what they are, but I do know that men like him are only interested in games of power. Have you noticed that Jesus is not like that?'

Her eyebrows drew together. 'But he is a very powerful man.'

'Yes.' Jair nodded his head. 'Will he use his power to overthrow the Romans, to establish Israel as an independent nation? Will he declare himself king and seat himself on David's throne in Jerusalem? Will he give his disciples positions of power around him? Will he make this man of yours one of his advisers?'

Mary didn't answer. They had been talking about ending Roman rule tonight. Judas had become very angry during a debate about whether Jesus was the chosen one, the Messiah, who would lead Israel. She hadn't really been interested in their political conversation. She had been preoccupied with the hand that gently rested on her leg under cover of the table. Old cravings slithered, curling round the small of her back. It had been a struggle to leave, but she'd realised Jair and Lila would be anxiously waiting for her. It took huge willpower to pull away from him, to refuse his offer to walk her the short distance back home. She knew he would pull her into some dark alleyway, that he would kiss her hungrily. She knew his hands would move fast, that it wouldn't take much to move the layers of clothing that hung between them.

She had walked away trembling, a cacophony of conflicting emotions raging in her mind. Now, seated beside Jair within the boundaries of the courtyard and his friendship, she could feel the oil and water of lust and desire separating and settling within her. She realised Jair was studying her face.

'Mary, these feelings are all good, but they are misplaced. He is not good for you,' he said, smiling gently.

She nodded sadly. No man of integrity would have touched her in that way before becoming engaged. She knew Jair was right.

'You've heard Jesus say his kingdom is not of this world, haven't you? I think he has come, not to free us from Roman rule, but to free and heal us of things that destroy us from the inside out. He is calling us into a better way of living with each other.'

Moonlight glistened on a tear escaping Mary's eye. 'But look at me, Jair. I'm not free. I have been driven tonight by old lusts. I could have so easily done things I used to do.'

'What stopped you?' he asked quietly.

She paused to think. 'Your faces – Lazarus and Martha's faces – Jesus' face.'

He reached over and squeezed her shoulder. 'We are family now. You are not alone in the world any more. The things you do or don't do matter now because you are loved. You see?' he patted her shoulder gently.

She wanted to lean her head on his chest, but she didn't. She sat there for a long time after he had gone in, until the moon was low in the sky. She remembered how Jesus had accepted her as she was, pouring out the tools of her trade on his feet. His words came strongly into her mind: 'Your sins are forgiven – go in peace.'

When she finally lay her head down the first traces of dawn were beginning to glow in the east.

※　※　※

Jair had invited Jesus to come to their local synagogue to teach on the Sabbath. Lila and Mary were sitting next to their neighbour in the women's section. Lila had brought raisins with her to keep the children quiet. Mary smiled at their neighbour, resisting the desire to lean over and rub her twisted and crooked back.

The scripture had just been read. It was about Jubilee. Jesus was sitting at the front, slowly scanning the crowded room before he spoke. Lila thought he was looking for someone in particular. She turned her head, trying to follow his gaze, but Joshua pulled her headscarf and it fell down onto her shoulders. She quickly put it back in place, hoping no one had been offended. When she looked up again, Jesus was looking directly at her, or so she thought. She felt embarrassed and confused.

'Woman,' he called out.

Lila mouthed 'Me?' pointing to herself.

Jesus shook his head, 'The woman next to you.'

How could he even see her? Lila thought. Both her and Mary leaned down at the same time to speak to their neighbour.

'He's calling you,' Mary said, excitement in her voice.

'Me? What does he want with me?' The woman tried to crane her head round to look at Mary.

'I don't know, but he's waiting for you, you better go. Do you want me to help you?' Mary had one hand under her elbow.

'Push me up,' she said and both Lila and Mary obeyed. The woman was suddenly on her feet.

'Come here,' Jesus beckoned. She shuffled her way slowly down the dividing aisle that separated the men from the women. A hush descended on the gathering as they watched her slow progress. She finally came and stood next to Jesus, her head at the level of his chest. He tilted his head to one side, looking into her face and smiling.

'How long has this spirit crippled you?' Jesus asked.

'Eighteen years,' replied the woman clearly. There was a chorus of agreement from those who obviously knew her well.

'I remember when it began,' called a woman in front of them.

Jesus had risen from his seat, remaining focused on their neighbour. Then he raised his voice and said, 'Woman, you are set free from your infirmity.' He laid his hands on her back, like Mary had longed to do, and she jerked violently like a jack-in-the-box, a cry of surprise escaping her lips. Everyone rose to their feet as one, craning to see. Mary ran down the aisle in time to see the woman straightening up, a look of profound shock on her face.

Mary propelled herself to the front and threw her arms round the woman who had begun to praise God in a wobbly voice. Her daughters joined them, hugging and kissing her, hopping and dancing round her, touching her once crooked back in wonder. Chaos ensued.

Lila wiped her eyes on Joshua's tunic as she watched Jesus face in awe. He was celebrating with the women, throwing his head back and laughing and singing. But then she saw the face of the synagogue leader and she felt that familiar sinking feeling in her guts. *Why is it always the same with religious people?* She watched him rise to his feet and clap his hands. She saw some faces lose their joy.

'There are six days for work. So come and be healed on those days, not on the Sabbath,' he bellowed, pushing Mary as he made his way towards Jesus. He took hold of the woman whom Jesus had healed by the arms and firmly directed her back to the women's section. Lila thought she saw him say 'you should know better.' She was glad to see that her neighbour was not perturbed by whatever he said. She came back to her seat next to Lila, hopping and skipping and singing under her breath. Everyone around them wanted to touch her, but they did so in a furtive way, glancing over their shoulders uneasily at the synagogue ruler.

'You hypocrites!' Jesus shouted, making Anna and Joshua jump in Lila's arms. She'd never seen him so angry. 'Doesn't each of you on the Sabbath untie his ox or donkey from the stall and lead it out to give it water?' He was glaring at the synagogue ruler and his cronies across the room. Their expressions were indignant. They did not reply.

'Should not this woman, a daughter of Abraham, whom Satan has kept bound for eighteen long years, be set free on the Sabbath day from what bound her?' Lila felt her neighbour's body begin to shake beside her. She looked and saw she was weeping. She took hold of her hand and squeezed it hard. Mary held her other hand, her face a storm of outrage.

The synagogue ruler looked around at his congregation for their loyalty – none was forthcoming. Humiliated, he and his supporters rose and filed out of the door behind him, avoiding Jesus' searing stare. When the last one had gone, celebration broke out again. People started singing a Jubilee song. Some started dancing the vine-step down the aisle, while others pushed their way through to congratulate and embrace the healed woman. Lila made her way over to Jair and Anna climbed into his lap, kissing his face several times with sticky raisin kisses. They lingered, watching their neighbour rejoicing with her friends and family. Lila realised she'd lost track of Mary and began scanning the room for her. Eventually she found her. She was dancing with Jesus.

10. ALL

The widow

Chloe was meandering through a farmers' market in a nearby town. It had almost been a year since the affair had started. She'd wanted to get away, do something different. She'd heard that the place had a good market on a Wednesday. The kids were at school, the house was all sorted and Mark was at work. She felt hollow. People brushed against her – brushes on a drum. She picked things up but didn't see them. She wandered aimlessly. Suddenly, she stopped still at the sound of laughter – his laugh. She came alive, every nerve on end, looking around frantically. Then she saw him, sitting having coffee with his wife outside a patisserie. She hid behind a stall and watched them – hungrily, furtively. He was totally focused on his wife. His eyes moved between her lips and her eyes as she spoke. He laughed at something she said. He leaned over to whisper in her ear and then kissed her earlobe, then down just behind her ear – like he used to do with Chloe. She had only discovered that spot with him, Mark had never found it. It had been one of their many secret pleasures.

His wife seemed to like it too. They could have been the only people in the place; a love bubble surrounded them, excluding everyone; excluding her. Chloe's hollowness turned from a drum into a bottomless pit. She clutched her stomach, wrapped her arms round herself and stared at the ground trying to decide what to do. A small plastic bag floated past on a gust of wind; it twirled as it passed her, dancing on her pain. Like an addict who knows that just one more fix may kill but reaches for the needle anyway, she looked again. Their foreheads were touching, both looking down at their hands laced tenderly together on the table. He stole a light kiss from her lips. Chloe realised she'd stopped breathing. Her lungs were burning. She took in a sob of air. The couple turned at the sound. His eyes locked on hers. She was a rabbit caught in headlights – rooted to the spot.

'You all right, love?' the stall owner asked, touching her elbow. It felt like an electric shock. She wheeled round wildly, unable to speak, horrified at coming undone in public. She shook off his hand, trying to smile as she moved away. But her body wasn't working. It was shuddering like a car that needed its wheels realigned.

'Chloe!' Tom shouted.

She looked back involuntarily, his voice pulling her. He was standing; his wife was still sitting holding one of his hands. They were both staring, different kinds of agony burning in their eyes. Chloe broke into a run, dodging shoppers with bags, prams and dogs. She didn't look back again.

She sat in the car for a long time, her mind tracing over and over every detail.

He loves her – that's good. They're okay – that's good. His boys won't lose their dad – that's good. Good for them – good for You. Is this Your way of helping me let go of what's not mine? If I'd known it would hurt this much, I would never have been so stupid to ask.

Shock. Then numbness. Now tears howling from the depths of the abyss within her. It felt the same as when her dad had chosen his eighteen-year-old mistress over a relationship with her. She rocked herself, banging her head on the steering wheel. She was tipping over the edge of sanity. She couldn't breathe through her nose. She looked into the abyss, but didn't fall. Somehow she was teetering on the brink. She slowed her rocking as the whirlwind blew itself out. She became aware of her surroundings again, squinting to see if anyone had been watching her. The car park was silent and still. She leaned her head back on the headrest and willed herself to get control.

Into the lull dropped a Bible verse: Job 5:18. She didn't know what it was. *Is that You?*

She reached for her small pink leather-bound Bible in her handbag. She held it in her lap for a while, rubbing the soft surface with her thumb and running her fingernail down the silver-edged pages.

'For he wounds, but he also binds up; he injures, but his hands also heal,' she read.

Her eyes welled with tears again, their source a different feeling. She blinked and focused to read the verse again. Beside it, in the margin, were some other references. She turned to Isaiah 30:26. Her eyes scanned down to the end of the verse:

'... the Lord binds up the bruises of his people and heals the wounds he inflicted.'

There were other verses she'd underlined on that page. Her eyes wandered over them with a growing sense of His presence.

'In repentance and rest is your salvation, in quietness and trust is your strength ... Yet the Lord longs to be gracious to you; he rises to show you compassion. For the Lord is a God of justice. Blessed are all who wait on him! ...Whether you turn to the right or to the left, your ear will hear a voice behind you, saying, "This is the way; walk in it."'

She was enveloped in living, breathing, warm, embracing grace – her car a sacred space.

She closed her eyes. Her nose was beginning to clear, but she still breathed through her mouth. A proverb she'd often drawn from when dealing with rebellious teenagers floated across her consciousness as she see-sawed between her pain and the comforting presence. 'My child, do not despise the Lord's discipline and do not resent his rebuke, because the Lord disciplines those he loves ...'

She relinquished; gave in; sea met sand.

She found herself forgiving her dad and asking for forgiveness for having held on to the hurt for so long. She then found herself forgiving Tom for offering her false hope and for failing her so badly. She let go of him and her unrequited love. The sea engulfed her, liquid heaviness filled her, displacing the emptiness, salving the pain, weighting her back into sanity. It rose and rose then spilled over her lips and to her amazement she found she was speaking softly in a language she did not understand.

Not done that before, she mused, listening to herself. She was distracted by the novelty of it, feeling the shapes her tongue and lips were making. She raised her fingers to her lips. She closed her mouth. Then opened it again. She could stop and start at will. She let

202

herself play with it for a while, feeling better than she had done for a long time. A rush of gratitude gurgled up and she was babbling, crying and laughing. The comforting presence intensified, glowing, radiating, exulting – saturating her.

So this is joy ... I didn't know it could be like this ...

※　※　※

'I saw him today,' Chloe said. Mark's back stiffened, but he didn't turn around. Slowly, he started scrubbing the saucepan in the sink again. She was sitting at the kitchen table, having just put the kids to bed.

'And ... ?' he asked, concentrating hard on a stubborn bit of burnt-on food.

'He was with his wife – at a café. I saw them kiss,' she said quietly.

'Oh.' He stopped his scrubbing and turned his head. It felt like the first time they'd really looked at each other in ages. The heavy rain of despair had washed the air clean between them. Everything was so much brighter, Chloe thought, and the colours seemed so much more vivid. There was something different about Mark's eyes. They were more open, more readable. She remembered how she felt the first time she'd looked into them. Sea blue-green – lighter at the centre, darker round the edges. They looked bluer tonight because he was wearing a light blue denim shirt. Windows to the soul: windows that had been veiled for how long? 'Are you okay?' he asked.

She was surprised by his concern for her. She had no right to it. 'You know, I think I am.' she smiled tentatively. She fiddled self-consciously with her wedding ring and then looked at him again. 'Do you want a drink?'

'Yeah ... okay ... I'll have a beer.' His lips curved slightly in reply. She went to the fridge as he finished clearing the sink. She returned with a can, a bottle of wine and glasses.

'So, what happened?' he didn't look at her while he poured for them both.

'Well, I went to that farmers' market that Val was telling us about the other day. I just wanted to get away someplace different. Then I heard his voice. I looked around and saw them, sitting wrapped up in each other at this little French café.' She sipped her wine. 'That's quite nice,' she said, nodding at her glass.

'I thought you'd like it,' he smiled. She felt a slight flutter in her stomach as she looked into his eyes again. There he was – unguarded, vulnerable – looking back at her.

'Anyway,' she tucked a loose strand of hair behind her ear and his eyes followed the movement, 'I made some kind of noise – not on purpose – I think I gasped or something, and they both looked up and saw me.'

'What did you do?' He was pensive, focused, leaning forward.

'I turned to walk away. He called after me. I panicked and ran all the way back to the car,' she sipped her wine again, 'then I lost the plot.'

He leaned back, imagining her crying in the car. 'Big sobs?' he raised his eyebrows.

'Yeah, big snotty sobs.' The tension broke as they gave themselves to laughter. In the lull that followed, they stared at each other, looking for the way back to how it used to be.

'I'm so sorry,' Mark said, his eyes glistening. 'I'm so very sorry for … '.

'Don't.' Chloe reached over and touched his hand. ' I've been such a fool,' he took her hand running his thumb lightly along her palm. It felt new. He lifted it to his mouth and kissed it.

'The most amazing thing happened in the car after I'd cried myself out,' she said watching his head bent over her hand. He lifted his eyes to hers, still cradling her hand in his. She hesitated, touching his wedding ring. He waited, drinking her in. 'It was like God came and sat in the car with me. It was amazing.' Her eyes were shining. 'I felt this – this overwhelming presence. I've never known joy like it. I started speaking in tongues – I was totally amazed. How could I go from utter desolation to such a high in seconds? Was I going nuts?' she paused. 'But it's not gone away,' she touched her chest, 'I can still feel the effect of it here.'

Mark leaned his chin on one hand. He had never wanted her so much in all their years together. Chloe saw and trailed the fingers of her free hand across her collarbone. 'Seeing them together today – it hurt so much, like surgery without an anaesthetic.' Her hand moved down to her heart. 'But it's gone – he's gone – I've let go. Not the way I would have planned it,' she smiled ruefully, 'but then the Lord's ways aren't my ways, are they?' Her hand moved up to her shoulder and her fingers twisted the strand of hair that had fallen from behind her ear again.

'No, not often,' he said simply. 'God, I've missed you. I've missed this,' he pointed at the space between them. 'I got so lost ... I want to be a better man.'

'What if you can't? I mean, what if this is as good as it gets?' She was trying to look pragmatic and worldly-wise.

'I've asked God to help me.' He leaned forward so their faces were close. The intensity in his eyes warmed her. 'I nearly lost you once, I don't ever want to lose you again,' he leaned in, crossing the remaining divide between them and brushed his lips lightly against hers.

A rush of pleasure went through her at the smell of his skin, his breath. 'I want to be connected to you ... the real you, not just the bits you let me see. I'd even watch porn with you if you like?' she tried to look nonchalant at the prospect with a sad little smile.

'No,' he shook his head, touched by her mercy. 'I hate what porn has done to me ... to me and you.' He leaned back, stretching out the nervous tension in his body and running his hands through his hair, leaving it looking tousled. Her eyes wandered from it down across his forehead, languidly exploring his features.

'C.S. Lewis hit the nail on the head with his Turkish delight in *The Lion, the Witch and the Wardrobe*,' he threw his head back laughing. 'I was reading that to Charlie the other night and it hit me so hard.' Chloe looked confused. 'You know when Edmund meets the White Witch and she gives him enchanted Turkish delight so he'll keep coming back to her for more? He can't get enough of it, could eat it 'til he explodes, but it never satisfies him. He betrayed the people he loved the most just to get more of it.' Light dawned in Chloe's eyes.

He leaned across the table again, taking both her hands in his, searching her eyes. 'I swear to you, I'm done with avoidance and deception. I don't want to touch it any more. It doesn't satisfy. I want you. I want sex with you, intimacy with you, not an impersonal spectator sport. I know I may sometimes be tempted by it, but I *will* tell you when I am; I swear.'

Chloe smiled and stood up. It had been a day of surprises. This was the last thing she thought she would be doing but she was in front of him now, still holding hands, swinging them uncertainly between them. He tugged her arms playfully and she responded by straddling his lap. Desire and insecurity vied for control as familiarity interfaced with the unknown. Slowly he leaned forward kissing her mouth, gently at first – tentatively – and then as she parted her lips, letting him in, his hands slid up her back to her neck, pressing her like an apple to his mouth. His want for her grew stronger than his fear of rejection. She responded to it and reached up, caressing his face, her fingers meandering into his hair. He worked to undo the clasp that held her hair. It fell away letting the rich, dark mass cascade around their faces. They pressed their foreheads together savouring the moment.

The strong current of hope pulled them towards how it could be again. She brushed her lips across his cheekbones; his nose; his eyelids; all the beauty she hadn't noticed for so long. Desire surged through him as he sensed the barriers had finally come down. He thrilled at being loved again. He kissed her neck up into her hair, breathing in the scent of her perfume behind her ear.

How did he know? A small wave had been building inside her and rippled out across her skin. He lifted her onto the table pressing his mouth into the softness under her jaw line. She let out a soft groan of pleasure. He moved their drinks out of the way as she pulled him to her.

'I've missed you too,' she said huskily. The urgency to be one again suddenly overtook them. Clothing got pushed, pulled, and thrown aside. He surfed her waves, waiting for her, holding back until he thought he couldn't bear it any more. They crashed together on the shore of the table, the solid oak creaking in harmony with them.

'I love you,' Mark rasped hoarsely into her hair, 'I love you so much.'

She turned her head to look at him. 'We're one again ... always be honest with me?'

'I will,' he said, his breathing slowing down as he pushed himself off the table. He looked down at her, 'I want all of you ... and I want you to have all of me.'

She reached up and brushed a damp strand of hair out of his eyes. 'How did you know about behind my ear? You never knew that before.'

'I don't know,' he smiled a post-coitus smile, eyelids heavy as he staggered back, looking down at the floor for his clothes. 'Must be God telling me – I'm so in tune.' He stuck his fingers up either side of his head like antennae. Chloe giggled.

❄   ❄   ❄

They were sitting at their favourite table in the Italian restaurant. Chloe was looking gorgeous. She was wearing a dark green silk halter-neck top, which showed off her tanned shoulders to perfection. Her hair was up in a loose, messy knot that looked carelessly thrown together and incredibly sexy. As usual she wasn't wearing much make-up, just some lip-gloss and something that shimmered on her eyelids. Watching her, Grace found herself wanting to experiment with make-up again, for the first time in years.

'You're looking … ' Grace scrutinised her, searching for the right words, ' … very alive, very sensual. You could be French!'

'Well the way things have been going,' she leaned in hiding her mouth behind the back of her hand, 'we could be starring in our own French film.'

'You and Mark?' Grace asked, just to be sure.

She smiled and nodded. 'Let's just say we feasted on love at our kitchen table.'

'Mmmmm.' Grace wrinkled her nose. 'How can I sit round it for a coffee now that I know that?' Grace hugged her. 'That's great news – I thought there was something different about you. Since when?'

'Since God turned up in my car!'

❄   ❄   ❄

Bishop Duncan rarely wrote letters in his own hand. He usually dictated them to his secretary, and only signed them. But this one had been brewing in his mind for some time and he knew it had to be written with pen and ink. The headed paper sat blank before him, the pen his mother had given him held poised in his hand.

'Gracious Father, enable me to skilfully minister as you have ordained me to do,' he prayed aloud, then put nib to paper. He loved the sound it made as it rode across the expensive surface; he loved the scent of the ink as it sank in. The words flowed eloquently:

Dear Chloe,

It is good to hear that you and your husband are still worshipping at St Matt's. You, Mark and your children have been much in my prayers. I trust that each one is beginning to find their place in your new home and in new schools.

It saddened me greatly when I first heard that one who represents me in this diocese had caused so much pain through unguarded frailty. I wanted to write to you to convey my deepest regret.

Please do not think for one moment that I would pay you the discourtesy of believing you to be totally innocent. I trust you have been working out your salvation with fear and trembling also.

However, these things grieve our Lord and we would be poor stewards if we did not enter into his anguish for his flock. The thief comes to kill, steal and destroy. But our Lord is the Good Shepherd who knows his sheep by name and they know his voice. My prayer is that all involved will listen to His voice. My hope is that each one will be healed and restored in God's good time.

I believe you know His voice,
Blessings,
+Duncan

※ ※ ※

When Chloe got the bishop's letter, she rang Grace and read it to her through jerking sobs. Grace had been writing the next chapter in her story, but had deleted several attempts at the first paragraph. She welcomed the distraction. Her heart swelled with admiration for her bishop when she heard what he'd done. What a man, what a leader.

'He gave time and thought to me – and to our family. Oh, it's like your story, isn't it? An important man like him taking time to be gracious to me?' Chloe blew her nose loudly. Grace held the phone away from her ear.

'Handwritten? He never writes letters himself,' Grace shook her head at the extravagance of it.

'The thing that really touched me was when he said, "I believe you know His voice." For him to say that after what I've done … well … '

she sniffed noisily. 'I mean … he's being really generous, putting himself on the line like that, isn't he? For all he knows, I could be the Jezebel the Archdeacon imagines me to be. That he'd hold out that hope and trust me again …' she started to cry.

'Oh Chloe – he's right, though, isn't he? You do know His voice, and you now know yourself a lot better too.'

'Uhuh,' she managed, after a big sniff. 'He didn't condemn me. Coming from him, that means so much.'

When Chloe hung up, Grace swivelled her chair round at her desk slowly and replaced the phone in its cradle. She smiled at her icon of Jesus. 'Thank you,' she prayed.

She returned to her writing, thinking about Chloe and Mark giving all of themselves to each other at last, trusting in God to be the third strand in the cord of their marriage that would not be easily broken. *How hard it seems to give your all; to trust completely; to depend utterly on grace …* She started to write:

❀   ❀   ❀

The passion in his voice was compelling. There was hardly any room to move, a sea of people surrounded him. He railed against the Jewish leaders of Jerusalem, the scribes and the Pharisees. He warned the people against their vanity; their selfishness; their blindness; their hypocrisy. He called them blind guides and 'play actors' who hid behind masks; haters of God, who were slamming the door of heaven in the face of His people.

'Beware – they like to walk around in flowing robes and love to be greeted in the market places, and have the most important seats in the synagogues and places of honour at banquets. They devour widows' houses and, for a show, make lengthy prayers. Such men will be punished most severely.' His eyes spat fire as they ranged across the faces around him. They rested momentarily on a handsome Pharisee. Aaron looked away quickly, unable to hold his gaze.

Jesus was standing by the altar, in the place where the leaders of Jerusalem had murdered the prophet Zachariah. Jewish legend had it that the blood of Zachariah had bubbled on the pavement of the temple court, the very place that Abel – the first martyr in the Bible – had been slain by his brother, Cain. Jesus accused the Jewish leaders, not only of the murder of Abel and of Zachariah, but of every martyr of God because they were not only guilty of slaying all the prophets but he knew they were about to kill the Son of God.

In a voice filled with pathos he continued: 'If you had known – even you, especially in this your day – the things that make for your peace! But now they are hidden from your eyes. For days will come upon you when your enemies will build an embankment around you, surround you, close you in on every side and level you, and your children within you, to the ground; and they will not leave in you one stone upon another, because you did not know the time of your visitation.'

Jair looked anxiously across at the stony faces of the Pharisees standing at a distance. He saw Aaron just as he broke eye contact with Jesus. The look on Aaron's face sent fear running down Jair's spine. A deep sense of foreboding gripped him as he listened, wondering what terrible future event it was that Jesus spoke of.

The temple guard had not yet stopped him; the chief priests and teachers of the law were afraid of the people, and the people were enthralled with him. Since they had ushered him into Jerusalem with cries of 'Hosanna', throwing their cloaks and palm fronds before him as he rode in on a donkey, expectation had been running high and the mood had been euphoric. But now the crowd seemed bewildered by these ominous words.

Jesus began to make his way through the people towards the entrance to the Court of the Women, where the great trumpet shaped receptacles stood to receive the people's tithes. The sound of clinking coins had been a constant background noise as he spoke.

They parted for him. Lila saw that he was weeping. He looked broken-hearted. She felt her own heart twist, remembering the last time she'd been here with him. In a loud voice he cried, 'O Jerusalem, Jerusalem, you who kill the prophets and stone those sent to you, how often I have longed to gather your children together, as a hen gathers her chicks under her wings, but you were not willing. Look, your house is left to you desolate. For I tell you, you shall not see me again until you say, "Blessed is He who comes in the name of the Lord!"' He ended on a ragged sob.

You gathered me, Lila thought.

He reached the huge archway and sat down heavily. A restless buzz of conversation grew among the crowd. No one understood what he was saying or why he was so upset. The disciples drew protectively close to him. Jesus leaned his head back against the wall and looked heavenward, tears rolling down into his beard. He wiped his eyes with the heels of his hands and then closed them for a time. Jair and Lila watched him helplessly.

He lowered his head, regaining his composure, then began looking around him as if searching for something. Lila wondered if he was looking for the disciples who'd been sent off earlier to get food. Her stomach growled at the thought. Breast-feeding made her so hungry. She knew Anna would tire soon of the raisins she'd been reaching up to give her while she perched happily on Jair's shoulders. Joshua was still asleep, tied in a shawl on her chest.

Jesus' facial expression changed – he'd found what he was looking for. Lila followed his gaze out through the archway, but she couldn't see what it was that had changed his expression of grief to one of tender love. She looked back at him to check she'd got the direction of his gaze right and then back to the area near one of the treasury receptacles. All she could see was a little old woman shuffling towards it. She watched her as she slowly lifted her gnarled hand and dropped two small coins into it. She looked back at Jesus and saw that he had tears in his eyes again. Did he know her?

Jesus didn't speak loudly, only loud enough for those nearest him to hear, 'I tell you the truth,' he said, 'this poor widow,' he indicated with his chin, 'has put two coins, the smallest amount worthy of being called an offering, into the treasury, but she has put more in than all the others.' The disciples turned to look at the woman whom Jesus was honouring. 'All these people gave their gifts out of their wealth, but she – out of her poverty – put in all she had to live on.'

The old woman was far enough away to be oblivious of the attention being paid to her, but she had stopped and was slowly turning, looking in Jesus direction, as if she'd heard him call her name. She stood still for a moment, just staring. Jesus' face broke into the smile Lila loved. He was an unremarkable looking man, but when he smiled like that it transformed his face – *a window that opens into heaven,* she thought. It wasn't wasted on the woman, because she responded in kind – her thin, frail features lit from some internal source. *They've known each other all their lives,* Lila mused, *but then why didn't he go and greet her?*

Lila thought of her grandmother as she watched the woman eventually turn away, making her way back through the Beautiful Gate. She realised that the pain which usually accompanied the memory was gone. Instead, she found herself thinking: *Two lepta – nothing – you couldn't even buy a piece of bread with that. But it was her entire fortune? All she had? Why hasn't Judas picked up on it and given her something? He's always going on about the poor.* She looked around, but couldn't see him anywhere.

'Jair?'

'Yes, my love.' He smiled.

'Can you give me some money?' she asked, holding out her hand.

'Are you going to get some food?' He looked pleased.

'No. I was going to give it to that old woman.' She could still see her walking away.

She made her way after her. The widow had stopped and had seated herself, resting against a wall, exhausted. Lila greeted her, 'Shalom.'

The old woman looked up with opaque eyes. Lila realised she was nearly completely blind. 'Shalom, sister,' she said, smiling. Something stopped Lila from immediately pressing the money she intended to give her into her hand. 'It is good – ' the widow gasped, 'to be in the – ' another gasp, 'house of the Lord ... is it not?'

'Yes, it is.' Lila sat down beside her, emotion catching in her throat as she remembered the last time she'd sat with grandmamma. She felt concerned at the laboured breathing of this woman. She felt no urge to speak, just to be with her. Lila had a growing sense of awe that a holy moment was upon them. She waited for the woman to speak.

'I have sought the Lord – here – all my life,' she confided haltingly. 'He has never forsaken me, though I have been on my own these many long years. He truly watches over the widow.' She was struggling to speak, her breath shallow and weak. 'Do you know the Lord?' The woman turned her blind eyes on Lila.

'I think I do.' Lila smiled looking back to where Jesus sat.

'There is nothing better – you can do – with your life – than to know him – through every season.' She touched Lila's hand, parchment on silk and gripped it for emphasis. 'Trust in the Lord – with all your heart – and lean not – on your own – understanding.' Lila squeezed her hand back, nodding at the familiar verse. It was one of Jair's favourites.

'Today – I have sensed – his presence – as never before. Perhaps at last – it is my time ... '. Her frail voice grew whispery. The woman leant her head on Lila's shoulder. Lila let herself cry silently. She knew what was happening now. After a little while she looked down, shifting slightly causing the weight of the woman's head to tip forward. She managed to catch her and pushed her back up against the wall. But the woman did not respond. Lila leaned closer, only to discover that she was no longer breathing. She shook her gently, but her body only slumped to one side. She stared at her. It seemed she had shrunk in size.

Lila stayed sitting with her, too moved as yet to seek assistance.

This must be the place where all women of God would wish to depart this life ... what more fitting place than here? Go – fly to Him. She gently placed her head against her shoulder, stroking her face tenderly. She felt all her childhood pain over her grandmother's death gather up and lift from her.

❋ ❋ ❋

Mary had not spent any more time with the group of Zealots. Since she had danced with Jesus at the crippled neighbour's healing, she had felt a change in herself. She knew now that her past had left her with drives and desires that would lead her nowhere fast, if left unchecked. It made her wonder about Judas and his friends. Was all their talk of freedom just a cover for wanting to do whatever they liked?

She'd seen a change in Judas. There was a brooding darkness in his eyes, which frightened her. She felt it creep over her whenever she was near him. She didn't understand it, but knew she didn't want to keep company with him any more. While everyone had been gathering in the city, Mary had spent more time at Jair and Lila's than at home with her brother and sister. Jesus had often been sad; his mood had affected the whole community of followers. Everyone seemed insecure, especially Peter.

Jair had spoken with Lazarus and had been keeping an eye on Mary. It had become very clear to both him and to Lazarus that they had to do something soon about finding her a suitable husband. She was a social creature, still very young. She was very different from her sister. Martha had never expressed an interest or desire to marry. She had even asked him not to arrange suitors for her because she wanted to stay focused on the business.

But Mary's past showed itself constantly in little sensual indiscretions. The difficulty was whether any God-fearing man would want an ex-prostitute as a wife. Jair had spoken to Jesus about the matter. 'We need a Hosea or a Boaz sort of man, someone who loves God and who will love her regardless.'

Jesus was thoughtful. 'Have you met Stephen?'

'No. Who is he?' Jair asked.

'He joined us when his aunt was healed – you know, the crippled woman in the synagogue near you?'

'Oh yes, that was something wasn't it?' Jair smiled at the memory.

'He has been with me ever since, eager to learn. I mention him to you because I noticed his expression in the synagogue when Mary danced with me.'

'Oh?' Jair raised an eyebrow.

'Yes,' Jesus smiled. 'Maybe a meeting with your neighbour would be the place to start?'

Jair smiled gratefully, knowing that there was more Jesus understood about this man Stephen than he would say. He felt a quiet confidence that Jesus' choice would be the best possible one for Mary – that is, if she would have him. He chuckled to himself.

As he had expected, Mary reacted badly at first. 'How dare you go behind my back? How many people know about this? Have you been talking with everyone about it?' her cheeks flamed red.

'No, no, no, Mary. We asked a few friends – Mary Magdalene, Joanna, Susanna. They love you too and want the best for you. But it was Jesus who suggested this.'

'Oh ... ' She looked nonplussed. 'Have you met him?'

'Yes, last night. He is a good man.' Jair smiled. Lila nodded a little too eagerly and Jair's smile turned to a frown, 'You noticed?' sarcasm laced his voice.

'Oh Jair – he's handsome. I'd have to be blind not to see it.' Lila playfully pushed him.

'That could be arranged.' he laughed and pushed her back into the couch.

She smiled, leaning on the cushions, her thoughts returning to the widow who'd given her all to God, whose physical eyes had failed her but whose spiritual eyes were keen and bright. She had gone to her burial, arranged by the temple priests that same evening. No one else had been present. Lila thought about something Jesus had said – something about the last being first and the first being last.

She pulled her wandering thoughts back into the present conversation as Mary asked her a question, looking for reassurance, 'So, not an old goat then?'

'Oh no – if you were blind, you'd still sense that he was a beautiful man. He has a heart after God,' Lila's eyes shone, 'a bit like you, my love.' She touched Jair's foot with her own. He looked at her appreciatively.

Jair quickly collected himself, turning to Mary, asking her if she would be willing to meet Stephen the following day. Mary agreed, 'But if I don't like him, I'm not going to marry him.' Jair sighed ruefully, marvelling that it hadn't occurred to her that maybe it would be him saying no to her. But then she had probably never had a man turn her down before.

※ ※ ※

Judas met with the chief priests, the elders and the officers of the temple guard to discuss with them how he might betray Jesus. Aaron was particularly delighted. His proposal, made as adviser to Caiaphas the high priest, was turning out to be a great success. The council were delighted too, agreeing to pay Judas thirty pieces of silver. He consented, and was dispatched to watch for an opportunity to hand Jesus over to them when no crowd was present.

'Do you think he'll come through for us, brother?' Caiaphas asked in a low voice, raising one heavy eyebrow.

'Without doubt, rabbi,' Aaron replied. 'He is disillusioned; what better cause for betrayal? It won't be long now.'

A fleeting thought swooped down on him – *you've been disillusioned all your life.* He swept it aside like driftwood on a current, running his hand down his beard. He bid his colleagues goodnight and bowed deferentially to Caiaphas. As he came out into the cool night air, he stood for a moment and breathed in with deep satisfaction. *Soon, very soon,* he smiled to himself, stoking the fire of hate that burned in him against the Nazarene. No one would ever humiliate him in public again like the so-called teacher had done that day in the temple with Lila.

As he made his way home, his thoughts focused like a magnet on Lila and the child; Lila flustered and surprised in the market place, the intoxicating smell of her skin – a deliciousness that had once been his. Their chance encounter had awakened cravings in him for her that he thought had died the day he had used her for higher purposes. He pondered the unreadable emotions in her eyes again for the hundredth time as she had tried to conceal the little girl with those familiar eyes, who peered from behind her skirts.

Jaw muscles clenched greedily as he came to the entrance of his home. He resolved that she would be his again, and the child with her. His wife could add the child to their six; she had eyes and heart only for children; one more would make no difference. He had long tired of her worn body and his newly-awakened craving for Lila made him feel alive and vital. Yes, there were prostitutes for the bored married man, but you could not buy what Lila had given him. *She had been so eager ...*

※ ※ ※

Mary was nervous. She'd always known the rules with men. But this man – this situation – was an anathema to her. What would he want in a wife? What did she want in a husband? It was only as she walked across the alleyway between their homes that she realised – what she wanted was something like what Lila had.

She didn't have long – it wasn't very far to their neighbours. She felt like she had done the first time she went to Hasmonean Palace; but she couldn't be Rahab here. She tugged at her headscarf, pulling it further down over her forehead for protection. She was walking behind Jair. He would keep her safe. She tucked herself in behind him.

'What are you doing?' Jair asked, turning his head.

'I – I – don't know how to be ... ' she stammered. Jair smiled affectionately.

He turned and took her by the shoulders, 'Remember our talk in the courtyard that night?' She nodded. 'This is a good man ... and if you find yourself warming to him, and him to you, then a miracle will have occurred! Let's just see what happens, shall we. Now stop hiding behind me.' She nodded more slowly. He squeezed her upper arms firmly, then turned and knocked on the door.

When they entered, the woman who'd been a cripple sat straight-backed on her couch next to her husband. To their right sat a young man. Mary looked at him through her translucent headscarf. He was looking at her quite candidly. She felt exposed and pushed herself in behind Jair again. Jair moved to sit down and reached behind him to pull her to his side so she could sit as well. She felt awkward.

Who would have thought that I used to brazenly dance for men? – she almost laughed.

Stephen's parents sat on his right, next to Jair. Mary closed the circle. Formal pleasantries were exchanged. Mary stole glances at Stephen and decided that she liked the way he looked at her. There was genuine appreciation in his eyes, behind a courtesy and kindness she'd not often encountered, other than in Jesus, Lazarus and Jair. But there was something else that was familiar about the way he looked at her … what was it? Finally she hit on it … *he wants me!* She felt a thrill run through her. Then she suddenly was faced with the question of whether she wanted him? She observed him talking with Jair and with his family. He had an attractive face, eyes wide set, short nose, thick, dark beard framing a full mouth, lean and muscled; he looked like he was used to hard work.

At that moment, Jair asked what trade he was in. Stephen said he worked with his father and brothers in the building trade. It was a good business and he could offer Mary security and stability. Suddenly into her mind came the image of the herbs she had planted by her front door. Underneath lay the four unnamed, miniature babies. Slowly she felt herself being sucked into the vortex of her recurring nightmare, down, down, down.

Jair touched her arm. 'Mary? Would you like to ask anything?' he was looking at her quizzically. She realised by the silence and the fixed expressions that he had probably asked her this more than once.

'No' she whispered, shaking her head.

When they left, Jair led her carefully across the alleyway to their home. 'Are you all right?' he asked, his brow furrowed with concern.

'I, I … ' she mumbled. He caught her by the elbow.

'Did you not like him?' Jair asked, concerned.

'I liked him well enough.' Her eyes stayed fixed on the ground where shadows from the tree in their yard danced with the night breeze.

'So, what's wrong?'

She fought against shame, dragging her eyes up to his. 'How can I marry him? I am soiled goods and I cannot give him children – if he knew, he would not want me,' despair tore at her young face.

Jair smiled a little, 'He does know – and he wants you still.'

Mary raised her head more swiftly this time in disbelief, 'He knows? How does he know?'

'Do you think we would try and deceive someone from among our fellowship on a matter as significant as this? Remember the day you danced with Jesus in the synagogue? He saw you then and wanted you from the moment he set eyes on you. He spoke with Jesus about you.'

Her cheeks flushed, 'So... ' she paused as she put the pieces together, 'He wants me just as I am?'

'Just as you are,' Jair smiled.

※ ※ ※

Judas was quicker than any of them expected. Like a door left carelessly ajar through which a gust of wind hurls itself against the warmth of candlelight, he snuffed out the flame of hope in every heart of every follower of Jesus of Nazareth.

On the first day of the Passover feast, Jesus celebrated with his disciples and then went out to a secluded place called Gethsemane. Judas came to Aaron's house to inform him. Messengers were dispatched instantly to the temple guard, to Caiaphas and to the various elders. Aaron dressed quickly and went with Judas to the high priest's house.

When everyone was assembled, Caiaphas addressed them: 'Be ready for anything. These men are dangerous. They have stirred up the people and deceived many, as Judas has confirmed for us. He is an eyewitness so guard him well. He will lead you to the man we want.'

'Yes, the one I kiss is the man; arrest him,' Judas said looking intently round the armed guard.

Aaron clapped him on the back, 'Well done, Judas.'

'You're coming with me, aren't you?' Judas asked.

'I would dearly love to, brother, but I have some other business to attend to.' Aaron embraced Judas firmly, giving him a reassuring look as he drew back. Judas squared his shoulders as he turned to go. 'Come and see me when it is done,' Aaron called after him.

Little did Aaron know, that this was the last time he would see his protégé.

11. RISE

The resurrection woman

Trevor took the Martin Christening. Grace was very aware of the time it was being held. Peter was paintballing with some friends all day, so she had no reason to go home for lunch. She waited in the parish office after the morning services and watched through the window as the guests arrived promptly at 12.30pm. The service only took twenty minutes and soon they were streaming out again into the Sunday afternoon sunlight for photographs. As she looked at James Martin, she realised her body was no longer reacting out of fear at the sight of him. She studied him with his wife and son as they smiled at the cameras and fussed over the long, lacy Christening dress in which they had put the baby. He seemed to be a genuine family man. She whispered the words she had heard Jesus say in her vision, 'Forgive him, Father ... I forgive him.'

She waited until she was sure that everyone had left before venturing over to church. She wanted to spend a few minutes in prayer, to get some final closure. Seeing the Martin baby disturbed her. She had been thinking about the one she had aborted – another one of his children. She wondered how many others there had been.

As she closed the door behind her, she leaned against it and breathed deeply. She walked slowly down to the communion rail and knelt down. She focused herself and began to pray. She didn't hear the door opening behind her, nor the expensive leather soled shoes on the worn aisle carpet. It was only when he knelt down next to her that she opened her eyes with a start and turned to see James Martin.

'Why didn't you take our baby's Christening?' he asked, not looking at her, but straight ahead at the cross on the communion table.

She stared at him, unsure how to answer. Eventually she said, 'I had a pretty full schedule – I thought it was best to pass it on to Trevor.' She looked away from him, seeing that her bluff had not worked.

'You don't like me, do you?' he asked, still not looking at her. 'I thought you priests were supposed to show the love of God to all people?'

'Whether I like you or not is neither here nor there,' she replied. 'However, as a priest, I believe that God does love you,' she said matter-of-factly and then briskly changed the subject. 'I thought you had all gone ... why have you come back? Don't they need you at the party?' She felt a growing alarm at being alone with him in the isolation of the church.

He cleared his throat and looked down at his hands resting on the rail. 'My wife knows I'm here. It's an answer to her prayers,' he laughed dryly. 'I don't deserve her.' He shook his head. 'Being loved by her and becoming a father has changed me – today's service especially,' he paused. 'I wanted to come back here on my own and give thanks for ... ' he stumbled and Grace looked at him again. The hard, calculating expression was gone. He looked troubled. 'I wanted to make peace ... and give thanks,' he repeated. 'I was prepared to do it on my own, but since you're here, will you help me? What is it people do? Make their confession?'

Grace's mouth opened slightly in amazement. 'We're not a Catholic church, you know,' she said.

'I know. But I want to make peace with – whoever – with the universe, with God I suppose. Isn't that what people do when they want to do that?' he turned and pierced her with a searching look.

Grace leaned away from him slightly, her internal struggle reaching a peak. *God, I can't believe this is happening. Do you really expect me to do this?* Silence was her stern reply.

James didn't seem to notice. He continued, 'Today as your colleague – is it Trevor?' she nodded, 'asked us if we rejected the devil and all rebellion against God – I can't explain it – but I felt something, something I've never felt before. I've never given religion a second thought all my life. Thought religious people, no offence,' he looked at her, but she didn't respond, 'were weak and needy. But today I – I actually felt ... afraid.' He sounded surprised.

He rubbed one hand over his face and cleared his throat again. 'When my son was born and I held him in my arms for the first time, I swore to myself I would change. But I'm realising I won't be able to do it in my own strength. I need …' he was searching for words, '… help.'

Grace was speechless. Conflicting thoughts swirled round each other. She was astonished to be in the situation. Nothing had prepared her for it. There had never been a course in theological college on how to do this. She realised that forgiveness wasn't a done deal just because she'd been able to pray the words. She wrestled with the fierce desire for justice. It wasn't much of a contest. She didn't really want to subdue it. She was in a position of power now, so different to all those years ago when he had been the powerful one and she had been helpless.

'I can't do this. Sorry.' She stood up abruptly. 'I'm going to call Trevor. You can do this with him.' Her voice was controlled and clipped.

She moved away from him as she got her phone out of her pocket, her anxiety levels continuing to rise along with an unnerving fury.

He rose to his feet with her, 'Why can't you do this with me? You're a priest, aren't you?'

'Of course I am, but this situation is not appropriate,' she said with some force, 'Hello, Trevor?' She spoke to her colleague on the phone, moving away from him.

She heard James mutter something about women priests. She ignored him.

When Trevor heard she was alone in the church, he said he would keep talking to her on the phone as he made his way to her. Grace felt momentary relief. She kept a safe distance from James, moving around the church as she talked to Trevor. He arrived in minutes (his house was only a few doors down from hers) and, after some pleasantries, Grace excused herself and left hurriedly.

She was drained of all energy. When she got home, she sank down onto the hall carpet, leaning up against the thickness of her front door . . she rested her head back and closed her eyes.

After some time, she lifted her head and opened her eyes. She felt dazed. Had it really happened? Was he genuine?

'I know I'm to bless those who curse me, but God I want him to suffer,' she prayed.

Into the silence that followed dropped a word. It was her name: 'Grace.'
Grace is the free gift of God.

She thought about that for a while.

I'm a minister of grace ... called Grace.

A wan smile broke onto her lips at the divine humour she had never seen before.

Am I wrong to deny that we have met ... about what happened ... about the abortion? Should I tell him? Should I challenge him to hand himself into the police for what he did? Do I have a duty of care to other women in this town, in this church, which I am not fulfilling by my silence?

She didn't know the answers. She was too exhausted to think any more. She picked herself up off the floor and decided to make herself some toast.

She'd take it up (theoretically) with the diocesan vulnerable adults officer.

But one thing she did know. She must find a way to forgive him, to make peace with herself, with God and with the unborn child she had aborted.

❋ ❋ ❋

'Can I come with you?' Grace asked Peter.

He looked up quickly from the weekend newspaper he was reading with his traditional mug of tea and marmalade on toast. 'To Helen's grave?' his dark eyebrows rose slightly as he said her name.

'Yes,' Grace replied simply.

'Why? I mean why now? You've never wanted to go before.' He laid the paper down on the yellow and white check tablecloth.

'I don't know …'. Grace twisted the gold chain she was wearing round her neck between finger and thumb. 'I'm not sure really.'

'That's not like you,' he said, studying her face for a moment.

'Can I?' she looked up at him tentatively.

'Sure – it'll be nice to have company on the long drive,' he smiled. She loved him for not pursuing it, for accepting her request at face value. She felt calmer.

'What time were you going to go?'

'About ten. Should be able to get there by about eleven-thirty, grab some lunch in the pub and be back in time for the rugby.' He folded the paper up neatly, stacking all the weekend supplements perfectly on top of it.

'I better get dressed then. Who's playing today?' She got up from the round table and wrapped her dressing gown more firmly round herself.

'England v the All Blacks,' he stood up and reached for her. 'You don't have to get dressed just yet, do you? It's only nine.' His hands dropped down to her hips and pulled her to him.

'What did you have in mind?' She looked knowingly through several ringlets and pulled at one of his pyjama top buttons.

They were on the road by 10.30am, having lost track of time. They got through the Dartford tunnel and round the M25 to north London, where Peter had lived his previous life, by 12.15pm. They made it through the Saturday traffic to the graveyard. Grace began to feel nervous again. What was more disconcerting was she couldn't put her finger on the reason why.

Peter led her through the graves, pointing out the ones he particularly liked. 'This is our row,' he said, over his shoulder. 'That one was the first new one after Helen's,' he pointed and slowed his pace. 'I hated it at first – it felt like an insult.'

'What do you mean?' Grace stopped walking altogether and pulled him to turn and face her.

He smiled and rubbed his face. 'It was like they were taking the attention away from Helen. Like their tragedy was worse than hers. But I love it now. Her family really care for it. I got to know them well. We'd meet up here and end up chatting for hours.'

'So this must be Helen's then?' Grace asked, stepping over to the next grave.

'Mmm.' Peter didn't speak. Grace didn't know what else to say. She stood reading the inscription on the stone, nervousness fluttering in her stomach like a butterfly.

Peter crouched down and brushed some grass clippings off the base of the stone. He picked up the pot that sat ensconced to one side of the base. 'I'll just go and fill this with water.' He nodded in the direction of where Grace assumed the tap must be. She nodded and hugged herself as if she were cold, but it was a warm autumn day.

She stared at Helen's grave. It was a waist high, cream slab of stone with a domed top. The engraved inscription was simple: her name and her dates of birth and death. Then beneath that: 'Dearly loved and deeply missed;

daughter, sister, wife.' It was so like Peter to keep it discreet, succinct and to the point. No embellishments.

Why am I here? She asked herself again.

Peter came back with the flowers he'd brought already arranged in the pot – cornflowers and white lilies. He placed it down into its inset. He stood up and viewed his work with satisfaction. Grace felt she was intruding. She began to edge away slightly, but Peter reached out for her and grabbed her hand. 'Don't go, babe,' he said, looking into her eyes. 'It's so good to have you here with me.'

Grace let him pull her close to him. She laced her fingers between his.

'It's been damn lonely coming here all these years on my own. At first, I'd come hoping to feel some kind of comfort, but it only heightened my sense of abandonment. I was so miserable. I never dreamed of you then,' he paused and then looked at her affectionately. 'She would have liked you.'

Grace looked back at him hesitantly. 'What do you believe happened to her after her death?'

'I thought we promised never to talk about religion.' His smile faded.

'Oh, Peter, this isn't about religion – it's about you, about her, about me. I want to know what you really think.'

'Sorry – I know, you're right. I shouldn't be so defensive.' He ran his fingers through his thick, greying hair.

Grace waited.

Peter looked at the headstone and let out a heavy breath, 'I believe that when you die, that's it – finished.' He turned and looked at her. Grace held his gaze, saying nothing. 'I can't believe in a good God, and heaven, and all that stuff you believe in. It makes no sense. How could a good God let a beautiful person like Helen suffer for years and then end her days not even able to relate to her loved ones because she was so spaced out on morphine?'

Grace squeezed his hand and leaned her head on his shoulder affectionately. She felt relief that he was expressing what she'd always suspected he believed. She was glad he was allowing her to hear his bitterness.

'It would be nice to think there was nothing more. I wouldn't need to think about what I'm going to say one day to my … my … to the baby I aborted,' she whispered.

Peter moved so she had to raise her head up again. He searched her eyes intently, 'Do you think about that? Oh darling, I had no idea.' He put his arm around her.

Emotion suddenly caught her off guard. 'I'm sorry, Peter, I have no right – this has nothing to do with your grief and loss.' Grace wiped a tear away irritably.

'Maybe that's why you wanted to come here,' Peter mused. 'It's okay, I don't mind. Maybe it's a good thing we're both talking about stuff we normally never say.'

'Yeah, maybe.' She gave a non-committal shrug.

They were both quiet on the way back.

When they got home Peter went into the living room to watch the second half of the rugby. Grace went to her desk and opened her journal. She started sketching something.

❊   ❊   ❊

'Mark and I would like to renew our wedding vows. Can we organise a service soon? It would be good to do it before Christmas.' Chloe was dipping a chip into some mayonnaise as she sat opposite Grace in their alcove in the pub.

Grace was having her usual chicken caesar salad. She didn't answer right away because her mouth was full, but when she'd emptied it she exclaimed, 'That's marvellous Chloe – that's so great!' Her eyes sparkled.

'I know – will you do it for us?'

'I'll have to ask Trevor, but I'm sure it will be fine with him. He knows I've been looking out for you guys. Anyway, he's getting less precious about ministry since that amazing service when we all felt God's presence so powerfully.' Grace stuck another fork full of lettuce and chicken into her mouth.

'Yeah, it's been so refreshing coming to church the last few weeks. I love it,' Chloe laughed.

'It's good to hear you laugh like that.' Grace smiled at her friend.

'God is good,' Chloe sighed.

'All the time,' responded Grace. Chloe noticed that she was looking at her in an odd kind of way.

'What?' Chloe asked.

'I'm going to tell you something that no one knows but Peter,' she said putting her fork down in her half-eaten meal. Chloe was instantly riveted – a chip hung suspended inches from her mouth as she waited.

Grace looked like she was having second thoughts, but then with supreme effort began to speak. 'You're not the only one whose made huge mistakes and been restored. So many times I've wanted to tell you, but have thought better of it because of my role in the church and what they teach you in college – not to get too close to parishioners, etc.' Chloe raised a dark eyebrow and stuck the chip in her mouth with some satisfaction.

Grace scrunched up her napkin and chucked it down beside her plate. 'Before I was a Christian, I made some bad choices which resulted in consequences I've had to live with.' she kept her eyes on her plate.

'Is that all you're going to say? Oh, please – you know all about me – come on, girl, give me the dirt.' Chloe was surprised at how euphoric she felt being in the refreshing role of confessor.

'Oh, Chloe – it's so hard for me – I'm ordained. You've asked me to do your re-affirmation of wedding vows. How can I? Forget it – sorry, I shouldn't … '

'Oh no you don't! Don't you dare stop now, Grace.' Chloe leaned forward and grabbed her friend's hand.

Grace looked up at her with tears in her eyes. She sighed and gave in. 'You know the story I sent you ages ago?'

Chloe nodded, looking confused at the tangent the conversation was going in.

'Well, it's became a book. It's been like a therapy for me – as I've meditated on stories of women encountering Jesus in the gospels, it's made me look at my own life – at stuff I'd just put behind me once I became a Christian.'

'Go on … ' Chloe encouraged, squeezing her hand.

'Well, Lila becomes friends with a girl called Mary – she's the woman who wept over Jesus feet and poured perfumed oil on them, wiping them with her hair.'

'Yes,' Chloe patiently nodded.

There was a long pause. Then softly, 'If Lila was like you … well, Mary is like me.' Grace looked up at her again, uncertainly.

'What do you mean?' Chloe asked wanting to be sure.

Grace waited for the penny to drop.

Chloe's eyes widened. 'Oh … '

Grace nodded, looking down at her plate. 'Yes, I paid my way through university by working for an escort agency.'

Chloe stared at her friend as the enormity of the confession sank in.

Grace continued quickly, 'I stopped when I got pregnant and had an abortion. I got an infection and it left me infertile. That's why Peter and I don't have kids.'

Chloe's lips parted slightly.

'I'm only able to tell you because I've just told Peter recently. It's all come about because of my writing.' She left out her encounter with James Martin. No one but Peter would ever know that, and he didn't even know his name. 'I became a Christian, married Peter and then started the whole process of going forward for ordination. Everything was so exciting. I'd been forgiven and thought I'd left the past behind me – and in a way I had to some degree. No one ever knew and I was being given a new identity. I was too scared to look at stuff from the past that needed healing. It was too huge. I mean – I thought the past was the past. I couldn't do anything about it. But I've realised that salvation is eternal, it works outside time – Jesus has redeemed and healed my past as well as my present. It's been amazing!'

A tear escaped Chloe's left eye and trickled down her smooth cheek. It meandered round the dark mole near her nose. She squeezed Grace's hand again. 'Thank you for trusting me with this – I've wondered what secrets you've kept so well hidden. Would never have thought it was this.'

'I know – pure, holy curate, eh?' Grace mocked herself dryly.

Chloe sat back in her chair and pushed her bowl of cold chips away from her, looking at Grace with new eyes.

'I feel more healed than I ever have – it's been so liberating. It's like that line near the end of *Titanic* when Rose says "He saved me in every way that a person can be saved". What God started in me when I first believed has been working its way through to the core of me. He's really been saving me in every possible way.'

'Glad you've worked out the theology of it,' Chloe said ruefully. 'Very important,' she nodded sagely.

Grace smiled. 'There's something I want to do to mark it – a bit like your re-affirmation of marriage vows. I was wondering if you'd help me?'

❋ ❋ ❋

It was 31 October – Halloween, or All Hallows' Eve. It was a Sunday. It was the Sunday that Chloe and Mark had picked to re-affirm their marriage vows. They didn't want a separate service but had opted for doing it as part of the normal family service at 11.00am. Chloe had said something about wanting to renew their vows before the whole community.

Chloe wore a dress in her favourite Mediterranean green and her hair down round her shoulders. Mark wore jeans and a jacket with his collar open at the neck. They walked to the front of the church during the third worship song, followed by their children. Charlie brought up the rear and proudly told his mum later that he had managed not to pick his nose the whole time.

Grace led them through their re-affirmation vows.

Val and Mo sat in the front pew, grinning broadly.

Mark couldn't take his eyes off Chloe. Love glowed between them, not a sentimental, romantic love, but a gutsy, humble one. When Grace came to the sentence: 'What God has joined together let no one tear asunder,' her voice failed her. Chloe and Mark looked at her, the emotion of the moment overwhelming them. They each reached for her hands and together they turned to the congregation.

Grace cleared her throat; 'Chloe and Mark would like to say something to all of you now. Mark?'

Mark looked like he wasn't going to be able to do it. He looked at the floor and then at Chloe who smiled reassuringly at him. 'Sorry, folks ... I'm not used to being up the front here.'

There was a general murmur of understanding, which he seemed to gain strength from.

'We want to thank all of you for your love and support over this last year. We would not be here today if it wasn't for you. What I want to say is that everyone knew what Chloe did and I'm sure had a variety of opinions on the matter. But what you don't know is that our marriage had grown cold long before ... and not by accident. It was through some deliberate choices and failures on my part.

'We both failed each other, our children and all of you, and we can never tell you how sorry we are for the pain we have caused. We've forgiven each other and I know you've forgiven us, but we both want to say thank you to you in this place, the place where we first made our vows, where many of you promised to hold us and help us keep them.'

As one, the congregation cheered. Hankies came out and Mark's prayer partners came and hugged him and then stood behind him, hands resting on his shoulders. The band started to play. People gathered round them, hugged them and kissed them. Grace marvelled that there was even some dancing – granted, just a mild hopping from one foot to the other, but still, it wasn't the English country village church thing to do. She glanced at Trevor, who was standing in his prayer stall, to see what he was making of it all. He had his hands raised slightly and his eyes closed in an even more un-English country village church sort of way. She laughed.

※　※　※

It was 1 November. It was Monday morning – All Saints' Day.

Grace sat at her round kitchen table, a small framed piece of embroidery lay in front of her. Peter sat next to her, admiring it: 'It's beautiful, Grace. When did you get the idea for it?'

'When I went to Helen's grave with you; I came home and drew it out in my journal while you were watching rugby. Chloe showed me how to do it. I've never done embroidery before – you know how she loves doing crafts with her kids. She was always doing stuff with the young people when she was the youth worker.'

Peter leaned in and kissed her cheek. 'Shall we go?'

'Yes – the service starts at 7.00pm. We've got twenty minutes to sit quietly before it begins.'

She picked up the embroidery and they went to get their coats.

They sat near the back of the church, partly because Grace was aware of Peter's self-consciousness in unfamiliar territory, but also for her own sake. She didn't want to be a leader tonight. She just wanted to be Grace. The church was in darkness except for the candles lit at the front. Slowly, other people made their way into pews. By 7.00pm the church was full.

Peter leaned over and whispered, 'Who'd have thought there were so many grieving people?'

In every pew, small candles had been placed alongside the Bibles. Trevor began the service by inviting people to come and light their candles from those that were already burning at the front and place them on the communion table beneath the cross. As they did, he asked them to give thanks for the lives of those they remembered and to leave any burden of grief and sorrow with God. He spoke of Jesus being the man of sorrows and familiar with grief, able to carry our burdens and give us His peace.

Grace was nearer the aisle than Peter. As she moved to walk down and light her candle, she became aware that Peter had followed her. She reached behind her for his hand and squeezed it. In her other hand was the candle and her piece of embroidery.

As she waited her turn in the aisle, she found herself becoming nervous. The enormity of what she had done all those years ago rattled her fragile faith. 'Oh God, meet me, help me,' she prayed.

She became totally focused on the candle as she lit it, willing it to catch quickly and not blow out as she moved. She thought of the life that she had snuffed out within her, and the subsequent consequence of infection and infertility. Guilt weighed heavy within her. She thought of James Martin, who would never know. She watched the flame grow strong and steady as she gently placed it alongside the many other candles.

I never acknowledged you, never owned you, never welcomed you. I've cursed myself with such a foolish choice. Tears were rolling down her cheeks. Peter stood beside her and placed his candle next to hers. He put his arm around her waist. She drew strength from him. *I commit you to God. I trust that you are with Him, that He will redeem the evil I have done and that one day we will meet. I'm so sorry.* She shook as she lost control of her emotions.

People came and went around them. Eventually she pulled herself together and placed the framed embroidery in front of her candle. She closed her eyes and gave thanks for the life of the unborn child she had once carried in her womb – what was it – for only fourteen weeks? She pressed her hand into her pelvis and blessed her womb, cleansing it from death in the name of Jesus. She felt warmth glow in her and knew she had done a powerful thing.

Into her mind came a clear image of Jesus holding a tiny baby in the palm of his hand. He breathed on it and it began to grow. Soon he was holding a fully-formed child in his arms. As Grace watched in wonder she realised it was a little girl. Rebecca – she thought instantly. The image faded.

She opened her eyes and looked down at her embroidery. The single white rosebud on its bed of green leaves now needed a name. She reached out, picked it up and took it back with her to her seat. Peter whispered, 'I thought you were going to leave it there?'

As she sat down in their pew she replied, 'I was, but I know what my baby's name is now – it's Rebecca.' She was overwhelmed with emotion again and buried her face in Peter's chest. He soothed her, stroking her hair gently. When she recovered, the service had come to an end and people were leaving quietly. They sat in companionable silence, watching the candlelight flicker beneath the cross. 'I want to put her name beneath the rose.' She looked up at Peter.

He nodded and gave her a sad little smile. 'Then it's finished.'

※　※　※

That night, Grace couldn't sleep. She climbed quietly out of bed and went to her office. She took the embroidery out of its frame and tenderly stroked the rose with her finger. Then she got out the embroidery things Chloe had given her, drew in 'Rebecca' and began sewing in chain stitch beneath the rosebud. She reframed it and then decided to hang it in place of a photo of her and Peter at her ordination above her desk. It looked right beside the icon of Jesus that Nana had given her. She sat staring at it for a long time. Peter came into her office, his hair tousled and one pyjama leg caught up above his knee. 'There you are,' he said sleepily. 'What time is it?'

'I don't know,' she replied. She opened her laptop and looked at the clock in the top right hand corner of the screen. 'Goodness, it's three – I'm sorry, I didn't mean to wake you.'

'You didn't. I just woke up and wondered where you were.'

She gazed up at him, but he was looking at the wall where she'd hung the embroidery. He seemed pleased that she had put it there.

'It's like having a headstone, isn't it?' he said, standing behind her and running his fingers through her curls.

233

'Yes,' she replied simply.

'Helen believed,' he said quietly. Grace turned around looking up at him in amazement.

He smiled sheepishly. 'I know ... I've never said. I've spent all these years being angry at the God she trusted in – who I thought had failed her.'

Grace pulled him close to her, wrapping her arms around him, 'What's changed that you'd tell me this now?' she asked.

'I'm not sure,' he frowned slightly. 'Today was good. That service ... it moved me. I felt differently, I can't explain it.'

She smiled, pushed her chair back and stood up to face him, 'So where does that leave you?' she asked, running a finger down the side of his stubbled face.

'I can't be an atheist any more ... I guess I'm an agnostic.' He looked slightly surprised at himself as he said it.

Grace kissed him.

'Come to bed,' he whispered, pulling the lapels of her pyjama top with both hands.

When their loving was over and Peter was asleep again, Grace crept out of their room and down to her office. She opened her laptop, knowing at last how she was going to end her story. She opened her Bible to John 20 and began reading and taking notes. The morning chorus sounded louder to her than she could remember hearing it before. She picked out the voice of a lark as the sky lightened outside her window. Then, with a deep breath she started to write:

Peter denied him three times.

The cock crowed three times.

All the disciples scattered.

Only the women and John followed Jesus' torturous journey to Golgotha and watched them nail his lacerated body to a cross.

They wept and waited uncomprehendingly for what seemed an eternity.

John held Jesus' mother in his arms. The enormity of the responsibility that had been bestowed on him focused his mind.

It kept him from falling into the gaping void that was opening up inside his chest.

When the sky grew unnaturally dark, Jesus cried out in a loud voice, 'It is finished!'

Mercifully, he breathed his last.

※　※　※

The temple curtain that separated the people of God from the presence of God was torn in two from top to bottom. The chief priest and the Sanhedrin chose not to believe the account of the priest who was on duty at the time. They blamed him for the damage done to the rich, thick curtain, disqualifying him from ever holding his sacred duty again and forbidding him from telling his story on pain of death. But he later found the frightened followers of Jesus and joined their number, such was his conviction.

※　※　※

Mary lay with Anna between her and Lila. The night pressed, thick and smothering, around them. Mary didn't think she'd slept, but she couldn't be sure. Minutes, hours, days and nights had blurred into one horrific nightmare. Her mind kept recoiling from the memory of her beloved teacher, almost unrecognisable, bloodied and bruised, dragging his heavy cross through the streets of Jerusalem.

Anna and Joshua had kept them tethered to routine; otherwise they may have come totally adrift.

'Are you awake?' she whispered.

'I haven't been asleep,' came the dull response. 'You were talking in your sleep.'

'Was I? What did I say?'

'I don't know – I couldn't understand you.'

Mary rolled onto her back. 'Do you think it's nearly dawn?' She rubbed her eyes, hoping that it would enable her to see some light coming from somewhere.

'I don't know.' Lila ran her fingers over Joshua's familiar features. He lay on the other side of her. He didn't stir. 'Joshua will let us know.' She pressed one breast and then the other to see which one was more swollen with milk. She couldn't remember which side she'd fed him from last.

'I wonder how the men are?' Mary thought aloud.

'I hope they found Peter.' Lila was thinking of Judas, fearing that in his despair Peter may have done the same thing.

An involuntary shudder ran through Mary. It disturbed Anna, who whimpered plaintively. She thought of the brooding darkness she'd sensed in Judas. For the umpteenth time she wished she had said something to him instead of avoiding him. She wished she'd had the confidence to challenge him, to make him talk to Jesus or if not him, then maybe to Peter or Jair – to anyone, rather than do what he'd done. It was too late now for repentance, but surely God would have forgiven his betrayal if he had turned? Her misery increased to an unbearable level.

'I've got to get up. I can't lie here any more.' Mary stealthily moved Anna's little hand from her chest.

'Where are you going?' Alarm sounded in Lila's voice.

'I don't know. I've got to do something or I'll go crazy.'

'Mary Magdalene and some others are meeting at John's house this morning and Joanna and Susanna are meeting them at the tomb. They are going to anoint his body. I suppose you could meet Joanna and Susanna at Hasmonean Palace or Mary at Gennath gate?'

'I know. When they spoke of it, I thought I wouldn't be able to bear it, but now I want to go with them. I want to anoint him one more time. Maybe it will help me accept that he really is … ' – she couldn't finish her sentence.

They froze as they heard the front door open and close downstairs; then footsteps. The women were on their feet as the bedroom door opened silently.

'Jair?' Lila asked the darkness.

'Yes.'

'Oh, Jair.' Lila stepped towards him, found him and held him to her, comforting herself with the smell of his skin. She was trembling.

'Is Peter all right?' Mary asked pensively.

'He's alive – if that's what you mean – but he's a broken man. We brought him to John's house where Jesus' mother and some of the other disciples are. The women are meeting there this morning.' His voice sounded bleak. 'The others are in Bethany.'

'I'm going to meet Joanna. I want to ... ' Mary's whisper crumbled as she began to cry with the relief of his presence.

'If you go now, you should be in time. It's nearly dawn,' Jair realised he was slurring his words slightly. Until Lila had held him he hadn't realised how exhausted he was. He hadn't slept for two nights.

Mary groped for their hands, found them, squeezed them and left their room. She went next door, lit a lamp and took a bottle of her perfumed oil off the shelf. She wrapped it in a cloth and pulled an extra shawl around herself.

※   ※   ※

Mary usually avoided going anywhere near Hasmonean Palace, and even now the cover of dark couldn't stop her skin from crawling as she waited by the familiar servants' entrance. Joanna and Susanna appeared moments after she arrived. As they turned from locking the door they both jumped and let out frightened cries on seeing Mary's shrouded figure.

'It's me, Mary – I had to come, sorry ... ' she reached out and touched Joanna's arm.

The women immediately embraced her. 'Come ... ' whispered Joanna and they made their way towards Ephraim gate as dawn light began stroking the eastern sky.

By the time they reached the burial garden, the edge of the sun was creeping over the horizon. They saw the other women ahead of them and ran to them. 'Where's Mary Magdalene?' Joanna asked breathlessly.

'Look,' Susannah said pointing, lost for words.

Mary looked in the direction she was pointing and saw the open, dark mouth of a tomb where she assumed Jesus' body must have been laid. Why was it open? A gasp escaped Joanna's lips. Mary had told her that soldiers had rolled a huge stone over the entrance only two days ago, and now it stood clear to one side. Where were the soldiers that had been stationed guard?

'Where's Mary?' Joanna asked again.

'She's gone to tell Peter and John that his body has been taken.'

'Did she look inside?' Mary asked.

No one replied.

Joanna stepped towards the tomb, closely followed by Mary. The others picked up courage and tentatively followed at a slight distance. Joanna hesitated at the entrance and then grasping Mary's hand, stepped down into the tomb. It took some time for their eyes to adjust to the gloom after the brightness of sunrise. They stood against the wall on the left, getting accustomed to the dim light.

It was empty, but for the grave clothes lying neat and flat as if the precious body they had contained had simply evaporated from within them. The head cloth lay folded to one side. The women looked on and then at one another in bewilderment. Mary thought it was her eyes playing tricks on her but she thought the light inside seemed to be getting brighter. Soon it got so bright, she found she was squinting. Suddenly two men in clothes that gleamed like lightning stood beside them. The women cowered in terror against the wall.

'Why do you look for the living among the dead?' They spoke in unison, their voices sounding like a gushing river. 'He is not here; he has risen! Remember how he told you, while he was still with you in Galilee: "The Son of Man must be delivered into the hands of sinful men, be crucified and on the third day be raised again."' The women pressed themselves against the cold, rough stone, transfixed as the light dimmed and the two figures slowly faded from sight.

Mary was trembling uncontrollably, her mind whirling. 'Did you see that? Did you hear them?' she blurted.

'Yes – did you?' Joanna asked stupidly.

'I thought it was just me,' Mary said, a shaky laugh escaping her mouth.

'What are we waiting for – let's go tell the others,' Joanna said in a wobbly voice. They stumbled out of the tomb, each one steadying themselves against the entrance as they exited, and made their way out into the morning light. Then they were running – joy, fear, adrenalin fuelling them. Mary was the first to reach John's house. Mary Magdalene opened the door to her, her face a mask of grief.

'He's not been taken; he's not dead. We've seen angels – they told us to come and tell you,' Mary blurted. The other women piled in through the door behind her, all talking at once.

Mary Magdalene looked at them uncomprehendingly. Mary grabbed her shoulders and shook her, 'It's true, it's true – they said he has risen!'

They were greeted with the same response from the disciples. Peter and John were tying their sandals when the women burst in with what sounded like hysterical nonsense. Mary Magdalene's account was far more plausible than this over-emotional report, but as they started walking out of the city, hope plucked at their smouldering faith and they began to run.

Young John was fitter than the middle-aged fisherman and he reached the tomb first. He leaned up against the entrance and peered into the gloomy entrance. Peter came up behind him a few moments later and pushed past him in his 'bull in a china shop' manner. He took the three shallow steps down into the tomb in one stride and stood staring at the grave clothes, his breathing laboured. Neither of them could understand it, but John began to believe what the women had said. As he entered behind Peter, he looked around hopefully anticipating his first sighting of an angel. He came out disappointed, but mystified by the grave clothes left so neatly. The two disciples walked past Mary Magdalene in a daze. She had followed them and was standing outside the tomb.

They passed the younger Mary at the entrance to the garden. 'We didn't see any angels,' John said, searching her face to see if she really had been truthful. She felt momentarily hurt that he would doubt her, but then joy washed it away.

'You'll see ... ' she smiled at him and waved as they made their way back to the city.

Mary started walking through the garden toward Mary Magdalene who still stood crying brokenheartedly outside the tomb. It made young Mary's eyes well up to see this strong woman so undone. As she watched her, she had a profound realisation that Mary Magdalene wasn't a strong woman at all – her strength had not come from within her, but from another. Without him, she had nothing. She hesitated, not wanting to disturb the older woman's grief. Mary began to pray for her friend as she stood watching her from a distance.

Mary Magdalene was bending over looking into the tomb. Mary heard her talking as if to someone inside, 'They have taken my Lord away, and I don't know where they have put him.'

Before Mary could think further she suddenly realised they were not alone in the garden. A man stood between her and Mary Magdalene. She involuntarily jumped, her heart pounding in her chest. The older woman was standing up and turning round from the tomb. Mary saw that her face wore a distraught look and was still wet with tears.

When the man spoke to Mary Magdalene, the younger girl felt a thrill go through her, 'Woman, why are you crying? Who is it that you are looking for?'

In a wretched voice Mary Magdalene replied, 'Sir, if you have carried him away, tell me where you have put him, and I will get him.'

There was a pause and then the man said, 'Mary.'

Mary could see the change come over her friend as she looked up at his face and cried out, 'Teacher!' She involuntarily reached out to him, grabbing his arms, falling down on her knees at his feet. She dropped her hands down to the ground and held his feet, pressing her face to them, kissing them again and again. Mary had fallen to her knees too, tears of awe and reverence poured down her cheeks.

'Do not hold on to me, for I have not yet returned to the Father. Go instead to my brothers and tell them, "I am returning to my father and your father, to my God and your God."'

Mary wiped her eyes and when she looked again he was gone. She rose to her feet unsteadily and made her way to Mary Magdalene who still knelt, shivering in the wet grass. She got down beside her and gently put her arm around her. Slowly the older woman looked up, her eyes shining, her face transformed. They didn't speak – there were no words for a moment like this.

❋ ❋ ❋

There had been many sightings of Jesus over the following month. Lila was frustrated that she had not been witness to any of them. For the first time in her life she found herself resenting being a mother of young children. *If only I could have gone with Mary that morning,* she thought again and again. The only thing she could console herself with was the knowledge that Mary hadn't been present for any other sightings, or for the final one either. John had told them how Jesus had led his followers out to the Mount of Olives, commissioned them and commanded them to wait in Jerusalem until he sent His Spirit upon them. John had described to them in detail how Jesus had risen into the sky and then disappeared before their eyes. Lila, Jair and Mary had listened in rapt silence.

They had been waiting in Jerusalem since, secretly meeting for fear of the Jewish leaders. Despite the wonderful stories of those who had encountered the resurrected Jesus, people were still fearful. The memory of the crucifixion was a traumatic and brutally gruesome reminder that there might still be a very real threat to the lives of those who believed in the name of Jesus. Many were still tormented by their own cowardice and powerlessness to stop the terrible events that had changed all of their lives.

They tried to carry on with life as normally as possible. Jair met with Stephen's family to arrange the wedding; Mary made two more bottles of perfumed oil, selling one so as to be able to buy fabric and embroidery thread for her wedding dress; Lila helped her to make it; they all celebrated Joshua's first steps on his first birthday; Anna played dress-up in the wedding dress as it was being put together; Mary and Lila played with her in the evenings by holding Jair's prayer shawl over Anna's head as she solemnly wrapped herself in fabric and peered up at them for approval.

It was one such evening, when Jair was at a meeting at John's house, that a knock came at the door. Mary had just got Joshua to sleep in her room and had come back down to play weddings. Lila lowered the shawl, letting it fall on Anna's head. She looked at Mary, wondering who it could be. Hesitantly she went to the door and asked who it was.

'Open up. We have a warrant.'

Lila's heart lurched in her chest. She turned to Mary whispering, 'Take her upstairs.' Mary bundled Anna up in folds of cloth and ran nimbly up the stairs with her in her arms.

'Put me down,' came Anna's irate voice. Lila could hear Mary hushing her.

Oh Father, please help Anna be quiet. Please don't let Joshua wake up. Make Jair come home.

'Open up!' this time the command was accompanied with banging on the door.

'Just a minute.' Lila tried to keep her voice level. She looked round the room, panicked and confused. What else could she do? She picked up an empty clay water pot lying on the floor. She clutched it behind her back as she turned to see the door crash into the room. Two temple guards heaved in on top of it and took their place either side of the doorway. She stopped breathing when Aaron walked authoritatively into her home.

Her throat constricted and her mouth went dry. Memories of him raping her overwhelmed her and she began to tremble, cowering against the wall. He walked over and stood a foot away from her, smiling as if to reassure a frightened child. 'Don't be so afraid,' he said. 'I apologise for the damage to your door – I didn't intend for that to happen.' He looked round disapprovingly at the guards. They stared ahead blankly, not meeting his eye.

'I'm sure you know why I am here?' He looked at her for confirmation. Lila still could not command her voice to speak. Getting no response from her didn't faze him in the least. He ran his hand down his beard slowly as he studied her face. 'You and I both know that she is mine.' He raised his eyes to the ceiling, indicating he knew full well where Anna was. 'I've come for my daughter.' He smiled again.

Something snapped in Lila. That fierce tigress instinct rose up from the pit of her stomach again. She stood up to her full height, fists clenched by her sides as she stared up into his face. 'Over my dead body,' she hissed.

'That would be such a shame – it's such a beautiful body.' He looked down at her chest as if he could see through her clothes.

Before she had time to think she had raised her hand to slap his face, but he caught her arm in a vice-like grip. 'Ah there's the passion I've been missing,' he mocked. 'You can come too if you like,' he laughed. 'I might let you share my bed again.'

Rage exploded in Lila and she began to kick, punch and bite him. The guards were on her instantly. They held her small frame between them as Aaron straightened his robes and smoothed his beard. Lila spat in his face and saw a flicker in his eyes that momentarily frightened her. She thought he would kill her there and then. But he calmly drew his sleeve over his cheek, wiping the spittle away, holding her stare with steely eyes. Then he moved to the stairs and began climbing them.

'No, no Aaron ... please, no. Don't do this. Take me, leave her – she is innocent. Please, Aaron,' she ended in a wail, knowing nothing she could say or do would change his mind. Aaron didn't hesitate. She heard a scuffle and a scream, Anna's scream. Lila fought against the guards holding her as Aaron returned down the stairs with Anna wriggling in his arms.

'Please, Aaron, please don't do this ... please,' Lila sobbed. Mary had come down the stairs behind him and lunged at his back but one of the guards pre-empted her move and sent her sprawling on the floor with one blow.

'You know where to find us,' Aaron said, smiling. 'If you want her you will have to come to me.'

'Mama ... ' Anna howled, reaching out for Lila.

'Anna ... ' Lila was suddenly focused on her daughter, talking in a soothing reassuring voice, 'don't cry, darling. We will come and get you. Don't cry, my love …'.

With a swirl of his cloak, Aaron was out of the door, the guards jogging either side of him into the night. Lila ran after Anna's pitiful cries as they faded into the night. She collapsed in the road, sobbing hysterically.

Joshua began wailing upstairs. Mary called up to him, reassuring him she would come to him, but first she went out into the street looking for Lila, holding her head as a trickle of blood ran through her fingers.

※　※　※

Jair was dumbstruck by the scene that greeted him on his return home. He was reminded of the day he'd brought Lila home from the temple courts; Lila bleeding and bruised, her clothes ripped and covered in dirt. Like then, there were no words to console the anguish. He tried his best to stay calm and comforting, but being so disempowered left him feeling exhausted and hopeless. Aaron was totally within his rights – Anna was his child. One only needed to look at her face to see it. A dark despair had crept into Jair, into the gaping void left by Jesus' absence. Secretly, he had doubted all the stories of sightings of the resurrected Christ. He had tried to hide it from Lila, but he knew she knew. He hadn't been able to get thoughts of him hanging on the cross out of his mind. It was as though he had reverted to the weak, uncertain man he had been before his encounter with Jesus in the temple. He hated himself.

'I told you this would happen and you wouldn't listen to me. Jesus said you would always have her to remind you of the grace we had received – well he was wrong!' Lila shouted at him.

Jair said nothing. He stared bleakly at the floor.

Mary was rocking Joshua backwards and forwards, trying to keep him from howling.

'What are you going to do, Jair?' Mary asked hopefully.

'What can I do?' he said picking up the broken door and setting it up in the doorway. His shoulders were slumped and his voice weak.

Mary felt righteous indignation ballooning in her chest. 'You cannot seriously be thinking of letting him take your daughter away – one of our family?' Lila's wailing grew louder as Mary spoke.

'She is his daughter,' Jair said flatly.

'No, she is not! You raised her, loved her, sang to her, clothed her. Jesus entrusted her to you!' Mary's voice rose.

Jair stared at her. 'You're right, I know. Pray for me – I have lost my faith. Oh God, help my unbelief.' He walked over to Lila who was rocking herself backwards and forwards on the couch, 'Forgive me,' he said resting his hand on her head. She slowed her rocking but couldn't stop her crying. 'Jesus was not wrong, Lila – he would not lie to me. Come, let's go to John's house. Everyone is gathered there praying through the night. Perhaps together we will know what to do.'

✻ ✻ ✻

They crept into the crowded room. The disciples were sitting together in the centre of the room and the other hundred or so were gathered around them, hands raised traditionally in prayer. At first, Lila wanted to shout at them all – to wake them up from their heavenly-mindedness to the horror of what was happening to her daughter. But as she knelt down, holding onto Jair with Mary and Joshua behind her, she focused all her attention on praying for Anna. She remembered Jesus' story of the persistent widow, who kept on knocking on the judge's door until she got what she wanted. As she petitioned God for the safe return of her daughter, a deep calm slowly descended upon her.

Mary felt it too. She reflected later that it was as if she'd entered another world where anxiety and fear could not go. Joshua who had been fretful up until that point, went very still in her arms.

Jair's head slowly lifted and his shoulders straightened as he raised his hands in prayer.

At first, the sound was soft and distant and then it grew louder and louder until it was like a roaring wind. Lila began to cry out, praying uninhibitedly. She realised she was not alone. Everyone was praying loudly, but she couldn't understand what anyone was saying. She realised she didn't understand what she herself was saying. The place began to shake. What looked like tongues of fire descended into the room, separated and came to rest on each of them. The noise was so loud and the shaking so intense, it should have been unbearable, but everyone seemed able to endure it. In fact everyone seemed to be enjoying it. To Lila's amazement she found herself singing and laughing. She turned to Mary and saw she was doing the same thing. The power and joy she felt was matched by a certainty that Anna was safe and that Jesus' words would prove true. Lila and Mary embraced in the small space they occupied, worshipping God as they had never worshipped before.

As the sun rose, a crowd gathered outside. It was the festival of Pentecost and many international Jews had returned to Jerusalem for the celebrations. The crowd grew, drawn by the sounds coming from the house. Peter had moved to an open window and saw the commotion outside. In his mind he heard the words Jesus had spoken to him the first time he'd seen him resurrected: 'Feed my sheep.' He was filled with a boldness he had never known, a boldness that steamrollered over the guilt and shame of his recent failures. He led the disciples and followers of Jesus out into the street. They came into the light dancing and laughing, singing and praying.

Mary could hear people asking each other, 'How is it that each of us hears them in our native tongue declaring the wonders of God? What does this mean?' She heard others jeering at them, accusing them of being drunk.

Peter stood on the steps that led up to the roof of the house and addressed the crowd, 'Fellow Jews, let me explain this to you; listen carefully to what I say.' Mary thought his voice had changed – there was authority and power in it. He sounded more like an educated man – a teacher, not a fisherman. 'These people are not drunk, as you suppose. It's only nine in the morning! No, this is what was spoken by the prophet Joel: "In the last days, God says, I will pour out my Spirit on all people. Your sons and daughters will prophesy, your young men will see visions, your old men will dream dreams. Even on my servants, both men and women, I will pour out my Spirit in those days, and they will prophesy … "'

It was glorious! Three thousand believed in the name of Jesus that day and were baptised. The river of God carried them along in its powerful current.

※　※　※

Jair found Lila and Mary after some searching. He had Stephen with him. In a purposeful voice he shouted above the noise of the crowd, 'Come – it's time to get our daughter back.'

Lila threw her arms around his neck. Something Peter had said at the end of his sermon came to her. She held Jair's face in her hands, kissed him and said, 'The promise is for us and for our children.'

※　※　※

Jair banged hard on the ornately carved door. Maternal urgency made it hard for Lila to stop herself from leaning past Jair and trying again when no response was forthcoming. Jair must have sensed it because he quickly banged again more forcefully. A small window opened and they saw two eyes look them up and down.

'Open up!' commanded Jair with authority, 'In the name of the risen Lord Jesus Christ.'

A change occurred in the eyes that looked out at them. The window shut abruptly. Then they heard the rattling of bolts, chains and keys. Lila could hear Stephen whispering in the tongue he had received earlier. She found she was doing the same.

The heavy door opened, slowly revealing a snowy haired old man. 'Have you come for the girl-child?' he asked.

'Yes,' they replied in unison.

'I have been instructed not to let you enter, but I too have believed in the name of Jesus. I have been waiting for the Messiah all my life.' His eyes sparkled.

'Brother!' Jair exclaimed stepping forward and embracing him. Instantly the Holy Spirit descended on them both. The old man exclaimed in amazement and began speaking in a language that sounded bizarre to Lila. She watched as he shook and wept in Jair's arms. It was Mary that urged them to move in through the door and out of the street, while she kept watch outside with Joshua.

Still shaken and praising God, the old servant led them through a series of corridors. Signs of wealth and privilege were everywhere. It was clear to them that Aaron had risen to the heights of power in the city. Stephen was busily recounting to the servant all that Peter had said in his sermon about the gift of the Holy Spirit that God had poured out on them that day. The old man was nodding his head excitedly as he walked and listened.

At last they came to a low door, behind which they could hear children's laughter. 'She is in here with my wife and the other children,' he turned to them, his hand on the door latch. 'You must be quick though; there are other servants present – I cannot vouch for their discretion.'

'We cannot thank you enough.' Jair held his shoulders.

'Yes, thank you – thank you so much,' Lila whispered.

The servant lifted the latch and pushed open the door. Lila let out an involuntary cry of joy as she saw Anna sleeping, cradled in an old woman's arms. The sound woke her with a jolt and she automatically opened her mouth wide and howled.

'Oh, my love, my sweetheart.' Lila rushed to her daughter, scooping her up into her arms.

'You must go now!' rasped the old servant. 'One of the servant girls has run to our master. You haven't much time.'

Stephen moved into the corridor followed by Lila, with Jair closely behind her. Anna clung to her mother. They ran through corridors, eventually coming to the courtyard and the outer door beyond which lay freedom. Stephen and Jair brought up the rear looking over their shoulders. Lila reached it first and began unlocking it.

'Hurry ... hurry ... ' Jair urged.

As she began to draw the last bolt a voice halted her, 'Stop, thief!'

They all turned to see Aaron standing flanked by several guards.

Determined, Lila returned her attention to the bolt and drew it back completely. She put her hand on the heavy latch and raised it. As she did a dagger thudded into the door, grazing her thumb. It shivered with the impact, firmly embedded in the glossy wood. As blood oozed from her skin everything went into a nightmarish slow motion. She was mesmerized by the swell of liquid trickling down her wrist as it caught the light in its sleek surface. It's the dream ... the dream she thought. Foreboding and despair suddenly made it hard to breathe. She tried to pray in the tongue she had joyfully received that morning, but couldn't. Fear had her in its grasp. Lila pulled on the door with all the strength in her one free arm. It resisted her efforts, standing aloof in judgement of her like her accusers so long ago in the temple court.

Jair and Stephen had turned to face their attackers. Lila tore her eyes away from the streak of blood on her hand, looking over her shoulder just in time to see Stephen lunging at Aaron. She saw one of the guards raise a spear. She turned back to the door, feeling every tendon and muscle crackle in her neck with tension. She pulled against its heavy mass, her lungs and throat burning. And then Jair cried out, his full weight fell on her.

Anna screamed.

Stephen turned from Aaron at Jair's cry. 'Oh, no,' was all he could say as he saw that the spear the guard had thrown was sticking out of Jair's shoulder at an angle. He crossed the space between them in two strides and lifted him off Lila and Anna holding him face down in his arms, with the long spear sticking up in the air.

Aaron and the guards were upon them.

'Leave him alone,' screamed Lila as one of the guards made to grab Jair from Stephen.

Aaron reached down and pulled Lila to her feet, with Anna wailing in her arms.

'Leave us alone, Aaron – don't you see it's over? Please stop,' she sobbed.

Jair was moaning in agony. Then the guard gripped the shaft of his spear and pulled it ruthlessly out of Jair's body. Blood gushed from the gaping wound. A scream escaped Jair's lips, ending in a pitiful sob. Stephen looked in horror at the ragged hole that was left. In seconds, Jair's tunic was saturated in crimson. Stephen turned him over and Jair's eyes rolled in his head as his face went ashen. Stephen pulled off his prayer shawl and began to unceremoniously stuff it into the wound, staunching the blood.

'Throw them outside,' Aaron commanded. 'But not these,' he looked at Lila and Anna, still holding her arm firmly in his grasp. 'Your leader is dead. What possessed you to think you could come here and succeed in your plan? You are powerless – like he was on the cross,' he sneered, inches from her face.

One guard dragged Jair up, but his body was like a puppet with its strings cut. The other wrestled to get a grip on Stephen.

An unnatural calm descended on Lila. She looked into Aaron's eyes and held his gaze. 'He is not dead, he is risen and he has sent us power from on high,' she declared.

Aaron's eyes flickered, his grip loosened slightly on her arm. The Sanhedrin had been in disarray at the news of the broken seal on the tomb, the Roman guard's dereliction of duty and the missing body. He had not slept well since the news.

'Let us go, Aaron,' Lila continued in a steady voice. 'I don't belong to you and nor does Anna. We belong to Jesus Christ, the Son of God. In His name, let us go,' she repeated with an otherworldly strength in her voice.

Aaron stared at her in amazement.

Stephen stopped struggling with the guard and stood breathing hard beside her. The other guard who held Jair's limp body against his chest looked at Aaron and asked, 'Now, Master?'

Lila was praying furiously.

'In the Name of Jesus, let us go,' Stephen reiterated.

It was as though Aaron was waking from a dream. Amazement turned to confusion. He let go of Lila and frowned, rubbing his hands over his face.

'Why are you tormenting me? You have done nothing but torment me since the day I met you. Go – get out of my house. I never want to see your face again.'

'Master?' the guard who held Jair exclaimed.

'Get them out of my sight,' he ordered and turning to the other guard who held Stephen, he barked, 'Let him go.'

The guards were baffled, but were trained to obey orders.

Stephen took Jair from the guard, picking him up and hoisting him over his shoulder in one swift movement.

Lila was staring at Aaron. She was realising that the balance of power had changed. The Spirit of God was with her, was within her. His power was greater than any man's strength, even this man. She found herself saying, 'I forgive you, Aaron. I forgive you everything. I hope you find the mercy of God that you so desperately need.' She was overwhelmed with an emotion she couldn't identify.

Aaron's black eyes bored into her, a look of loathing contorting his features, 'Get out!' he yelled, backing away from them.

One guard pulled the heavy door open. Without looking at Aaron again, Lila ducked under his arm seeing Mary standing in the street with Joshua in her arms and ran to her. Stephen followed with his heavy burden. They heard the door slam behind them but didn't look back. They went down several streets and alleyways before Lila had to stop and put Anna down.

From there they moved more slowly, as Anna's little legs could not keep up the pace.

When they finally reached the safety of John's house they were all utterly exhausted. Those who were still there gathered round them. They laid Jair out on a table. He was still breathing, but he had lost a lot of blood. Lila spoke softly to him, 'Jair, can you hear me?' Jair?'

Jair's head rolled to one side.

Lila looked anxiously at Stephen, 'Will he live?' she asked.

'Only God knows,' he replied reverently. 'Let's lay our hands on him and pray, as Jesus taught us. Surely Jair has not lived out his full number of days?'

John agreed and those who were there gathered round the table began to pray.

In the silence that followed Lila watched with joy as the colour crept over Jair's cheeks like sunrise over a landscape.

❀ ❀ ❀

'Do you think it's true?' Peter asked nervously.

Grace couldn't reply. She was so tense with anticipation that she felt if she spoke she might shatter. She just nodded and tried to smile at him as he drove them to the hospital.

When it was their turn, he ushered her in front of him into the scanning room. She lay down on the examination bed and the nurse squirted cold gel on her flat belly. Grace held her breath as the scanner was pressed into her pelvis. Only then did she realise how badly she needed to pee.

And suddenly there it was on the screen – a tiny baby; arms and legs moving vigorously, its heart pumping furiously. Grace burst into tears, 'Thank you Jesus, thank you!' she cried, not caring in the least if her expression of faith was inappropriate in a secular environment.

'Your baby is fifteen weeks,' said the nurse coolly. 'How come you didn't come for your twelve week scan?'

'We didn't know we were pregnant.' Grace laughed shakily through her tears. 'It was only after missing my third period that I really began to wonder,' she sniffed and squeezed Peter's hand.

He was still staring at the screen dumbfounded. Eventually he turned to Grace, tears running down his face, 'We must have conceived on All Saints' Day!' he whispered.

In response, Grace reached up, wiped his cheek with her thumb and pulled his face towards hers. They kissed passionately, forgetting about the nurse until they heard her politely clearing her throat.

❋   The End of Book One   ❋

BABE'S BIBLE II
SISTER ACTS

From the safe distance of the bench she watched the blonde, willowy woman pushing her son on a swing. His dark curls alternately covered his face then flew behind him like tendrils of smoke. He squealed with anticipation as he rushed towards his mother again and again. She watched each face pensively to see if either would tire of the repetitive game. Neither did. She marvelled.

She shifted in her seat, beginning to feel uncomfortably hot in the May sunshine. She slid across the bench into the shifting shadow cast by a chestnut tree and lit a cigarette.

Doesn't matter. She thought, pressing her free hand against her belly. But through the smoke she continued to gaze hungrily at mother and child.

※　※　※

Grace turned at the scent of cigarette smoke. Its seductive earthiness reminded her of heady adolescent days: missing lessons; lying hidden in long grassy fields surrounding her boarding school; gazing up through swaying stalks; watching clouds expand and change against endless blue through the forbidden, mysterious haze she exhaled through her mouth and nose.

She smiled at the young woman on the bench and then looked back to Zack who was shouting 'Mummy!' demanding that he alone have her attention.

'Yes, love, I'm here,' she replied patiently. The wind caught a corkscrew of hair, throwing it into her face. She scraped it away and tucked it behind her ear.

'I want to go on the slide now.' Zack kicked his legs, making the swing wobble and lose its rhythm.

'Okay, but just wait 'til I get you out.' His little body was twisting now, one knee half out of the confines of the swing seat and harness. 'Wait, Zack!' Grace's voice rose, warning him of the danger he was in. He stopped struggling. Grace moved towards him and caught hold of the chains, slowing the swing safely. Then she helped him out and set him on the ground. No sooner had his feet touched down than he was off towards the slide.

Grace followed. *He's not even four but already he's so sure of himself.* She shook her head thinking of the pleasure this character trait gave Peter. It disconcerted her, but she loved it too. She shoved her hands into her jeans pockets feeling her hipbones jutting out. She hadn't needed to stick to salads since Isaac had been born; she burnt calories just watching him. She liked not thinking about what she ate; she liked not thinking about herself. He really had fulfilled his name and surprised them both with laughter. Never in all her days had she hoped to be as happy as she'd been in becoming his mother.

※ ※ ※

The watching woman took a last drag and then stubbed her cigarette out on the side of the bench. She leaned across the gap towards the rubbish bin and flicked the butt on top of the overflow of crisp packets, ice-lolly sticks and soft drink cans. She noticed a doll's head, one eye missing, lips pursed and pink, with a few tufts of blonde hair still intact, lying on top of a crumpled newspaper. She shuddered involuntarily and got up, walking quickly away. Her eyes followed the boy as he hurtled down the slide into the waiting arms of his mother. Their laughter hurt her ears.

※ ※ ※

Grace's eyes followed the woman as she walked away. She was holding Zack upside down, tickling his tummy and making him squeal with delight. She felt something, something that had become familiar over the last five years. Like wind tugging at a kite. She stopped tickling Zack and concentrated hard on the diminishing figure.

'Mummy!' demanded Zack, slapping her thighs.

'Sorry, honey,' she turned him right way up and plonked him on the rubber surface of the play area. He ran back to the slide's ladder. She followed, pondering the sense she had. She found she was praying in the language she often used when she didn't know how to pray. She babbled quietly, a collaboration of river over stones, worn smooth by the flow of rushing water.

'Wat'cha doing, Mummy?' Zack pulled back from the shoulder he'd snuggled into after landing in her arms again. He touched her lips with his chubby fingers.

'Praying,' she smiled.

'Why?' he pulled at her lower lip.

'Not sure,' she caught his hands in hers and kissed them. 'Shall we go home for some lunch?'

He nodded vigorously.

※　※　※

The watching woman lay on the operating table and stared hard at the ceiling.

The anaesthetist leaned over her with the gas mask in his hand. 'Please count from ten down to one for me.'

As he placed it over her mouth and nose she began to count in English but by the time she got to 'six' she was speaking in another language. She faded out at what must have been 'four'.

When she came round she was in a ward with others. She vomited, wishing she was alone. Someone called a nurse, who huffed and sighed as she changed the top sheet and blanket. Dull throbbing pain oozed through the morphine barrier. She turned her head towards the wall, yearning not to exist.

When she next opened her eyes, someone was shaking her. Confused thoughts scattered like glass marbles on the stone floor of her brain. She squinted to focus on the face leaning over her. Dread fear sucked her down. Her whole body recoiled into the bed away from him.

'All done?' he asked brightly, his gruff voice mirroring his shaved head and the tattoo that wove its way up his neck and around the back of his left ear. She nodded, eyes down.

'Good girl. So – you be out today? Gotta get back to work you know. Can't have you lying around here not making money.'

Overhearing him, the nurse came alongside. 'She's lost a lot of blood. She's going to need to stay in for a few days just until we've stabilized her.'

He looked annoyed, but then quickly cloaked his expression. He was now the charmer, surprised and concerned over the blood loss. The nurse looked anxious but left them.

He leaned down and stroked her hair, feigning affection and whispered into her ear, 'Three days – no more. Don't even think about trying to escape. I have eyes and ears everywhere. You're mine and I always get what's mine.' He pretended to kiss her forehead, pressing his teeth into her skin. As he pulled away he was smirking. Then he was gone. Her body began to shake.

The nurse returned and took her temperature. As she waited at the bedside, their eyes met briefly. 'Is there anything I can do for you?' she asked, concern furrowing her brow.

Rescue me! The internal scream did not reach her eyes, which were well practised in the art of subterfuge. 'No – thank you – I sleep.' She noticed her accent was stronger, perhaps the effect of anaesthetic. As the nurse walked away she remembered the mother and son she'd watched earlier in the park. She rolled onto her side, pulling her knees up to her chest as silent tears soaked through the frayed pillowcase edge and pooled on the surface of institutional plastic.

To be continued ...